CUPID'S FOLLY

Harriet was alone with Alasdair MacKyle at last. He stood breathtakingly close to her in the darkened garden.

"This is a dangerous business." h̶ and dropped his hands to b̶ ger- ous," he said nto hers.

After their de ly thrust her fron

Harriet smiled. s you have less dislike for English ladies than you claim," she said, her voice shaky with passion.

"Liking has nothing to do with the matter," MacKyle said coldly. "One can feel as much lust for the lowest-born whore as the highest English lady."

Harriet trembled with rage . . . at this insuffer- ably stiff-necked gentleman . . . and at her own hungering heart. . . .

MELINDA McRAE holds a master's degree in European history and takes great delight in researching obscure details of the Regency pe- riod. She lives in Seattle, Washington, with her husband and daughter.

THE
HIGHLAND
LORD

by

Melinda McRae

O
A SIGNET BOOK

SIGNET
Published by the Penguin Group
Penguin Books USA Inc., 375 Hudson Street,
New York, New York 10014, U.S.A.
Penguin Books Ltd, 27 Wrights Lane,
London W8 5TZ, England
Penguin Books Australia Ltd, Ringwood,
Victoria, Australia
Penguin Books Canada Ltd, 10 Alcorn Avenue,
Toronto, Ontario, Canada M4V 3B2
Penguin Books (N.Z.) Ltd, 182–190 Wairau Road,
Auckland 10, New Zealand

Penguin Books Ltd, Registered Offices:
Harmondsworth, Middlesex, England

First published by Signet, an imprint of New American Library,
a division of Penguin Books USA Inc.

First Printing, December, 1992
10 9 8 7 6 5 4 3 2 1

To my father,
Forbes William McRae,
for introducing me to the
delights of bagpipe music
during my formative years.

And to Rich Hill,
for help with the Gaelic.
Mo buidheachas.

I

AUTHOR'S NOTE:
There is no MacKyle clan or Earldom of Kintail.
Loch Kyle and the Falls of Lochalsh are real, but
are not known by those names. Some may understand the connection.

What we commonly think of as a Scottish accent
is the language spoken by the people of the Borders
and the Lowlands. Burns and Scott were masters of
this dialect. Highlanders speak Gaelic, an entirely
different language. In 1822, ninety-nine percent of
the population of the Northwest Highlands were
Gaelic-speaking, and less than twenty percent spoke
English with any skill. Because of their isolation,
the English that they used bore more resemblance
to the King's English than the language spoken
among the Scottish Lowlands.

1

In the cause of Right engaged,
  Wrongs injurious to redress,
Honor's war we strongly waged,
  But the heavens deny'd success.

Robert Burns,
Strathallan's Lament

Lock Kyle, Scotland, 1822

"Marbhfaisg air!" Alasdair MacKyle swore aloud. Flinging the letter onto his desk, he stalked across the tower chamber. He had counted on the willingness of the Marquess of Egerton to sell Keppoch back to the MacKyles. What use were a few square miles of heather and hill to an English lord with estates in nearly every shire? But no, his bloody Sassenach lordship wished to keep the land "in the hope that it might eventually be put to some useful purpose and increase in value."

What would Egerton ever know of the value of this land, sitting in his elegant house in London? His ancestors had not fought for it, shedding their blood in a vain effort to free themselves from the tyranny of a forced union and a foreign king. No Egerton had been exiled to the Continent and seen his family stripped of its land and titles, Alasdair thought bitterly. Even if determination and money had won back most of the MacKyle losses over the last three generations, there were still two things missing. For Alasdair MacKyle, the great-grandson of the 4th Earl of Kintail, was only a plain "mister" in the eyes of the English, instead of holding the title of earl. And the wild, heathered hills to the south, where one could look down upon Kintail Castle and across the waters of Loch Kyle—the hills of Keppoch—were in the hands of an English marquess. *"Rugadh an diolanas e."*

"Alasdair!" The dark-haired young lady sitting before the window chastened him.

He looked chagrined at his sister Katrine's reproof. "A well-bred miss would not admit to recognizing those words."

"You say them often enough," she retorted. "What has you so upset now?"

"Egerton," he said. "He will not sell the land."

"Oh." Eighteen-year-old Katrine MacKyle did not share her brother's obsession with restoring the portions of the MacKyle estate lost in the previous century. She was far more concerned with the advent of spring and the Edinburgh Season that would be starting in a month. Last year she had made her debut, and Katrine looked forward to this new Season with eager anticipation. Winter in the Highlands was long and dark.

Alasdair shook his dark head. "I fear I will not be able to accompany you to Edinburgh this spring," he said with feigned reluctance. "It looks as if I will have to go to London."

"London!" Katrine squealed, clapping her hands in unalloyed delight. "Oh, Alasdair, really? I cannot think of anywhere I would rather go."

"I did not say I was taking you."

"You must! You know how I am dying to see London. And in the spring, during the height of the Season. It will be heaven."

"I am not going to London for the social season," he reminded her. "This will be purely a business trip. Although Egerton will not sell the land, he offers encouragement on my petition for the restoration of the title. He says it will assist matters greatly if I can be there myself to promote my own cause. And in person, perhaps I can plead a better case for his selling the land."

"But London? Alasdair, you must let me go with you!"

"For what reason do you need to go to London?" Alasdair eyed his sister with a teasing look. "All you would do is spend money and flirt with every young man you saw. You are to be betrothed to Robbie Ferguson before the year is out."

Katrine's face took on a mulish expression.

"I will not be forced into marrying anyone simply because you wish it so," she snapped. "Robbie Ferguson is a mere child."

"It is a grown woman that you are?" he countered.

She sighed deeply. It was an old argument. "How shall I ever know my heart if I have no comparisons to make?" she asked. "Everywhere I turned last year in Edinburgh, Robbie was there. He frightened all the others away."

Alasdair grinned in spite of himself. Once the lad had set his mind on Katrine, he brooked no opposition. Few men were willing to argue with the giant man who had the temper to match his red hair.

"Besides," Katrine cajoled, "if I am to marry Robbie, I will need to build my trousseau. 'T'will be the envy of all if it comes from London."

"We know few people in London," Alasdair warned her. "I fear you will be sadly bored. I want to restore the title, not watch you make a splash in London society."

"They say London is mad for things Scottish these days. Drape yourself in the plaid and we shall gain entry to all the right houses."

"I do not care to see our heritage mocked by the affectations of the English." Even if it meant it would help his task.

"Edinburgh is so dull," she protested. "Please, Alasdair?"

"You will need a chaperon . . ."

"Mrs. Fraser would come with us," Katrine said with eagerness.

"No doubt," he responded dryly. He knew Katrine had her chaperon wrapped around her little finger. Still, it might do. He could not fault Katrine for wanting to see London, even if for all the wrong reasons. He had resigned himself long ago to his sister's disdain for history, politics, and the pride of the clan. Her fancy boarding school might have turned her into a lady, but it had removed some of the Scot in her as well. He shrugged.

It was not her fight. And he knew he would not have a moment's peace if he did not take her with him.

"You may come with me," he said, gazing at his sister with a fond expression. Alasdair nearly lost his balance as she flung herself into his arms.

"Oh, thank you, Alasdair. It will be so wonderful! You are the best of brothers."

"One condition," he cautioned. "If you truly do not wish to wed Ferguson, I will not hold you to that obligation. But be warned now that I will never countenance marriage to an Englishman. Flirt all you like with them, but do not lose your heart, Katrine, for I will not tolerate it."

"I am not foolish enough to do any such thing," she replied, then gave him an impish grin. "But is it so certain you are that you can resist the charms of the English ladies?"

She laughed at the thunderous scowl on his face and danced out of the room.

English ladies. Alasdair gave a derisive snort. He would no more take one to wife than he would a kelpie. They were brainless, simple-minded creatures concerned only with their own comforts, ill-educated, simpering misses whose one purpose in life was to snag a husband. They might be packaged in an attractive manner, but inside they had as much substance as tea cakes. He would have no difficulty giving them a wide berth. When he felt the need to marry, it would be with a woman who shared his love for Scotland.

Alasdair looked longingly out the window at the sunlit dappled waters of the loch. How he longed to be there instead of in his office, going over the account books to make certain all would be in order before his departure to London. The process was made all the more difficult by the uncertain times that lay ahead. How could he continue to improve the estate when the prices of meat and kelp dived so low?

His face broke into a wry smile. Well, if Egerton refused to sell the land, there was a tidy sum that could be added back into the estate accounts. It would more than offset the cost of taking Katrine to London. He wanted to be generous with her shopping money.

With one last regretful glance at the loch, Alasdair turned his attention back to the books. There were so many things that could go wrong. Bad weather, rough seas, more unrest among the cottagers on other estates . . .

"Alasdair?"

He waved his steward into the room.

"Don't even tell me, Dougall," Alasdair said, taking in the man's grim countenance. "Disaster."

"It is not so bad as all that," Dougall replied. "More evictions in Keppoch."

"Damn Egerton. How many?"

"Only ten this time."

Alasdair swore loudly. "Families?"

Dougall nodded.

"I shall see them," Alasdair said reluctantly. He dreaded the upcoming conversation. As much as he wanted to, he could not help them all. He had taken as many families as he could onto his own land. Now he could only help the new ones find other homes.

After hastening down the spiraling tower stairs, Alasdair walked down a short corridor and entered the arched, high-ceilinged entry hall. On the far side of the room stood two men wrapped in shabby, faded plaids, their weariness evident in their faces.

"I welcome you to Kintail," Alasdair said in Gaelic.

"We have come to offer you our services, Lord Kintail," one of the men replied in the same language. "We have been ousted from our homes, all for some sheep. Everyone in the Highlands knows of your generosity to the Gael."

"We are hard workers," the younger man added. "We have a bit of the fishing as well. And my wife is a skillful weaver of the plaid."

"I am appreciative of your offer," Alasdair said. "You are welcome to stay with us for a few days, to eat and rest. But I cannot take on any more tenants, not without jeopardizing my own people's survival."

The two men looked at each other. "Is it Glasgow, then," the elder one said.

"Do you really wish to live in the city, where the air is black and foul, and you will be crammed together in a filthy rookery?" Alasdair asked.

"Where else are we to go?" the younger man asked bitterly.

"Upper Canada," Alasdair replied.

"We do not have the money to pay the passage for our own selves, let alone that of our families," the elder man protested. "And I will not sell myself into bonded servitude to another man for any reason."

"I think it will be possible to arrange your passage," Alasdair said. "You will have to make your way to Greenock on foot, but if you can manage that, there is money to pay your way on the ship."

The two men looked at each other again. "We shall need to discuss this with our families, especially our sons," one said.

"Think on it well," Alasdair told them. "In Canada there is land beyond imagining."

"It is a long and dangerous trip," the other man pointed out. "Few people die on the road to Glasgow."

"Yet more people die after they reach the city," Alasdair said. "In Canada you will be among your own kind, with your own language."

"But to leave Scotland . . ." The younger man's voice trailed off.

"In Canada there is still much that is Scotland," Alasdair said, hoping to persuade them. As much as he sympathized with their apprehensions, it was the best course open to them. "Those who have gone before have founded towns with names like Stirling, Bannockburn, Ineverary, and Glencoe. You will find welcome there among the Gael."

The men nodded, as if considering his words.

"Talk with your wives and your sons," Alasdair urged them. He turned to Dougall. "See that they are fed, and sheltered for the night. If they have questions, answer them."

"We are grateful for your help, Lord Kintail," the elder of the men said. "You have our gratitude."

"I thank you," said Alasdair. "And may God help you

in your decision." He bowed and left the men in Dougall's capable hands.

What a choice, he thought as he wearily climbed the stairs back to his haven. Slow starvation in the city, or exile forever from Scotland. He had no illusions that the thousands of Scots who fled in despair to the New World would ever come back. The mere thought of never seeing Scotland again tore at him. He was not certain if he could endure such a life. Yet he was asking these people to do that very thing.

What else could he do? It was difficult enough to keep his own tenants solvent, what with crop failures and lowered prices. But he could not stand by and watch impassively while Englishmen like Egerton tossed the Highlanders off land they had worked for generations. He cursed the owners who thought nothing of the ruined lives that followed. Profit was their only guiding force. And sheep cost less than men.

It was exquisite irony that he had been born in 1792. *Bliadhna nan Caorach*. The Year of the Sheep. The year all hell broke loose in the Highlands, and a way of life was gone forever. He was powerless to stop the change, except on his own lands. But he felt obligated to do what he could to enable his fellow Scots to find some kind of life for themselves. If they chose to go to Canada, he would scrape together the money to send them there.

Restoring the title was more important than ever. Not only for his own pride, but for what it would mean to others. As an earl, his words would have more influence. He could speak out against the evictions, and use his own lands to demonstrate that it was possible to run a profitable estate in Scotland. And if he regained Keppoch, he could stop the evictions there as well.

The trip to London was more important than ever.

Highbury Hall, Kent

"You are all packed and prepared for the journey?"

Lady Harriet Winterbourne planted a fond kiss atop her father's balding head. "As ready as I ever shall be," she announced, perching gracefully upon a corner of his massive desk.

"And is this the Season you finally decide upon a husband?" He arched a quizzing brow.

"Perhaps," she replied coyly.

The Marquess of Egerton shook his head in mock dismay. "Your mother would be shocked to see you still unwed at two-and-twenty."

"Mama would say 'twas better to remain unwed than to wed unhappily," Harriet said. "If she had not placed so much emphasis on marrying for love, I might have wed years ago."

"Foolish woman," he said, with a fond smile for his deceased wife. "So I suppose it is to be another Season of balls and breakfasts and exorbitant bills from the dressmakers?"

"And the milliners and the glove makers," she added.

He sighed. "Perhaps I shall be forced to take this back, then," he teased, bringing out a flat jeweler's box from his desk drawer and setting it in her lap.

Harriet lifted the lid and gasped in pleasure. "Papa, they are beautiful!" she exclaimed, tilting the box so the diamond and sapphire necklace, with matching earrings, sparkled in the light.

"I thought you might have some use for them," the marquess said gruffly.

"Oh, I shall," she said, hopping off the desk to give him an exuberant hug. "I will save them for the opening ball at Egerton House. With a blue gown to match . . ."

"You will outshine everyone there, as usual." He smiled. "Now, leave me to my business, girl. I still have a few matters to take care of before we leave in the morning. And be certain you have everything you want— I will not be sending a footman back for some forgotten trifle."

"Yes, Papa," she said, knowing full well he would if she asked. After another kiss to his cheek, she retreated from the study. Marie would have to repack the jewel case.

With that task taken care of, Harriet donned a cape and slipped from the house onto the back terrace. The gardens were only beginning to throw off winter's cloak. An occasional splash of color marked a patch of early-flowering bulbs. In a few weeks the gardens would be ablaze with every hue of the rainbow. But by then she would be in London.

This was the first year that she could honestly say she did not look upon the Season with anticipation. There were no longer any surprises in store for her; after three years as the reigning toast, there was little she had not seen or heard a hundred times over. Oh, there would be new girls, nervous and eager, looking to make a brilliant catch. A few new men would add their names to the list, seeking heiresses to repair their fortunes, a young miss to tend their motherless children, or a prized ornament from the Season's beauties. A few would find lifelong happiness, a few would consign themselves to an endless hell. And some would go home in failure.

In the last three years she had seen so much, yet remained remarkably impervious to it all. Like the others, she had looked upon her first Season with a mixture of terror and anticipation, nurturing her foolish dreams like all the other young ladies making their debuts. But the magic departed long before the final waltz of the last ball.

It was not that Harriet disliked the Season, for she did not. She reveled in the parties, the sly and witty gossip, the dancing and flirtations. And yet, despite the countless waltzes, carriage drives, moonlight walks, and even stolen kisses, her heart remained unmoved by the most eloquent pledges of love and admiration. She could look with fondness and even affection on many of her suitors, but that indefinable line between fondness and love was something she had been unable to cross.

There were nights when Harriet railed against her mother for filling her head with notions of the lifelong happiness a love match could bring. Books had been flung across the room in fits of disgust when the heroine fell joyfully into the hero's arms. What was wrong with her that she could not fall in love like everyone else?

But through three years there had not been even the faintest intimation that she had met the man she wished to marry. Harriet was beginning to think she would be forever unwed—or would have to settle for a marriage of friendship. But what if she did, only to later discover her "grand passion"? Which was the worse fate—never to marry or to marry where there was not love?

She knew her father wanted to see her married and settled. She frowned. What would he do with himself when she left his house? He and Tris would rattle around the estate like lost souls.

She smiled at the thought of seeing her cousin Tris in London. Even if he was barely a year her junior, Harriet could not stop thinking of him as the family baby. Why did society dictate a woman should marry young, while a man waited until he was mature enough for the responsibilities of a wife and family? As if a girl of seventeen were any more prepared!

Harriet shook her head and breathed in the clean, cool country air. It was only another Season, she reminded herself. Yet she could not rid her mind of her father's teasing words. "Is this the Season you finally decide upon a husband?" Would it be?

She knew she should marry. It was expected of her. It would please her father. On the spot she made a vow to herself. She *would* marry this year. If no new man caught her fancy, she would accept her most patient suitor. The amiable Lord Hanover had never made any secret of his desire for her. The merest encouragement on her part would have him at her feet. Perhaps it was this very thing that kept her from favoring his suit. But if no one turned her head, Han it would be. At least they were friends.

The matter now decided, Harriet turned her steps back toward the house. But deep in her soul she uttered a small prayer. *Please let me find him this year.*

2

A mighty mass of brick, and smoke, and shipping,
>   Dirty and dusky, but as wide as eye
> Could reach . . . and there is London Town!

> Lord Byron,
> *Don Juan*

Alasdair surveyed the main drawing room of the house in Upper Berkley Street with resignation. It would do. It would more than do, in fact. With London fast filling for the Season, he could not afford to delay longer. He would have preferred a lesser house, with a lesser address. The agent assured him that the terms were generous, even if the rent was four times what a comparable house would have cost in Edinburgh. Still . . . he had Katrine to think about, and a house in this section of town would be advantageous for her.

He gave the agent an approving nod. "We shall take it."

Katrine clapped her hands in glee. "Thank you, Alasdair."

With a reluctant smile, he turned back to the agent. "When may we take possession?"

"The housekeeper assures me they can have the house completely ready in two days," the man replied. "I can also see to the hiring of additional servants and a cook."

Alasdair nodded again and looked at Katrine. "I shall leave the domestic details to you, my dear. Make a list of everything that needs to be done, and what you shall need for staff."

Katrine, who had been running the house in Scotland since she was twelve, did not think this commission onerous. She immediately went in search of the housekeeper

17

to find what more was necessary to prepare the house for their arrival.

After signing the house papers and seeing to the agent's departure, Alasdair sat back in the library chair, sipping a glass of claret and reflecting upon their new situation. Not for the first time he wished he could have transacted this business from Scotland. He particularly wished he had left Katrine behind. Entertaining her would no doubt consume more time than he wished. But what was done was done, and he would have to make the best of things now. As long as he was in London, he would do all that was in his power to promote his case with Parliament, the Privy Council, and the king. The restoration of his family's title and honor was surely worth some sacrifice on his part.

Of course, to Katrine it was no sacrifice at all. Visiting London was the dream of a lifetime for her. He hoped they could make their stay short. Despite his admiration for her common sense, he feared that too long a sojourn in the capital would erode her Scottish sensibility and she would begin to resemble the pallid, witless London ladies who led society. It would be well for their business to be accomplished quickly so they could depart before any damage was done.

There was also the matter of Robbie Ferguson. Katrine would have to make up her mind on that head. He had meant what he'd said earlier—he would not force her into an unwanted marriage. But Katrine needed her own establishment. She had kept house for him long enough. Time for her to settle in a home of her own and start a family. She deserved a more lively existence than the Highland isolation he preferred. After all this business was done and they returned to Scotland, he would encourage her to accept someone's suit. They would even spend the winter in Edinburgh, if need be, in order to help her make her choice.

But for now they were in London. The shops would keep her busy for hours, there was the theater and the opera for entertainment, and undoubtedly they would receive enough invitations so as not to consider themselves social outcasts. Perhaps, when the first flush of excitement from the visit to the metropolis faded, Katrine would grow less enchanted with the Sassenach capital.

Setting his glass down on the desk, he rose to go in search of his sister. There was still much to be done before they moved from the hotel to this house. Katrine would require the use of a town carriage, and he should like to have a horse. London parks were uncrowded in the morning hours and he could find some escape from the press of humanity there. If only one could smell the scent of the sea there as well.

"I shall race you to the far trees," Harry called over her shoulder as she urged her chestnut mare into an unladylike early-morning gallop through Hyde Park.

"Unfair!" her cousin Tris shouted back, spurring his own mount. "You have the advantage."

She laughed gaily and urged her horse into a full-tilt gallop, heedless of the impropriety. The park was virtually deserted at this hour, and the Season was still young. There would be few to see her here. In truth, she did not care. Tales of a wild ride in the park would only enhance her reputation.

Tris was gaining on her as they reached the line of trees, but Harry had judged her start to perfection and managed to edge out her cousin.

"You win again, dash it all!" he exclaimed. "How do you always manage to do that to me, Harry?"

"Practice," she retorted.

Harry reined in her horse, slowing the mare to a sprightly trot and then a sedate walk, affectionately patting the sweating neck. She had loved the mare from the first moment she had seen her two years ago, a birthday present from her father. The animal had fire and spirit, which exactly suited Harry.

Tris brought his horse alongside and they rode at a more decorous pace to the other end of the park.

"Someday I will beat you," he vowed with a grin.

"I would not lay good money on it," she retorted. "Better confine your wagers to easier-won prizes."

"Give me an early start next time, then" he suggested.

Harry eyed him with glee. "Tristan Winterbourne asking for an advantage over the weaker sex? I own I am shocked."

"The only person who would be shocked would be your father if he saw you racing your horse like that in the park," Tris said.

"He has far more important things to worry about."

"Like marrying you off," Tris said with a challenging stare.

Harry quelled him with a dampening look. "Perhaps I should tell the matrons *you* are on the lookout for a wife," she said.

"Pray, no!" he cried in mock horror. "A fate worse than death!"

She laughed. "For the poor girl, you mean."

It was Tris's turn to look askance at Harry. "So that I can make the proper choice, who is to be the leading diamond of the season this year?"

"You are not planning on hanging out for a wife!" Harry exclaimed.

"No, but it would be good for my consequence to at least be among her court."

"I have heard that Lady Slipwell's daughter is quite a catch," Harry said, wrinkling her nose as she tried to recall all the gossip and rumors about the new Season's beauties. "It is difficult, you see, for one never quite knows what will be in fashion. Shall it be fair-haired ladies or dark brunettes this year? You may well have to wait and see what society determines."

"Pity I could not be amongst your court," he grumbled.

"No one would ever seriously believe such a thing," she replied with an impish grin.

"Only because you have the odious habit of calling me 'little brother,' " he complained. "Half the *ton* thinks I am your brother."

"*That* would improve your consequence far more than dangling after the latest toast," she informed him archly. Tris responded with a noise that sounded very much like a snort of derision. Harry turned her gaze to give him a good-natured setdown, but her attention was arrested by the sight of a lone rider coming down the path.

She lowered her voice. "Tris, who is that man over there?"

"Which man?"

Harry frowned in exasperation. "The only other person besides ourselves in the Park," she said.

"Can't say that I recognize him," Tris said at last. "Nice bit of blood there. Good day," he greeted as the stranger neared.

The man nodded a brief acknowledgment but did not slow his horse.

Harry did not know why her gaze was drawn to the unfamiliar man. She was not in the habit of staring at perfect strangers, and she was quite certain that she had not seen this man before. Nothing about him was the least bit familiar.

She scrutinized him carefully as he drew closer. His hair was dark and he wore no hat; his face had been exposed to the sun more than was fashionable. But it was his eyes that held her attention. They were the darkest ones she had ever seen, a deep, rich brown that was almost black. They swept over her quickly with a look that was a mixture of anger and disdain. It irritated her immensely. As much as it intrigued her.

Harry did something she rarely did—at least unintentionally. She blushed. To her annoyance, the stranger fixed her with an even cooler stare as he rode past.

"I want to know who he is," she confided to Tris when they were out of hearing.

"Deucedly unfriendly, I thought," Tris said.

Harry could not master the impulse to twist around and stare at the man one more time. A sudden shiver raced through her, almost like premonition. Who was he? She would put all of her energies into finding the answer to that question.

It suddenly looked to be a most interesting Season.

"Oh, look, Mrs. Fraser, Hatchards!" Katrine's eyes lighted with anticipation at the sight of the bookstore. "Do let us go in."

"Haven't you bought enough for one day?" her companion grumbled, but followed her young charge into the store.

Despite a full week of shopping, Katrine had not yet lost any of her enthusiasm for London's shops. She glanced around eagerly at the well-filled shelves, searching for Mrs. Opie's latest novel. Perhaps she could find something even Alasdair would enjoy. Leaving Mrs. Fraser perusing the latest issue of the *Ladies Monthly Museum,* Katrine wandered toward the rear of the shop.

There were far too many choices, she decided many minutes later. She hoped Alasdair would be pleased with the new edition of *Letters From a Gentleman in the North of Scotland.* But Katrine could not decide between a book from Mrs. Opie and one from Louisa Sydney for herself. Alasdair would approve of neither, but that mattered little. Mrs. Opie it would be, she decided at length. Carefully juggling the four volumes, her gloves, and her reticule, Katrine had just turned to join Mrs. Fraser at the front of the store when a man collided with her, sending everything she held flying.

"I am dreadfully sorry," the young man said, stooping down to pick up the dropped possessions. Katrine bent to retrieve her belongings and they reached for a book at the same time, their hands touching. Both drew back instantly.

"Allow me, please," the man said.

Katrine stood, knowing her cheeks were undoubtedly as red as the ribbon trim on her pelisse. Here she was in London acting like a veritable provincial, bumping into strange men and dropping her possessions all over the floor. Whatever would he think of her?

She dared a glance at the man crouched at her feet. His hair was golden blond and his clothes fashionable. Her heart sank. She had certainly disgraced herself in front of a member of the *ton*.

"How horridly clumsy of me," the man apologized, rising and reaching out to hand her the gloves and reticule. Their eyes met for the first time.

"Oh," he said, his gaze locking on hers. He stood there awkwardly, holding the books in his hands.

"Thank you," Katrine whispered as her fingers convulsively clenched her gloves. The man standing in such discomfort before her was so blindingly handsome she could barely breathe. He was nearly as tall as Alasdair, and looked all that was fashionable in his tailed coat and striped trousers. But her gaze was drawn to his eyes. They were the bluest of blue, like the Highland sky on a cloudless summer's day. And they were staring at her in rapt attention.

"Tris? Are you ready to come away?"

Katrine's heart sank as she saw the woman who walked up to them. She was dressed in a pelisse that must have come directly from the pages of *Ackermann's*, with an exquisite cottage bonnet trimmed all in roses, and Katrine sensed she was in the presence of a dasher. She felt suddenly very drab in her Edinburgh clothes.

"I am apologizing to this lady," the man explained, his eyes still focused on Katrine. "I quite clumsily managed to knock all her belongings to the ground."

"Oh, no, please, I was at fault," Katrine blurted out. "I was not attending."

Harry laughed. "I know Tris, and I am certain he was the one at fault. You are lucky you did not land on the floor as well." She looked expectantly from one to the other.

"My books . . ." Katrine said lamely.

"Oh, my goodness," Tris said, thrusting the volumes into her hands. "How foolish of me, Miss . . . ?"

"MacKyle," Katrine replied, waiting for the inevitable reaction. If her speech had not given her away, her name certainly would.

"Oh, how lovely," said Harry. "Scottish, is it not?"

Katrine nodded.

Harry held out her hand. "I am Harriet Winterbourne. And I am certain my cousin did not bother to introduce himself. Tristan Winterbourne."

Katrine's heart leapt at the knowledge they were only cousins. Looking carefully, she saw the resemblance in their blond, blue-eyed looks. She smiled demurely at Mr. Winterbourne.

"You must be in London for the Season," Harry said,

instantly curious about this young lady who had captured Tris's attention.

"My brother is here on business," Katrine explained. "But we have taken a house in Upper Berkley Street and I hope . . ." Her voice tapered off. "My brother is not much for society."

"How dreadful," said Harry with a laugh. "For what is London without society? You will allow me to pay you a visit, will you not? Shall you be receiving callers tomorrow?"

Katrine nodded and gave her the direction.

"Good." Harry smiled. "Now, Tris, if you are quite finished, we do need to be going. I still have to stop at the jewelers to retrieve Father's watch."

"It was a pleasure to make your acquaintance, Miss MacKyle," he stammered.

Blushing, Katrine nodded shyly. She stood where she was, watching him and his elegant cousin until they exited the store.

Outside, as Tris handed her into the carriage, Harry chided him fondly.

"I thought you had quite forgotten your tongue," she teased. "Do not tell me it is love at first sight?"

"Of course not," he said with excessive indignation, taking up the reins. "It was merely a momentary embarrassment. A rather awkward way to make a young lady's acquaintance, I can tell you."

"She seems a rather appealing miss," Harry observed. "It might prove amusing to further the acquaintance. I shall decide tomorrow, after we visit."

"We?"

"Well, certainly, you did not expect me to pay a call to her by myself? Not after the way you stared at her like a mooncalf for the entire exchange. No," Harry said emphatically, "you will go with me tomorrow."

Tris offered no argument and Harry smiled. It would be amusing to watch him in the throes of an infatuation at last.

While Tris skillfully negotiated the carriage through the traffic-clogged streets, Harry's thoughts drifted back to the stranger they had seen in the park that morning.

She could not forget those piercing dark eyes—nor the condemning look in them. She was unaccustomed to seeing anything but appreciation in a male glance, and it intrigued her that there was at least one man in London who did not view her favorably. She doubted it was a personal animosity—the man was most unfamiliar and hence could not have known who she was. Did he look at all women that way? Or was there something about her that particularly irritated him?

Curiosity was one of her besetting sins, Harry reflected. Poor Tris would grow tired of the park, but Harry resolved to ride there daily until she discovered the identity of the mysterious stranger.

Yet what if she never saw him again?

3

My Heart's in the Highlands,
My heart is not here,
My heart's in the Highlands,
A-chasing the deer;

Robert Burns,
My Heart's in the Highlands

Alasdair attempted to quell his nervousness as he was ushered into Lord Egerton's study. So much depended on this man, yet to Alasdair he represented everything that was hateful about the English. He was one of the rich absentee landlords who raped and plundered the Scottish countryside with no regard for the people who had lived there for generations. He took and took and gave nothing in return.

But Egerton, as a member of the Privy Council, wielded enormous power, and his support was critical to the restoration of the Kintail title. Alasdair would sleep with the devil himself to regain the right to use "Earl" with his name. Straightening imperceptibly, Alasdair prepared to meet the man who held the future in his hands.

A tall, elegantly dressed gentleman with silvery hair rose from behind the desk and stepped toward him. "Kintail," he greeted.

In spite of his aversion, Alasdair found himself smiling at Egerton's use of the attained title. It boded well for a favorable outcome to his petition. Alasdair gripped the proffered hand. "Egerton."

"Take a seat." The marquess gestured to a chair and crossed the thick Aubusson carpet, halting before a side table. "Brandy? Or there is Scots whiskey, if you prefer."

"Brandy would be fine," Alasdair said. Accepting the glass, he waited with well-covered impatience until the marquess was seated.

"I am pleased to see you took my advice and came to London," the marquess began. "You find your lodgings acceptable?"

Alasdair nodded.

"I imagine your sister is enjoying her visit to town. Women love to shop."

"That she does," Alasdair said with a wry smile. "Much more than I wish."

Egerton laughed. "I have a daughter, myself. My sympathies are with you." He raised his glass in salute. "Now, as to the matter of your petition . . ." The marquess drew a sheet of paper from his desk and handed it to Alasdair. "I had my secretary draw up a list of all the fees involved in introducing private legislation. T'would be an easier process if one could merely place a sum of money on deposit and have each person draw his share, but unfortunately, it will not work that way. You can make the payments yourself, if you wish, or you could leave a draft with my secretary and he will take care of things."

"That would be satisfactory," Alasdair replied. He leaned forward, trying to still his eagerness. "What do you think the chances are?"

Egerton rubbed his chin. "I have spoken to a few Privy Council members—privately and unofficially, of course—and they do not anticipate any difficulties. I think the events of the last century are long forgotten."

"Is anyone else petitioning for the same cause?"

"None that I am aware of." Egerton smiled wryly. "I imagine they will wish to see how your own petition fares."

"I certainly appreciate your assistance in this matter," Alasdair said, while wishing it had been possible to enlist the support of some other lord—any lord, as long as he did not have holdings in Scotland. He wondered if he dare bring up the subject of Keppoch again.

Before he could speak, Egerton extended an engraved

card. "There is a ball next Thursday at Egerton House," he said. "I should like you and your sister to attend."

"Thank you," Alasdair said with well developed politeness. Katrine would be thrilled. He was not. He was here to regain the title, not waste his time at social gatherings.

"There will be several people there it would be wise for you to meet," Egerton continued. "Sometimes it is easier to make these introductions in an informal social setting."

Alasdair nodded, instantly resigned to the necessity of attending. He realized he had been naive in thinking that he could conduct his business on a purely formal footing. London would be no different than Edinburgh, where business transactions took place in both government offices and drawing rooms. He only wished he were more adept at the social graces. "I look forward to attending."

"Do not mistake matters, you will be under scrutiny," Egerton warned him. "As I mentioned, no one seems opposed in principle to your request. But it will be their personal reaction to you which will most influence their decision. Your sister will be an asset as well. Naturally, in escorting her about, you will have the opportunity to meet people."

"Can you venture a guess as to how long the matter will take?" Alasdair was filled with dismay at the thought of interminable months in London.

"Difficult to say," Egerton mused. "You will probably have to wait and gauge the full reaction to the bill when it is proposed to make any judgment." He leaned forward across his desk. "That is why it is imperative that you use your time here in town to good purpose. Cultivate the influential. I cannot tell you enough how critical it will be for you to have the support of the Scottish lords."

Alasdair's heart sank. He was not on the best of terms with most of them. He had made his views on how they should run their estates all too clear.

"I'll take you around to my clubs, of course," Egerton said. "Would not hurt if you joined as well."

"That is generous of you," Alasdair replied, groaning inwardly. This was going to be a far more challenging project than he had anticipated. But he had no doubt of the final outcome. Alasdair was determined to restore the family honor—and the title. He could certainly endure a few months in London in pursuit of that goal.

Egerton stood, indicating the interview was at an end. "I will have my secretary prepare the initial papers and send them round for your signature," he said, walking Alasdair to the door. "As soon as we have your bank draft, we can begin the process."

"I thank you again." Alasdair shook hands once more.

Egerton nodded in dismissal.

Retrieving his hat and coat from the butler, Alasdair stepped out into the brisk March air.

This trip to London was going to be as unpleasant as he could ever have imagined. He shook his head glumly as he carefully avoided a rather nasty-looking puddle. He would have to toady to every lord in town, ingratiating himself with men he despised while he enlisted their support for his petition.

What was worse, he could see the expenses of the visit mounting as well. He would have to do a creditable job of presenting Katrine, and if their visit lasted as long as he feared, she would need thrice the clothing even she had planned. It seemed an extravagant waste of money to dress a sister only to make a favorable impression when the money could be more wisely spent in improvements on the estate.

If there was a purpose to Katrine's presence here in London, he would not be as upset. But he had no intention of wedding her to a Sassenach. If her heart was not set on Robbie, there were many equally fine Scottish lads who would do. But by succumbing to Katrine's blandishments and bringing her to town, he was now committed to making her visit an unexceptional one. That would involve allowing her to cut a dash in town society.

Still, he reflected, as he stepped around a fresh pile of horse dung that the crossing sweeper had yet to clear away, he did not think it would be terribly taxing. He knew few people in London. It had been a kindness for Egerton to invite them to his house, where they could meet the people he needed to know. Katrine, perhaps, would strike up friendships with some suitable young ladies. They might go out once or twice a week. It would not be an onerous burden. And if he was very lucky, they would be on their way back to Scotland before late spring.

Katrine fussed and fidgeted over her wardrobe in the morning, choosing then discarding gown after gown. Her clothing was all well and good for Edinburgh society, but after only a week in London she knew that her wardrobe was sadly wanting in style and dash. Although she had not minded much yesterday, it suddenly became of the most critical importance that she look her best this morning. Just in case *he* came.

Even if he did not, she looked forward to seeing Harriet Winterbourne again. Katrine had acquired many friends during her stay at Miss Sampson's Select Seminary for Ladies in Edinburgh, keeping in close contact with many by letter, and visiting them when possible. But the isolation of the Kintail estate had worn on her in the last months. Now she found herself in London, the city of her dreams, without a friend or acquaintance of her own age anywhere. Knowing Alasdair, he would make no effort to amuse her. The meeting with Harriet Winterbourne yesterday had been providential.

For a moment Katrine wished she had someone in London to guide her. For she knew that one did not usually strike up conversations with total sttrangers in shops, although Harriet had not seemed the least forward. But Katrine wondered exactly who Harriet was—and why she had been so eager to pay a visit today. Was she perhaps not quite suitable for a young lady to know?

The thought was ridiculous. Katrine knew a well-bred lady when she met one, and Harriet Winterbourne was certainly that.

Her high opinion of that lady was in no way influenced by her interest in the lady's cousin, Katrine assured herself.

At a point where Katrine had nearly worn herself out with a combination of anticipation and dread, Finlay stalked into the room in his typical unbutlerish manner and announced the arrival of the Winterbourne cousins.

"Oh, I am so glad you came," Katrine said, leaping to her feet and crossing the room to greet her guests. Then she blushed. "That is . . ."

"I quite understand," Harry said, amused by the girl's innocent enthusiasm. "You are newly arrived in the city, do not know a soul, and even a chance-met stranger looks like manna from heaven."

Katrine nodded.

"Well, I shall do what I can to rectify that situation," Harriet said emphatically. While removing her gloves, she quickly sized up the situation. Fashionable address. Dutiful chaperon. House undoubtedly rented for the Season. Katrine's clothing, while not quite up to London standards, was stylish enough.

"It is a pleasure to see you again, Miss MacKyle," Tris said, bowing gallantly. Katrine offered him a shy smile.

"Let me make you known to Mrs. Fraser," Katrine said, leading her guests over to her widowed companion. "Harriet Winterbourne. And Mr. Winterbourne."

Mrs. Fraser nodded a greeting, her eyes barely lifting from her sewing.

Katrine and Harry took seats on the sofa, while Tris sat in a nearby chair.

"Are you to be in town for the entire Season?" Tris asked.

"I am not certain," Katrine replied. "Alasdair—my brother—is presenting a private bill to Parliament, so we will remain for as long as it takes to achieve its passage."

"Which can be dreadfully slow at times," Harry said. "But I doubt that shall disconcert you," she added with a twinkle in her eye. "I imagine you are quite pleased to be in London."

Katrine nodded enthusiastically. "It is marvelous," she said. "I have only been here a week and I cannot bear the thought of ever leaving again. There is so much to see. And the shops . . ."

"Perhaps we can throw a spoke in your brother's plans and have his bill delayed until you have enjoyed every last minute of the Season," Harry said with an impish grin.

"Could you do such a thing?" Katrine asked.

"My father could," Harry replied airily. "But that is neither here nor there. The first object is to widen your circle of acquaintances. Do you have any connections in town?"

Katrine shook her head. "Alasdair has a few friends . . ."

"Then you will come with me tomorrow when I pay my calls," Harry said with a decisive nod. "By the end of the week you shall have many new acquaintances. Things Scottish are all the rage; you will be quite the attraction. And we are having a gathering at the house next week— I shall send a card for you and your brother."

"You are too kind," Katrine said.

Harry laughed. "That is one of the few adjectives that is rarely applied to me. No, I assure you, Miss MacKyle, that kindness is not one of my better qualities. But I am, I confess, rather at loose ends these days, and am sadly in need of a diversion. London may look wonderful and exciting to you, but the excitement pales with time, I assure you. I was not certain how I was going to endure another Season."

"I cannot imagine being bored in London," Katrine said.

"I know, it is a sad reflection upon my character that I am, is it not?"

"I shall have to mark this down in my book," Tris said, roused from his silent contemplation of Miss MacKyle's charms. "Harry admits to having a fault."

"I never claimed to be faultless," Harry said archly. "But I hardly think that *you* are qualified to point out my character flaws, Tris."

"Do you live in London the year round?" Katrine asked, amused by their teasing banter.

"Heavens no," Harry said. "Only in the fall, for the Little Season, and the spring. We then rusticate at home in Kent, or traipse about the country visiting friends."

"Where is your home in Scotland?" Tris asked Katrine.

"In the Western Highlands," she replied. "I doubt you have heard of it. We are near the Isle of Skye."

"And do you reside there year round?" he asked.

"For the most part," she replied. "My brother prefers it. He is not fond of city life."

"I have never been to Scotland," Tris said. "I should like to see it sometime."

"Perhaps Father will hire you as estate manager," said Harry dryly, who had never hear Tris utter one word of interest in Scotland until this moment.

"Oh, does your family have property in Scotland?" Katrine asked.

"A few scattered acres," Harry replied. "I have never been there myself, either. Should I like it, do you think?"

To Katrine it was unimaginable that a lady such as Harriet Winterbourne could find anything in Scotland to enjoy. "It is very . . . scenic," she said.

"Perhaps I should ask your brother. He would probably give me a more glowing description." Harry smiled.

"That he would," Katrine said. "He would never set foot off the estate if he could help it. He loves tramping about the hills or sailing in the loch. I would not see him for days if there was not so much business to attend to."

"I am interested in meeting this outdoorsman," Harry said.

Katrine smiled weakly. She could only imagine Alasdair's reaction to Harriet Winterbourne. It would be a miracle if she could persuade him to attend their ball.

"I had planned to do some shopping today," Harry said. "Should you care to come along? Tris, I fear, will leave us as soon as we reach Piccadilly, but I think we can contrive to manage without his help." She nodded to Katrine's companion. "Mrs. Fraser may accompany us, if you would be more comfortable."

"I would like that very much," said Katrine. "Grant me a few moments to retrieve my bonnet and cloak. Mrs. Fraser, shall you join us?"

The lady nodded while she stowed her sewing in the voluminous bag at her feet. "Your brother would never forgive me if I allowed two young ladies to wander about London alone. Begging your pardon, Miss Winterbourne. Miss Katrine's brother is something strict."

"I quite understand," said Harry. "I am certain my

papa would rather I was better accompanied. Tris does have the annoying habit of abandoning me, even when he has promised to be my escort for the day."

Tris shot her a disparaging look.

Katrine and Mrs. Fraser went to gather their cloaks, leaving the two cousins alone.

"You did not tell me you planned to take Miss Mac-Kyle shopping with you," Tris complained.

"I did not think it was of concern to you," Harry said with a mischievous grin. "I know how much you detest shopping, Tris. I did not want to ruin your day."

"It is only shopping with *you* that I cannot abide," he said glumly.

"Ask her to drive in the park with you tomorrow," Harry suggested. "I am certain you shall enjoy that better."

"I will," said Tris with a decided air.

Katrine very much enjoyed her shopping expedition with Harriet, even though she found only a few things to purchase. It was enjoyable to go about with another young lady. She was in high spirits when Alasdair returned to the house in the late afternoon.

"Is it busy you are keeping yourself?" Alasdair asked, as he poured himself a glass of claret and settled comfortably in front of the fire.

Katrine nodded.

"And have you spent all our money yet?" he asked with a teasing look.

"Not quite," she replied. "But I am trying. Oh, Alasdair, I met the loveliest lady quite by accident at Hatchards yesterday. She paid me a call today and we went shopping. She says she will take me up with her tomorrow when she goes calling so I can meet some people."

Alasdair eyed her critically. "And what does Mrs. Fraser think of all this?"

"Oh, she was quite impressed—Harriet's father is in the government, you know. And we are to be invited to a party at her house next week."

"Oh, I quite forgot. Egerton is having a fete as well and has condescended to invite us. Tuesday, I believe."

Katrine's eyes gleamed. "Two parties in one week! Thank goodness my new dresses will be ready."

"Egerton has offered to introduce me about," Alasdair said reluctantly. "So I imagine there will be a few more invitations forthcoming. I anticipate you will be tolerably entertained."

"Did he know how long matters would take?" she asked with an apprehensive look.

Alasdair shook his head. "Parliament works to its own schedule. The bill could sit in committee for weeks. And once it is passed, it still must go to the Privy Council for approval. And then to the king."

"It sounds like it could take ages," Katrine said, her eyes dancing at the prospect of an entire spring in London.

"Which suits you," Alasdair teased. "By the time I get you home you will have forgotten you are even a Scottish miss."

"Oh, that I doubt," Katrine retorted. "Harriet said that things Scottish are all the rage now."

"Thanks to that infernal Walter Scott," Alasdair complained. "I imagine half of London expects to see us wrapped head to toe in plaid."

"Perhaps a cloak?" Katrine ventured timidly.

Alasdair gave her a despairing glance. "Next you will have me believe it is high fashion."

"Oh, but it is," Katrine protested. "You should have seen all the lovely plaid ribbons at the milliner's. There was one which looked so much like the Kintail . . ."

"At least you have a right to wear it," he said, "unlike all the Sassenach dandies who are merely bowing to the whims of fashion."

"Then I can have a cloak made in the plaid?" she asked eagerly. "It will be ever so warm on windy days."

"If you wish," he said, shaking his head at the thought.

"And a bonnet to match," Katrine mused, pretending not to see the look on her brother's face. She did not mind if her heritage was suddenly all the crack.

* * *

Katrine was delighted when Harriet arrived in the morning to take her up for the morning calls. She came in an elegant town barouche, which Katrine admired greatly. Alasdair had rented a carriage for them, but it was a rather plain thing, without any style.

"I have brought your invitation to our rout next week," Harry said as Katrine settled next to her on the seat. Mrs. Fraser looked across at them with a placid expression. "It is on Tuesday evening."

"Oh dear." Katrine's face reflected her disappointment. "We are promised to another party that evening. At Lord Egerton's."

Harry laughed. "My dear girl, Lord Egerton is my father."

Katrine stared at her wide-eyed. "He is?"

"I forget you do not know London society that well. I just assumed you knew who I was." Harry laughed again. "See how puffed up with my own consequence I have become?"

Katrine colored. "I am sorry—"

"I am not," Harry replied. "Well, I am glad there will be no conflict. Your brother will be attending as well?"

Katrine nodded. "Alasdair will be there." She was not at all certain what her brother would say when he discovered that Har—Lady Harriet—was Lord Egerton's daughter. It would be just like Alasdair to raise a fuss over the only friend Katrine had. She resolved not to tell her brother until it became absolutely necessary. Until the night of the party.

"I am curious to meet your brother," Harry said. "Are you two much alike?"

"Not at all," Katrine admitted. "Alasdair is much more concerned with managing the estate. He loves the country. While I would rather live in the city."

"You find London to your liking, then?"

"Oh, yes," Katrine said with an enthusiasm that brought a smile to Harry's face.

"I shall make certain, then, that your visit will be memorable," Harry promised. She looked up as the carriage slowed. "Here is our first stop. Lady Charlotte Deaning is a dreadful bore, I am afraid. But her mama is a great gossip. The news of your presence will be all over the *ton* by this evening."

Katrine was not altogether certain she wished to be so widely known. But she was far too polite to protest against Harry's plans. She obligingly followed her new friend into the house.

4

I pray, sir, tell me, is it possible
That love should of a sudden take such hold?

William Shakespeare,
The Taming of the Shrew

Katrine darted a quick glance at Alasdair, sitting stiffly beside her on the carriage seat. She prayed he would not make a scene when he discovered her little deception. She was not at all certain what he would say when he discovered Harry was Egerton's daughter. But Katrine did not allow her apprehensions to dim her anticipation of her first formal ball in London.

The Egerton house in Grosvenor Square blazed with lights, and more than one carriage waited in line to drop its occupants at the door. Katrine saw Alasdair's frown. Not for the first time did she wish she had a brother who entertained more interest in the social amenities. He would much rather be tromping around the estate in muddy work clothes. But she could not fault Alasdair. He worked hard to make the land profitable for themselves and their tenants. And he had brought her to London. She only hoped he would get some enjoyment from the visit.

Upon entering the hall, Katrine cast a quizzical glance at her brother, hoping to see some sign of reaction. But he took in the formal magnificence of the hall without a whisper of response. Twin staircases curved upward from the marble-tiled entry floor; the massive crystal chandelier that hung between them blazed with light. And to think Harry described the London house as a "rather paltry affair." Their country seat must truly be something to see.

When they reached the first-floor drawing room, Katrine anxiously scanned the crowd for a familiar face. Particularly Harry's. Or Tris's. She recognized one or two young ladies she thought she had met over the last few days, but their names eluded her. However was she to be introduced to any dancing partners if she did not know anyone here? With Alasdair himself knowing nary a soul, she could spend her entire evening standing beside him in silent isolation. Katrine nibbled her lower lip in vexation.

"I see Egerton," Alasdair whispered in her ear. "Let me make you known to him."

Katrine dutifully followed Alasdair as he threaded his way across the crowded room until they stood in front of Lady Harriet's powerful father.

"Egerton," Alasdair began, "I should like to introduce my sister, Katrine."

"It is my pleasure, my dear," the marquess said, taking her hand as she executed an elegant curtsey. "I understand you have already made the acquaintance of my daughter."

Alasdair shot a surprised glance at Katrine. She had said nothing to him about meeting Egerton's daughter.

"She has been most kindhearted," Katrine murmured.

"She and Mrs. Roberts have promised to take you under their wing tonight," Egerton continued. "I am certain your brother is anxious to be freed of the burden of sorting out all the eager young men who will wish to make your acquaintance."

Katrine blushed faintly at the compliment.

Egerton turned to Alasdair. "I trust you will not mind if my daughter's duenna performs the same service for your sister."

"Not at all," Alasdair said, pleased to know he would not have to keep Katrine under his watchful eye all evening. Nothing was more tedious than watching the young men vie for his sister's attention. The lady's assistance would free him to pursue his own ends.

"I believe they are in the dancing room," the marquess said, offering his arm to Katrine.

Alasdair fell in behind them, wondering why the marquess was being so helpful. Alasdair could view Egerton's assistance on the petition as a political matter. Yet this treatment of Katrine was clearly a personal favor. It drew him further into the debt of a man he did not want to like.

Egerton halted in front of a diminutive lady dressed in soft gray. "Mrs. Roberts, here is our Katrine MacKyle."

"I am pleased to meet you," Katrine said.

"It is kind of you to agree to look after my sister," Alasdair said.

Mrs. Roberts smiled gaily. "Think nothing of it. It is a delight to have another young lady to introduce into society. Lady Harriet no longer needs my guidance and I feel sadly unneeded."

Lady Harriet? The paragon about whom Katrine had talked incessantly for the last week was Egerton's daughter? Before he could question his sister, the marquess gestured for Alasdair to follow him into the card room.

"Oh, look, Tris, there is Katrine." Harry eagerly started across the floor at the end of their dance. "I am curious to meet her brother."

"I am not," Tris muttered under his breath as he followed Harry. Katrine had made her brother's views on the English—and Englishmen in particular—all too clear.

"Katrine, it is so marvelous to see you." Harry kissed her cheek, then stepped back to critically eye the younger girl's gown. "Very nice. And I like the flowers in your hair. They look so springlike—a welcome sight in March."

"Thank you," Katrine said, pleased her new dress met with Harry's approval.

"Is not your brother here?" Harry asked, looking at her with surprise.

"He is," Katrine replied, "but your father has already carried him off." She wrinkled her nose. "Business."

"How like Father," Harry commented dryly.

"You must let me be the first to solicit your hand for a dance," said Tris gallantly. "The quadrille is starting."

"A quadrille?" Katrine asked with a nervous smile. "I am not very skilled at that, I fear."

"Neither am I," Tris said with a grin. He held out his

arm. "Shall we create chaos upon the dance floor, my lady?"

Katrine giggled. "Certainly."

Harry absently watched their progress across the room. She was far more interested in Katrine's mysterious brother. "Did you meet Mr. MacKyle?" she asked Mrs. Roberts.

"A nicely mannered man," the matron replied primly.

Harry shot her a dubious look. "Why does that remark make me suspicious?" she asked. "Katrine tells me he is a saturnine soul."

"Quite stylishly dressed," Mrs. Roberts added with a nod of her head.

Harry sighed in exasperation. She would have to contrive a meeting with the man sometime tonight. Katrine's brother piqued her curiosity. He was a man uninterested in London society, who was content to remain in the country. An uncommon attitude. He might be a refreshing change from her usual acquaintances.

Hearing her name called, Harry turned and saw Lord Hanover coming toward her. She smiled brightly, but inwardly she sighed. Why could she not like Han more? He was handsome, rich, and heir to a dukedom. A lady should be flattered by his attentions. Why was she not?

"You are looking lovely tonight, as always, Harry," he said, bowing low over her head.

"And you look quite handsome yourself," she replied, surveying his well-favored form with approval.

Han gazed at the dancers. "Who is the young lady dancing with your cousin?"

"Katrine MacKyle. From Scotland. She is visiting London with her brother."

"You still have some dances free for me?" he asked. She nodded, handing him her card.

"A waltz? And the quadrille? And a—"

"Han . . ." She began warningly.

He smiled. "Three dances would scandalize the matrons, would they not? They would have the wedding planned before the musicians ended."

"I told you that I do not wish even to think about such a thing this early in the Season," she said, touching him lightly on the arm. "You may meet the woman of your dreams at a ball next week."

"I do not think that likely," he said with a quiet smile. "But I shall refrain from mentioning the matter again. For a time."

"Thank you," she said, and gave him her hand to lead her across the room to some waiting friends.

"You have spoken untruthfully to me, Miss MacKyle," Tris said as he stepped through the lively patterns of the dance.

"I have?"

"You said you were not very skilled at the steps of the quadrille. On the contrary, you dance it quite well."

Katrine smiled. "You flatter me, Mr. Winterbourne. I am much more accomplished at the reel."

"Alas, I do not think Harry thought to request one tonight. Perhaps you will honor me with the supper dance instead. I believe it is to be a waltz."

"That is most kind of you," Katrine said, struggling to contain her joy. Supper with Tris!

Then gloom descended upon her. Alasdair was sure to spot them. Whatever would he say? Katrine raised her chin defiantly. There was nothing unexceptionable about sharing supper with a personable young man. Alasdair could not expect her to starve, could he? Unless he could find her a Scotsman in London, she would have to associate with Englishmen. Even her brother could not be so unreasonable. After months in the Highlands of Scotland, she deserved a few weeks of enjoyment. She would not allow Alasdair to dampen her pleasure.

Confident Katrine would be properly chaperoned, Alasdair allowed Egerton to introduce him to selected guests. It was an inevitable part of promoting private legislation, he told himself, although he felt more as if he were riding into battle rather than merely chatting with government officials. One more necessary step to the achievement of his goal. Once he had the title back, he could go home to Scotland—forever.

Fastening an interested smile upon his face, Alasdair

trailed after Egerton, exchanging pleasantries with the men he met. He credited Egerton for his sincerity, for he made a special effort to bring Alasdair to the attention of Lord Eldon, the Lord Chancellor, and Lord Bathurst, one of the Cabinet Council. Those two men were key to the success of his petition. The conversations carefully skirted political topics, but Alasdair had no doubt the men were carefully evaluating him. He worked to be at his most gracious.

Realizing at last how long he had been gone from the ballroom, he excused himself from the knot of Parliamentarians and threaded his way back to where he had left Katrine. He wanted to make it clear to everyone that her brother kept a watchful eye. He did not trust these English libertines.

He spotted Mrs. Roberts seated at the side of the room, chatting amiably with an elderly matron. He made his way to her side.

"Mrs. Roberts." He bowed in acknowledgment.

"Your sister is doing quite well, Mr. MacKyle," Mrs. Roberts said. "I believe she is dancing with young Tewksbury at the moment. She has barely had a moment to catch her breath since you left."

"She will appreciate the supper break, then," he said, intending to take Katrine down himself.

Harry, chatting sweetly with her dancing partner, Lord Taine, glanced in Mrs. Roberts's direction and nearly stumbled over his feet in surprise. The man from the park! She could not mistake the dark hair, those piercing eyes—and that imperious mien. Her heart beat quicker at the sight. How fortuitous that he should be a guest here tonight. She had looked for him every place she went, and had begun to despair of seeing him again. No matter how indecorous, she would have to contrive a meeting. She prayed the music would end quickly so she could hasten to Mrs. Roberts's side.

Harry virtually left poor Lord Taine standing upon the floor the moment the music stopped. Willing her racing heart to still, she strove to compose herself before she reached Mrs. Roberts. Harry smiled winsomely at the strange man, and gave her chaperon an expectant look.

"Harriet, dear, here is someone I know you wish to meet." Mrs. Roberts smiled smugly. "Mr. MacKyle, Lady Harriet Winterbourne. Lord Egerton's daughter."

Harry could not say which of them was more surprised. This magnificent man did not fit Katrine's description of her older brother. Far from appearing the bucolic farmer, he was stunningly attractive in his formal attire. His well-fitting clothing looked elegantly fashionable and skilfully tailored. This Scotsman was quite one of the handsomest men she had ever met. Her gaze locked on those magnificent dark brown eyes.

"Lady Harriet." Alasdair bowed politely.

Embarrassed by her obvious discomposure, Harry belatedly extended her hand. "It is a pleasure to meet you, Mr. MacKyle. Your sister speaks highly of you."

"Yes, I understand you have made her acquaintance," he said with distant politeness. "I thank you for the interest you have shown in her."

"It is no more than the courtesy my father is extending to you," she replied, noting the faint accent to his English. "How are you finding your stay in London?" she asked quickly, hoping to divert him long enough to more closely take his measure.

"Highly enlightening," he said. "There is no other city in the world like it."

"Oh?" she asked, with a hint of amusement. "Have you traveled much, then?"

"Enough to make such a comparison," he said. His eyes quickly scanned the room, then he bowed again. "If you will excuse me, Lady Harriet, I need to find my sister in order to take her to supper."

"I believe she has already promised that honor to my cousin," Harry said. She took a step toward him. "If you would care to escort me, Mr. MacKyle, we can join them."

Harry saw the initial surprise in his eyes fade into a glint of what looked to be amusement.

"It would be an honor to take you to supper, my lady." He extended his arm.

Harry placed her gloved hand lightly on his arm, almost afraid of her reaction to physical contact. She felt the rigidity of his muscles beneath her fingers and realized he was as nervous as she. Interesting.

While diminutive had never been a word applied to her stature, it was exactly how Harry felt alongside this towering Scotsman. She should have guessed he would be so tall, judging from the horse he rode in the park that day. Harry liked tall men.

She espied Tris as soon as she entered the supper room, and led Alasdair to the table. "I have found your brother, as you see," she said to Katrine, who looked to be doing her best to hide her dismay at the sight of him. "Mr. MacKyle, my cousin, Tristan Winterbourne." The two men nodded briefly, then Harry turned to MacKyle. "I am quite partial to lobster patties, sir. And a glass of champagne, if you please."

Alasdair nodded at her command. After seating her, he walked toward the serving tables.

"I must own, Katrine," said Harry with a mischievous smile, "I was thoroughly shocked when I met your brother."

"You were?" Katrine gazed at her with dismay.

Harry laughed. "Yes, indeed. He is not at all what I expected. I had imagined a rather fusty man with ill-fitting clothes and a distinct paunch. You thoroughly deceived me on that matter."

"He *is* fusty," Katrine said defensively. "And I certainly think thirty is quite old."

Even Tris laughed at that. "We men do age less graciously than the ladies."

"You begin to make me feel positively ancient," Harry complained with a teasing smile.

Katrine colored. "I did not mean—"

"Alas, I am well aware that at two-and-twenty I am well on the way to being in my dotage," Harry said with a dramatic air. "It will only be a matter of time before I shall need an ear trumpet and a bath chair."

"You are getting rather long in the tooth," Tris teased.

Harry shot him a baleful glance. "One year makes little difference, coz. And as you said, men age less graciously. Why, you are surely the equivalent of a lady of seven-and-twenty at least. Nearly middle-aged, according to Katrine."

They all laughed.

"Here you are, Lady Harriet," Alasdair announced as he set plates and glasses on the table. "I hope my selection is to your liking."

"Thank you," Harry replied, barely glancing at her plate. "We were just discussing whether men or women grow old more quickly. Tris has totally contradicted himself by accusing me of being ancient, as I am one year his elder, then claiming men grow old faster than women. Which view do you take, Mr. MacKyle?"

"It is a matter that, I assure you, will be of less concern once you leave your youth," he said with a dampening look.

Harry bridled at his words. According to his sister, he was merely eight years older—what right did he have to call her a child? For that was what he certainly had done. There was a world of experience—and four years—between her and Katrine. It would be well for him to remember that in the future.

"I think that men grow older faster, at least in their attitudes," she said with a devilish gleam in her eyes. "It seems that once they reach the hallowed age of five-and-twenty, they become positively set in their ways." She smiled across the table at Tris. "At least there is still hope for you, coz." She sat back in her chair and took a sip of champagne, confident she had properly chastened Mr. MacKyle for his impertinence.

Pointedly ignoring Lady Harriet, Alasdair turned toward Katrine. "Is it enjoying yourself you are, *a phiuthar bheag*?"

"Oh, yes," Katrine said. "I have danced nearly every set and met ever so many people." She smiled shyly at Tris. "Lady Harriet and Mr. Winterbourne have been ever so kind to introduce me to their friends."

"How thoughtful," Alasdair said.

"Is *phiuthar bheag* your pet name for Katrine?" Harry asked. She was not accustomed to being ignored by any man. Particularly one in whom she was interested.

"It means 'little sister' in Gaelic," Katrine explained quickly.

Harry cast a curious glance at Alasdair. "Do you speak the language?"

"Yes."

"Say something else for us," she requested.

Alasdair fixed her with an unfathomable expression. "What would you have me say, Lady Harriet? That your eyes are like sapphires? Or your hair like golden wheat?"

Harry laughed. "Nothing so grand, if you please. How about 'good day' or 'how are you?' "

"Latha math," he said. *"Ciamar a tha thu an diugh?"*

"And what do I reply?" she asked with a smile.

"That depends on how you are feeling tonight, Lady Harriet," he explained.

"Oh, I am feeling very well," she replied with a smile.

"Tha mi gu math, tapadh leat," Alasdair said with slow deliberation.

"Ha mi gu ma, tapa lat," she repeated. "Is that right?"

"Very nice," said Katrine. "We shall have you talking like a Higlander shortly."

"I fear that would take more time than either of you has," Harry said ruefully. "My governess always despaired that I did not have an affinity for languages."

"You need not worry, Lady Harriet," said Alasdair with a short laugh. "I doubt you will have much need of the Gaelic."

"How is it that you are so fluent?" Harry asked. She watched his eyes darken.

"Gaelic is the language of my countrymen," he said.

"It must be an asset when talking with your tenants," she said. "Was it difficult to learn?"

"Not if it is the only language you are exposed to as a child."

"Oh," Harry replied, looking at him with increased curiosity. "I understand you are here to promote some private-bill legislation. Are you having any success?"

"It is too early to say," Alasdair replied. "Your father is optimistic, however."

"Alasdair is trying to get the family's title restored,"

Katrine explained. "Our grandfather supported the Stuart cause."

"Oh, you are a Jacobite, then?" Harry asked.

"The Stuarts did our family and our country much damage," Alasdair said with a pained expression. "I merely wish to regain that which belongs to our family."

"I wish you success of your venture," Harry said. "I will make certain my father gives it his utmost attention."

"Will not the dancing be starting again soon?" Katrine asked.

Alasdair smiled at his sister. "You do not want to miss a minute of it, do you?" He stood and bowed to Lady Harriet. "I thank you for the opportunity of sharing supper, my lady." He nodded to Tris. "Come, Katrine, I shall take you back to the dancing."

Harry watched them depart, a puzzled expression on her face. She stared at the untouched lobster patties on her plate. She had been much too interested in studying Katrine's brother to eat. With a sigh she turned to Tris. "An enigmatic man, is he not?"

"He is rather odd," Tris agreed. "No wonder Ka—Miss MacKyle is so thrilled to be in the city if she is shut up in the same house with him."

"Yes," Harry repeated, as if to herself. "A most interesting man. An acquaintance I should like to pursue, I think." For despite his polite words, she had the dampening feeling that he had been laughing at her the entire time. She wished to know why.

During the return trip to Upper Berkley Street, Katrine sat gingerly on the carriage seat, half dreading what her brother would say now that they were alone. After that awkward supper, he had behaved in a most pleasing manner with the people he met. He had even danced with her. She had been surprised at how late he allowed her to stay. Was he actually enjoying himself?

But now they were on their way home, and she anticipated a tirade on the character of Lady Harriet, her cousin, or both.

Yet his continued silence was even more ominous.

"Was the evening helpful to you?" she asked at last.

"I expect so," he said. "Egerton introduced me around and I talked with a few Privy Council members. But there is still a great deal more to be done. Clubs to join, societies to patronize, connections to make. It is all highly ridiculous."

"What societies did Lord Egerton think you should patronize?"

"Anything with a whiff of Scotland," he replied with a rueful shake of his head. "The Scottish Hospital, to show my interest in the less fortunate, the Caledonian Society, the Highland Society . . . The list is endless."

"You will be far too busy to escort me to any more assemblies," Katrine teased, hoping to lighten his mood.

"Never fear, I shall find time somewhere for that," he said. "We do not need to be more beholden to the Egertons than we already are."

"I do not think Mrs. Roberts minded," Katrine said. "She positively delighted in introducing me to people."

"Do not allow your enthusiasm to carry you away," he cautioned her. "We will probably not often be moving in such elevated company."

"I am certain everything will be enjoyable," she said, directing her gaze out the window. She could be grateful he had not said anything more about the Winterbourne cousins. From the way Alasdair had glared at Tris and snapped at Harry during dinner, she had feared he would encourage her to cut the connection.

But that, she reminded herself, was absurd. Alasdair was no fool. He could not afford to antagonize Lord Egerton. Which meant he would not dare come between Katrine and her new friends. With a smug smile she rested her head against the cushion, closing her eyes and reliving that wonderful supper waltz.

Harry lay awake long after the last guest had departed the Grosvenor Square mansion. It had been a most disturbing evening. All because of one provoking Scotsman. Alasdair. That was his name. The Scottish version of "Alexander," Katrine had said.

It had certainly been a new experience for Harry to be virtually ignored by a handsome gentleman. It had the ridiculous effect of piquing her interest in him. What would it take to make him look at her with the worshipful, adoring expression of all the other gentlemen of her acquaintance? It could be quite a challenge to elicit that response from him.

But she had not been the toast of four Seasons for nothing. If any woman knew the powerful effect of a smile, a word of praise, a nod of interest, it was she. She had been managing men for years—first her father, then Tris, then her many admirers. One rather puzzling Scotsman would prove no more impervious to her skills in the end. It would give her a rather large mote of satisfaction to wipe that smug condescension off his face. She would have the amusement of bringing that handsome Scotsman to heel, and he would go home with a little more respect for the powers of Englishwomen.

It was precisely his lack of interest that caused her pulse to race and her heart to pound every time she pictured his handsome countenance. Tris would jokingly accuse her of being in love, which was absurd. One did not fall in love with a man at first sight—or second sight, if one added that encounter in the park. And particularly not with one as prickly as Katrine's brother.

Yes, he was different from the usual run of town gentlemen, to be sure, but that mattered little. Certainly, he was handsome, well-dressed, and of trim physique, but so were a dozen other men of her acquaintance. Those compelling brown eyes were in no way unique. She needed both hands to count the number of men with his height. There was absolutely nothing to make him stand out from all the other men she had met and flirted with over the years.

Then why was his face so difficult to clear from her mind?

5

Let the maids of the Lowlands
Vaunt their silk and their hollands,
In the garb of the Highlands
  O give me my dear!

  William Ross,
  The Highland Maid

Alasdair guided his horse through the deserted park. The early-morning mist turned the trees lining the pathway into eerie, ghostly shapes. The stifling dampness muffled all sounds from the surrounding metropolis, and it was almost possible to imagine he was back in the Highlands. But memories of the previous evening intruded on his mind, firmly reminding him that he was in London.

It had been a surprise to find out that Katrine's new friend—Lady Harriet—was none other than Egerton's daughter. His own reaction to her had been an even worse shock. There had been no mistaking the initial attraction he felt—until he discovered who she was. Then attraction had turned into dismay.

It was a ticklishly awkward situation—a *gnothuch cio-gailteach*. He dare not offend the Egerton family; the marquess's support was critical for the success of his petition. Yet Alasdair wanted nothing to do with Lady Harriet. Even if her appearance was stunning, he judged she was the type who would wield her beauty like a weapon. Egerton himself had admitted she was spoiled—the only daughter of a doting father. Had she not proved it by her shameless flirting last night?

Alasdair thought he had judged her well on first sight. He recognized her as the woman from the park, who had perused him so brazenly that morning. He was convinced there had been a coldly assessing look in her eye then, as there had been last night. She was measuring him, wanting to determine if he was of any value to her. He was certain she would decide he was not. He did not want the responsibility of having to dampen her pretensions.

Englishwomen, with their bold and brassy manners, held little interest for him. Her very forwardness in suggesting he escort her to supper had only reinforced that view. In fact, had it been any other woman, he would have been highly amused at her attempts to set out lures. But because she was Egerton's daughter, he must grit his teeth and behave with excruciating politeness to Lady Harriet.

Deep in his heart, he had a foreboding about her that was all out of proportion to their short acquaintance. The very fact that her face and form haunted him throughout this ride was a disturbing sign. Certainly no other woman had discomfited him like this on such short acquaintance.

She inspired a dangerous mixture of desire and apprehension in him. The first he could control. The second was more difficult. He had come dangerously close to flaring at her in anger last night when she treated him like some nine days' wonder. For a moment he had truly wanted to knock her off her pedestal of privilege. Then reason prevailed.

It was odd to be so affected by a woman. Normally, they usually inspired little emotion in him. Occupied with his relentless pursuit of the title and his work on the estate, he had no time for dallying with the fairer sex. He never had the urge to lash out at one in anger as he had at Lady Harriet. He had wanted to tell her that while she dined on lobster and champagne, people were starving on her father's land. That families who had spent generations in the Highlands were being uprooted in favor of animals.

But what would she care, the daughter of privilege? As long as her pleasure remained unaffected, he knew she would pay little heed to the plight of others. Her wealth insulated her from worry. She could flit from ball to ball, dripping in jewels and costly silks, marry an equally blind aristocrat, raise suitably blinded children, and never know a thing about the world around her.

Unless someone showed her.

Alasdair shook his head at the absurdity of his thought. She would not wish to be bothered. There were far more important things to concern her—routs and Venetian breakfasts, the theater and the opera. A woman like Lady Harriet would not wish to have her perfect world show the slightest bit of tarnish.

He eyed his surroundings with a deepening frown. This damnable city. He hated it with every fiber of his body, yet he had no choice but to remain while his petition was carefully shepherded through Parliament on its way to the king. Everything that reminded him of the task felt his displeasure—Lady Harriet included.

With a muttered oath at the amount of time he had wasted thinking about that inconsequential woman, Alasdair spurred his horse forward into a breath-snatching gallop. He had to cleanse his head of thoughts of that lady.

Katrine was delighted with the deluge of invitations and visitors that followed her introduction to the *ton*. Each post brought the promise of new delights, and Alasdair positively tripped over Katrine's guests every time he ventured into the drawing room. Mrs. Fraser beamed like a proud mother at her charge's success, but Alasdair was not so certain he liked this turn of events.

"Is every idiot Englishman visiting our house?" he demanded of Katrine after the day's guests had departed. To his relief, that blasted Winterbourne cousin had been nowhere in evidence on this occasion.

"Only some," she replied.

"What about that creature in the pink waistcoat?" Alasdair shuddered at the memory. "How could anyone think an *easbalair* like that is any match for a true man like Robbie Ferguson?"

"Give me credit for *some* sense, Alasdair," Katrine protested. "Even I can see there is no comparison. But Mr. Lawford is amusing, nonetheless."

"I would think it easier to find amusement in London than in your own home," he said. "You are out every afternoon—is that not enough? You must have visited every sight in town."

"But there is so much to see! Today we are going to view the exhibit of the Laplanders and their reindeer at the Egyptian Hall."

"Fascinating," Alasdair drawled. He did not want to ask who her escort was—no doubt Tristan Winterbourne. He was beginning to have concerns about that relationship. Katrine spent far too much time in his presence, even if Lady Harriet usually accompanied them. It was fast approaching time that he spoke with his sister.

"Lady Harriet has asked us to accompany her to the theater on Saturday," Katrine said with an off-hand air.

Alasdair was not particularly interested in seeing Lady Harriet again. "Do you not feel you have spent enough time with Lady Harriet this week?" he asked. "She will soon grow weary of your company at this rate."

"It was Harry who extended the invitation," Katrine replied. "You are certainly free to decline if you wish. I can attend without you."

"I think not," he said.

"Alasdair, just because you resent having to deal with her father is no reason for you to insist I ignore Harry. She is my friend."

"And have you ever given a thought as to why Lady Harriet Winterbourne, the toast of London, the daughter of one of the leading lords of the land, is interested in a friendship with the granddaughter of an attainted lord from Scotland?"

"Because she is tired of London society," Katrine replied. "And the other young ladies resent her, because all the men favor her."

"Why has she not wed one of them, then?"

"Lady Harriet is waiting for *true love*," Katrine told him.

Alasdair laughed. "If she told you that, she is even more of a fool than I thought. True love indeed. More likely she is waiting for the largest purse."

"She has no need for that, Alasdair," Katrine said smugly. "Lord Egerton is quite rich, you know. I am surprised you have not considered courting her. I imagine her dowry would go far in restoring the estate and providing work for the cottagers."

"I will move the entire estate, rock by rock, to Upper Canada before I would take a Sassenach bride," he retorted. "I think the foul air in the city has touched your brain, Katrine,"

"No more than it has yours," she said, pouting. "You are determined to have a miserable time, and so you shall. But I do not think it fair that you insist I be miserable with you."

Alasdair threw up his hands. "Fine. Accompany Lady Harriet about like a tame lapdog. Do as you wish. But do not be surprised if she drops you like a hot brick the moment some other whim catches her fancy."

Katrine closed her lips in a thin line. "I shall tell Lady Harriet that you will not be free for the theater on Saturday," she said stiffly.

"On the contrary," he said. "I shall be certain to accompany you."

Katrine glared at him angrily as she stalked out of the room.

Alasdair stared glumly at the toes of his boots, knowing he had once again alienated his sister. He was deeply troubled by this unusual friendship between Katrine and Egerton's daughter. Katrine was young and impressionable, and spending so much of her time in the company of one of London's belles could only be to her detriment. After experiencing the delights of London, would Katrine ever be content in Scotland? The innocuous visit to the city he had planned for her was being rapidly undermined by those blasted Winterbournes.

He was half tempted to talk to the lady himself, to ask her to cut the connection with Katrine, for his sister's sake. But he was strangely reluctant to initiate a conversation with Lady Harriet. Despite his best intentions, he had not been able to get the English beauty out of his mind. If he did not know himself better, he could almost believe he was infatuated with her. The thought, of course, was highly absurd.

He did not want to spend an evening with her at the theater, sitting in the close confines of the elegant Egerton box. He much preferred a crowded assembly, or a rout, where only the most commonplace pleasantries could be exchanged. At the theater he would cause talk if he was not properly attentive. It was too *intimate* an evening to spend with a woman who disordered him so.

He reminded himself firmly that he was here to regain the title, and he must pay attention to the social amenities. Let Lady Harriet flirt with him all she wished— he would remain impervious to her wiles. If he had to accompany her to the theater, he would. Surely his business here would not take more than a month—two at worst—and he and Katrine could leave London. They would return to Scotland, where they belonged, and they would never see Lady Harriet again.

Harry found herself looking forward to the evening at the theater with more than usual anticipation. She hoped Mr. MacKyle would be well-pleased with her efforts. Harry had been on nervous edge ever since he and Katrine accepted the invitation.

Once again, she had ridden every morning in the park in the days after the rout, hoping to encounter the elusive Scotsman. But Mr. MacKyle had not appeared. Nor was he present when she paid her calls on Katrine, or accompanied her shopping or to the lending library. If Harry had not known better, she would have sworn he was not even in London. It was obvious she needed to adopt a more direct method of furthering their acquaintance. Hence the trip to the theater. He would be quite unable to avoid her there.

It was odd how the thought of him crept up on her at such unexpected times. She could recall his every expression: his daunting frowns, and the faint smile that brought an mused glint to his dark eyes. If she were a foolish miss in her first Season, Harry would imagine herself in the throes of an infatuation, but she was far beyond such silliness. Alasdair MacKyle piqued her curiosity, nothing more.

It would be interesting to discover what he thought of the planned entertainment. She smiled in anticipation as she fastened her sapphire ear drops. Perhaps tonight the icy Scotsman would begin to thaw.

"What are we to see tonight?" Katrine asked her hostess. The four were settled comfortably in the Egerton town carriage, on their way to Covent Garden.

Harry shot an arch look at Alasdair. "An entertainment I thought you should particularly enjoy, Mr. MacKyle. *Rob Roy Macgregor.*"

"How clever of you, Lady Harriet," Alasdair said in a cool tone. "I find Walter Scott's works highly entertaining."

Harry realized with a sinking sensation that he thought no such thing, and all her carefully constructed plans fell into a heap around her. She had thought an evening devoted to his homeland would give him inordinate pleasure. What a perplexing man!

"I think it will be wonderful," Katrine said, filling the awkward silence. "I have heard such marvelous things about the London theaters."

"We shall have to see that you visit them all while you are here," Tris said eagerly.

"I should like that above all things," said Katrine with a shy smile.

In the dim carriage interior, Harry saw Katrine's brother frown. Did he dislike all theater? Was he one of those strict Scot Presbyterians who thought the theater was the devil's own work? But surely he would not have consented to this evening unless he approved. Maybe, like many men, he simply could not abide the theater. Although after spending months in the isolation of the Highlands, she thought he would appreciate any pleasant diversion. What exactly would it take to bring a smile of pleasure to Alasdair MacKyle?

Alasdair watched Katrine's wide-eyed gaze take in the delights of Covent Garden from their vantage point in the Egerton box.

"This is beyond belief!" she exclaimed, marveling at the opulence that surrounded her. "I have never seen such elegant appointments."

Alasdair glanced around. Four tiers of boxes rose on either side of the oval pit, curving at the top toward the gilded ceiling. An enormous chandelier hung from the center, its two circles of gaslights illuminating the entire auditorium. The Egerton box was separated from its neighbors with a floor-to-ceiling partition, providing an illusion of privacy in the enormous theater. He had to admit it put Edinburgh's main theater to shame.

While Katrine and Tris chatted eagerly about the theater, Alasdair seated Lady Harriet.

"Do sit, Mr. MacKyle," she said, indicating the chair beside her. "I have a feeling you are not fond of theater. I am sorry to have forced you to attend."

"I am rarely forced to do anything I do not wish," he said, taking his seat.

"Except come to London when you would much rather be back in Scotland?"

"Estates do not run themselves," he explained. "Spring is a critical time."

"Is not your steward competent?" she asked.

"More than competent," he said. "But . . ."

"You cannot stand not being there yourself to oversee each and every last detail." She supplied the words. "Katrine has told me much about you."

"Katrine has yet to learn the value of judicious silence," he said with a wry grin.

"She is merely eighteen." Harry cautioned him. "Do not dampen all her high spirits before she has had a chance to enjoy them."

"She will have plenty of time to enjoy them once she is wed," he said succinctly.

"Is she betrothed?" Harry asked in some surprise.

"Nearly."

"Does she wish to marry the young man *you* have chosen for her?" she asked coldly.

"Do not think I would force her into a distasteful alliance," he said, a note of protest in his voice. "Katrine is free to make her own choice."

"As long as he is not English," Harry said.

"I feel she would be happiest with a man from her own country," Alasdair said, casting a stern glance at the whispering couple beside them. "A matter your cousin should be apprised of."

Harry laughed. "Tris is a bit of a flirt, but I assure you, Mr. Mackyle, that he is in no way eager to wed at one-and-twenty. Katrine is quite safe with him."

If Tristan Winterbourne was any bit as accomplished at flirting as Lady Harriet, Alasdair did not trust her reassurances. He had seen the way the lad stared at Katrine in a seemingly love-struck daze.

"It seems to me that you are the one who should be looking to wed," Harry said, rather surprised by her own boldness. "When you lose Katrine, who will keep house for you?"

"My staff is competent."

"Yes, but it has been my experience that it takes a lady's attention to detail to make things runs smoothly," she said.

"Your great experience?" he asked. What did this spoiled daughter of privilege know about responsibility and work?

She flushed. "My mother died when I was twelve, sir. I took on as many of her duties as I could. I run both the London house and Highbury."

"I am sorry, Lady Harriet," said Alasdair, glancing at her in surprise. Her words brought back the memory of his own grief at the death of his mother. The thought that they shared that experience made him uncomfortable. He did not want to share anything with Lady Harriet. "I am certain you run your father's house well," he said abruptly.

The beginning of the play forced them into silence, for which Alasdair was grateful. He was more ill at ease with Lady Harriet than ever. He did not want to look upon her kindly, yet he found himself wondering if he had been overly hasty in his judgment of her. He suspected she was an incorrigible flirt, but she was also intelligent. He could not deny her beauty. A dangerous combination.

But he could not forget that she was Egerton's daughter. There were far too many complications with that relationship to make him feel any sort of comfort in her presence. Once again Alasdair wished he was back in Scotland instead of the treacherous depths of London. He understood himself at home.

Harry and Tris both urged the MacKyles to accompany them to Lady Waterton's rout after the evening at the theater, but Alasdair was adamant. He and Katrine would go home. Harry swallowed her disappointment and bade them both a good evening, promising to call on Katrine on the morrow.

The evening had not been a total disaster, she reflected in the safe darkness of the carriage, but it was not far short of it. Tris and Katrine had, of course, been oblivious to the situation between herself and Mr. MacKyle. However, she could not shake the feeling that he had taken her in instant aversion from the moment he laid eyes on her in the park, and she truly could not understand why.

His behavior was most provoking. She had invited him to a play about Scotland, thinking it would be a pleasure, and he had been less than grateful. She had gone out of her way to be charming and witty this night, to no avail.

She was not so puffed up in her consequence to think that every man adored her, but it was a very new experience to find someone who was so impervious to her charms. It was of little matter of her—he need not be included in any future invitations she extended to Katrine. Harry was not about to waste her time entertaining a man who did not wish to be entertained. Lord Hanover was a much more amenable companion.

But as hard as she tried, she could not get Alasdair MacKyle out of her mind. He was so alarmingly different from any other male she had known—unimpressed by the wealth and importance of her family, scornful of her place in society, and disparaging of the very society she belonged to. He was an aloof, withdrawn Scotsman who probably deserved to be banished to his faraway estate, where he could romp about the barren hills and frolic in his stupid loch. She hoped the house was freezing cold in the winter, and no warmer in the summer.

She giggled. Perhaps that was his problem—he was as frozen as the Scottish weather. Was it possible to unthaw one such as he? Her lips curved into a sly smile. It was increasingly clear that it would be quite a challenge. But one she thought she would win.

6

Every day English vile
In our ears a long while!
From our sires 'twas our style
    To speak the tongue of the Gael.

Alasdair Macdonald,
A Birth Place Song

"It all looks so . . . peaceful," Katrine said as she surveyed the inner yard of the Tower.

"It is almost hard to believe that so many people lost their heads right over there," Tris said, pointing to Tower Green. "Cannot you imagine the tension that ran through the crowd as they watched the person mount the scaffold, knowing such a one only had but a few more minutes—"

"Tris!"

He stared into Katrine's white face and suddenly remembered her family history. "Oh, my Lord, I did not mean . . . ! Was your grandfather . . . ?"

Katrine smiled weakly. "My grandfather escaped to Belgium and lived to the ripe age of five-and-eighty," she said. "I only thought about those poor ladies, Queen Anne and Queen Catherine. . . . What a monster the king was!"

"I imagine George only wished he still had such power," Tris said dryly. "He would not have minded disposing of the late queen in such a manner."

Katrine grimaced. "Let us look at something less gruesome," she said.

Tris glanced at Harry and Lord Hanover, who were deep in conversation. Deciding not to interrupt them, he obligingly led Katrine to the Jewel Office. He paid the required fee and soon Katrine was gazing with awed wonder at the gem-encrusted coronation crown and the other regalia. The State Sword, made especially for the new king's coronation, with its ornamentation of a rose, thistle, and shamrock, dazzled their eyes.

"How I should have liked to see the coronation," Katrine said. "Did you go?"

Tris shook his head. "Take it from my uncle, it was a dry, dull affair."

"Even if George is not the most decorous monarch, still, he *is* the king," she said wistfully. "I am afraid I will expire from excitement next week when I am presented."

"Another dull and boring affair," Tris assured her.

"You sound as bad as Alasdair," she complained. "He is attending the Levee tomorrow and all he can do is complain about it."

"With good reason," Tris said, shuddering at the memory of his own presentation. "All the bother of court dress, in order to stand in line for hours, in return for less than a minute with the king. Once was enough for me." Katrine's crestfallen expression warned him of his error. "That is not to mean you will not enjoy *your* presentation," he said quickly. "It will be different for you. Ladies like that kind of thing."

"I am sure I shall," said Katrine saucily.

"Shall we go view the Menagerie?" Tris suggested, hoping to redeem himself in her eyes. Katrine nodded.

"Where have you been?" Harry demanded when they returned to the yard.

"We went to look at the jewels," said Tris defensively.

"Kindly tell me when you are going to run off," said Harry with exasperation. "I thought you had left."

"I would not do that," Tris protested. "Katrine would not have a chaperon."

"May we look at the animals?" Katrine asked hopefully, wanting to avoid an argument between the cousins. Harry should know she was perfectly safe with Tris.

Tris nodded and took her arm. They followed Harry and Lord Hanover toward the Lion Tower. The Menagerie was a disappointment to Katrine, however. "The poor animals look so forlorn," she said.

"Not to mention that they smell," said Tris, wrinkling

his nose. "Why, the pig sty at the house in Kent is more elegant than this."

Katrine giggled. "This smells worse than the seaweed when it is drying in the fields on a hot summer's day."

"Does that smell?" he asked.

Katrine pinched her nose. "Dreadfully."

"Why do you dry seaweed?" he asked as they quickly left the Menagerie. They exited the Tower and strolled along the edge of the moat.

"For fertilizer," she explained. "It was one of our better crops—until the prices dropped. But oh, how it smells!"

"How terrible that your gentle nose was exposed to such an offensive odor," he said gallantly, chagrined that their visit to the Tower had not gone well. He would send her a bouquet of fragrant flowers to atone for his error. And they could take a drive through the park before he took her home. Harry would certainly agree to that.

Alasdair returned the next day from the Levee at the Palace in Pall Mall with a fearful headache. The interminable wait for his presentation, and the obsequious words he spoke to the king, had not sat easy with him. Yet it was all part of the game he must play to foster his petition.

He shuddered at the remembered image of the king, his fat, beringed hand pale and clammy as he extended it to Alasdair. Groveling before an English king was not Alasdair's idea of a welcome experience. Yet he had smiled and looked appropriately grateful at the great honor extended him. Anything to regain the title.

Mo Dhia, he hated this city. The interminable social games sapped one's energy and no amount of rides in the city parks could provide the country exercise he preferred. Even on Hampstead Heath one could not escape the teeming metropolis in the distance. He would not be comfortable until he was home again.

"Alasdair?" Katrine's voice drifted in from the hall.

"I am here," he replied.

Katrine entered the library. "How did you find the

Levee? What did he say to you? Does he look enormously fat?"

"Boring, very little, and yes."

"Alasdair," she chided. "Do tell me. My presentation is next week and I simply must know what it will be like. I am already in a quake."

"A dead bore," he elaborated. "You will stand in line for endless hours waiting for your few seconds in the presence of the great one. It took an hour alone just to get out of the carriage."

"At least I do not have to wear hoops," she said with a giggle. "Harry had to wear them for her presentation and she said they made her feel like a rather large balloon. You had to practice wearing them for days to learn how to walk, and trembled in the greatest fear that you would trip on your way to the king. It is ghastly enough having to deal with that train."

"I doubt tripping over it will cause social ruin," he said.

"How like a man to say such a thing! You have no idea how important this is, Alasdair. I am to be presented to the king! Do you think the *Chronicle* will describe my gown?"

"Undoubtedly," he replied.

"I do wish the Drawing Room was to be at St. James instead of Buckingham House," she said. "Is the interior lovely?"

"Unimpressive."

"Oh, Alasdair." She scowled. "I refuse to allow you to ruin the occasion for me." She plopped down onto the sofa, glancing at him with a speculative look. "Were you wishful of attending Lady Wentworth's rout?"

"When?" he asked wearily.

"Wednesday next," she replied. "I should very much like to go, but Harry said I could go with her if you did not wish to go."

Did his sister ever go anywhere without her Winterbourne escorts? "I should be delighted to attend," he said.

"Oh, good." Katrine smiled. "I shall tell Harry we will accompany her."

"I will escort you myself," he said distinctly. She had been spending far too much time with Tristan Winterbourne. It was time he looked into the matter more closely.

"But why—?"

"I am capable of escorting my sister to a rout," he said. "Surely you are desirous of my company, or you would not have asked me to go."

Katrine frowned but did not argue.

Harry was quite pleased to discover Alasdair had escorted Katrine to the party at Lady Wentworth's. She had not yet been able to contrive a reasonable excuse to see him again. That awkward trip to the theater had shown her the folly of extending personal invitations to him. In the future, she would have to devise a way to converse with him in a more public setting. Like tonight. He would be less wary, less guarded. Perhaps she could get a glimpse behind his impassive facade.

She casually touched Lord Hanover's arm. "Come, Han. There is someone I should like you to meet." She guided him across the floor to where Alasdair stood, looking at the dancers with a disinterested expression on his face.

"Mr. MacKyle, I should like to introduce my friend, Lord Hanover. Alasdair MacKyle. A true Highlander."

"Pleased," said Lord Hanover politely. "Think I saw you at White's last week with Egerton. Planning to become a member?"

"Lord Egerton is assisting me with the passage of some legislation," Alasdair said, then remembered Egerton's suggestion. "I have some hopes of joining."

"Good, good," said Lord Hanover, darting a puzzled glance at Harry. She smiled encouragingly at him. "Be my guest on Tuesday evening. I can introduce you to some fine fellows."

"That is generous of you," Alasdair replied.

Harry lay her hand on Lord Hanover's arm. "Han, I hear the music starting again. You will excuse us? I have promised this dance to Mr. MacKyle."

She thought for an instant Alasdair would refuse her offer, but then he formed his features into a rigid smile.

"My pleasure, Lady Harriet."

On the dance floor he held her stiffly. Harriet wondered whether he was worried that she would either break or drape herself over him if he did not. Although his steps were sure and graceful, it was clear he was decidedly ill at ease.

"You do not like me, do you Mr. MacKyle?" she inquired boldly, deciding that plain speaking was her best tactic.

"I do not think our acquaintance has been of such a length that I could form such an opinion," he replied, rather disconcerted by her question.

"That is precisely why I wonder why you have taken me into such dislike," she said. "I puzzle over what I have done to earn such enmity. Or do you merely despise all ladies with light-colored hair?"

"There is nothing amiss with your appearance," he said.

That was probably the closest thing to a compliment she was likely to get from him. She arched an inquiring brow. "Then what, pray tell, is it? Do you disapprove of my friendship with your sister?"

"Katrine is not accustomed to such exalted company. I do not wish for her head to be turned by the life she is leading here in town."

"I hardly think a few months in London will be enough to ruin her forever," Harry said. "She strikes me as an eminently sensible young lady. I think you have little to fear on that head."

"She is young and impressionable," he insisted.

"As were we all at eighteen," she said. "Although I admit I find it difficult to picture you in that role. I suspect you were never young."

He bit back an angry retort. There had been no time for frivolous pursuits when he was eighteen. In an attempt to control his temper, he concentrated on the steps of the dance. But that only made things worse. For it made him more conscious of the slim figure in his arms, how well she moved, how smoothly they danced together.

It did not help at all that Lady Harriet was a damned attractive woman. He had not ever particularly cared for blond women, but her golden hair exactly suited her coloring. She was agile and light on her feet and he suspected she would be more than adept at the dizzying steps of a Scots reel. And her form . . . she was tall and delightfully shaped, with a waist that a man could long to wrap his hands around. . . .

With a start, he snapped back to attention. Nothing could disguise what she was—the spoiled daughter of an English lord. One whom, no matter how charming, he was firmly determined to resist.

He dared a glance at her and saw what he thought to be a self-satisfied smirk upon her face. She had been quite aware of the pattern of his thoughts. Berating himself for his lapse, he held her with renewed formality. He had no intention of falling under her spell.

"The waltz is perhaps a dance not to your liking?" she asked. Something had been going on behind that inscrutable facade. She had felt it in the way he relaxed, how his hold on her waist tightened ever so slightly. Then something had jolted him back into his rigidity.

"I find it rather tame after the dances of my country," he said.

"One does dance an occasional reel at some parties."

"I was referring to the Gillie Colum," he said.

She arched a questioning brow.

"It is danced over swords," he said. "And not for the faint-hearted. A single misstep can be painful."

"And have you ever made such a misstep?" she asked.

"Never," he said with a smile of pride.

"I should like to see such a dance. Do the dancers wear skirts?"

"*Philabeg,*" he corrected. "The little kilt."

"Is it true, what they say about Scotsmen and their kilts?" she asked with an impish twinkle in her eye.

"What, precisely, is it that they say?" he asked, daring her to further boldness.

"That an errant breeze can be highly revealing," she said, meeting his challenge. She was no milk-and-water miss; it was time he realized that.

Alasdair smiled in spite of himself. He gave Lady Harriet credit for her imperturbability. "The next time you meet a man in a kilt, I suggest you ask him."

"I shall do that," she replied. She tilted her head to one side and regarded him with a bold look. "Do you ever wear a kilt yourself, Mr. MacKyle?"

He nearly choked at her brazenness. He realized once more that his opinion of the London ladies had not been misplaced. A well-bred Scottish young lady would not even hint at such a thing!

"Oh, dear," said Harry. "Now I have shocked you. I extend my apologies, Mr. MacKyle. I never know whether to play the demure miss or lady-of-the-world with you; you seem equally provoked by either pose."

"I find women who play at any sort of games equally distasteful," he said bluntly.

"And you have me marked out as a gamester, have you not?" she asked lightly. "How perceptive of you! I can see there is no way I can pull the wool over your eyes. If that is the case, I can only be myself with you."

"I doubt you even know what that is," he said.

"Oh, but I do. I am the spoiled, pampered daughter of a marquess, undisciplined and overbold in my speech and, of course, on the hunt for a husband." She smiled cynically at him. "Have I left out anything? Oh, perhaps eager to corrupt the morals of innocent young ladies from Scotland."

She was all that, he thought, and more. But he was forced to admire her spirited self-analysis—and wondered just how much of it she truly believed. "You do yourself an injustice," he replied.

"And you are a poor liar, Mr. MacKyle," she said. "You have looked upon me with nothing but condescension from the first moment you laid eyes upon me—in the park, your recall?" She stared at him boldly. "So do not tell me it is my demeanor or my speech that has set up your back. You abhor me simply because I am English, am I not correct?"

And because she was a shameless flirt and Egerton's daughter, he added to himself. "I do not dislike you, Lady Harriet," he said. "I merely suspect you are piqued

because I am not as worshipful of you as you would
like."

She laughed lightly. "As if I had need of another
suitor. I fear you think too highly of yourself, Mr.
MacKyle."

"Perhaps I do."

If it were possible to lead her off the floor in the
middle of the dance without making a scene, Alasdair
would have done so in a moment. But he suspected
that Lady Harriet was trying to goad him into an un-
seemly display of temper, and he gritted his teeth
against the impulse. Instead, he gripped her fingers
tighter and swirled her about in the pattern of the
dance.

"Is your pursuit of the title progressing?" she asked.
"I imagine you are eager to be free of London."

"I hope to return to Scotland quite soon."

"A pity," she said. "The Season is barely begun.
Think of the delights you and Katrine shall miss. Why,
Vauxhall will not open till June."

"One more delight I have to deny myself," he answered. As if he would ever have allowed Katrine to set
foot on the grounds.

"Tell me, what will you do once you return to your
home?"

"Work," he said. "Unlike most men of your acquaintance, I take an active role in managing my lands."

Harry fumed at his words, but knew she could not
allow her anger to flare. It would be exactly what he
wished. She had started this conversation; now she must
endure it until the dance ended. But then . . . she had
an overwhelming desire to find herself private with Mr.
MacKyle so she could tell him exactly what she thought
of him. In words that no lady should use.

He did not quite leave her in the middle of the floor
when the music ceased, but it was the next thing to it.
Harry covered her discomfort by walking over to where
Lady Dunberry sat among the dowagers. After the arrogant Scotman's insults, it would be a welcome relief to
hear the latest simpleminded gossip.

*   *   *

Alasdair hastened from Lady Harriet, scanning the crowded room for a glimpse of his sister. He wanted nothing better than to leave immediately. But he did not spot Katrine before the next set formed, and he dared not interrupt her now. He carefully let himself out a side door and eagerly breathed in the fresh air of the garden while he willed his temper to cool.

He was certain he had not come off best in that interchange with Lady Harriet. He had prided himself on how well he had kept his feelings in check these last weeks. Why was he unable to retain his control when he was with her?

Because she was too damned attractive. Her soft golden curls, creamy skin, the lithe shape were worthy of an appreciative male glance. He remembered again how even he had been momentarily distracted when he held her in his arms, his hand lightly on her waist, her fingers curled around his. . . .

Wincing at the memory, he acknowledged that there was much to be attracted to—in a physical sense—with Lady Harriet. Now that he had fully acknowledged the attraction existed, he could conquer it and ignore it. Lady Harriet was not important to him.

Still, it would be best if he could avoid her altogether. When that was not possible, he would keep himself under firm control when in her presence. Next time, he would not allow himself to be cajoled by that enticing smile. He would politely but firmly decline any future suggestions that they dance. Dancing was far too dangerous an activity with Lady Harriet. For in the midst of the music it became too easy to forget who she was. He could not afford such a lapse in concentration again. It was far too disturbing to his peace of mind. Lady Harriet had a knack for challenging his calm assurance, and he had no doubt that she did it deliberately. She was testing him, probing him, looking for a way to gain the upper hand. It was as if there was a contest between them. But what was the prize?

He shrugged in deliberate indifference, relieved that the dance had ended and Katrine was being escorted off the floor. He stepped forward to intercept her and take her home. They had been here far too long already tonight. It was time that they were both safe in their beds. Lady Harriet would have to find a new target to draw her attention.

7

Can I behave, can I behave,
Can I behave before folk,
When, wily elf, your sleeky self,
Gars me gang gyte before folk?

Alexander Rodger,
Behave Yoursel' Before Folk

Alasdair stared with indecision at the note in his hand. Every instinct told him to refuse, for what could be gained by another encounter with Lady Harriet? He had firmly resolved to avoid her whenever possible. Yet here was another polite invitation: "Accompany my cousin and myself to Hampton Court." He would liefer dance on a table in the House of Lords. With a sigh, he tossed the note back on his desk.

He was tired of London, tired of society, tired of play-acting. Thoughts of Scotland beckoned to him like the songs of a Greek siren. He could not wait to get back to Kintail. Away from London. Away from society. Away from Lady Harriet.

He did not want to admit to himself how badly he wished to see her again. Every time they met he forgot his intentions of treating her with polite disinterest. He had no difficulty maintaining that attitude with the other women he met, but not with Lady Harriet. Why was it so difficult with her?

Because he did not respect those other ladies. They were exactly what he expected of Englishwomen—artful, flirtatious misses without an ounce of sense. Yet he was rapidly discovering that Lady Harriet was not like all the others. She was, he was forced to admit, as intelligent as she was beautiful. Her conversation might be bold, but it was witty and entertaining.

She did not match his expectations, and it was that very thing that so confused him. He did not know how to deal with her. If she had been unexceptional, he could easily dismiss her. But he could not. And that made him angry.

He would use this trip to Hampton Court to prove to himself that he was still firmly in control. He would treat Lady Harriet with the same degree of aloofness that he treated other English ladies. He would show them both that she was of no importance.

Alasdair sat in detached silence for the length of the trip to Hampton Court. The three other occupants of the carriage blithely ignored him, which he did not regret at all. In fact, the journey ended much too soon to suit him. He had the uncomfortable feeling that it was going to take every ounce of his strength to carry out his plan. Lady Harriet looked exceptionally lovely today, dressed in a shade of blue that matched her eyes.

"Shall we view the State Apartments or would you prefer to stroll the grounds first?" Tris asked when they alighted from the carriage.

"I should like to see the maze," said Katrine excitedly, hastening down the pathway.

"Do you wish to try your hand at the maze?" Harry asked with an amused look at Alasdair after Katrine and Tris disappeared into the greenery.

"No," Alasdair said.

"Then perhaps we can stroll down the Broad Walk," she suggested. "Katrine will be quite safe with Tris, I assure you."

Being alone with her once again was not at all what he wished. But he could not bolt off into the greenery in a frantic search for his sister. He held out his arm. Harriet placed her hand lightly on his sleeve, and they turned their steps toward the river.

He was acutely conscious of the feel of her gloved hand resting on his arm, and it grew highly difficult to treat her with disinterest. His muscles tensed with the effort of fighting his attraction and his steps quickened.

After only a few moments, Harry found herself nearly

running to keep pace with his stride. "Mr. MacKyle, please. I asked for a stroll, not a gallop."

He reluctantly shortened his steps. "Of course, I forget. English ladies are not accustomed to brisk exercise."

"Is it your aversion to the Hanovers that colors your opinion of we English?" she asked bluntly. "If we had a Stuart on the throne, would you look upon us with more toleration?"

"I owe no allegiance to the Stuarts," he said. "They cost my family greatly. And I do not think Scotland would have fared better under the Stuart yoke than the Hanoverian. The Bonnie Prince would have established his court in London, and ignored the north. Scotland has been doomed ever since the union."

"But surely union with England has brought economic gain to Scotland," she countered.

"Economic loss," he told her. "The country is impoverished."

"But you cannot blame the English for that," she protested. "Scotland is not a rich agricultural nation. It is foolish to attempt farming when the land is more suited to sheep."

"How is it that you are so well acquainted with what is best for Scotland?" he demanded. "Or is it your father's words you are parroting?"

Harry clamped her mouth closed and put on her sweetest smile. "Perhaps we should avoid all talk of politics and economics today," she suggested demurely. "Tell me about your home instead. From Katrine's description I cannot decide whether it is an enchanting mansion or a dim and dark castle. It is near the water?"

Alasdair frowned, his lips compressed in a thin line. He wanted to argue with her, to show her the folly of her English thinking, not discuss Kintail. "It looks out over the loch," he said.

"I have little experience with the sea—other than crossing the Channel, and the beach at Brighton. Is it similar?"

The very thought made him laugh. "Comparing the two is like comparing apples and oranges. The Channel is like a placid lake compared to the waters off Scotland.

The winter storms are wild, powerful things. And to call the sands at Brighton a beach . . ."

"You have been to Brighton?" she asked with surprise.

"Often enough," he said curtly, relieved she had interrupted him before he could say more about Kintail. He did not want to discuss his home with Lady Harriet. It meant nothing to her and everything to him.

"I rather enjoy Brighton," she said, ignoring his abruptness. "The Pavilion itself is fascinating. Have you been inside?"

"I regret to say I have missed that experience," Alasdair replied glibly. "But tell me, Lady Harriet, of your home. It must be a grand place."

She did not miss the sarcasm in his voice. "Oh, there are few houses in the country that can match it," she said airily. "Blenheim, perhaps, and Castle Howard. But we find it very comfortable."

"Indeed."

"Perhaps you can visit there before you return to Scotland," she said with an inviting smile. "I know my father would love to have you as our guest. And I am sure Katrine would appreciate the opportunity to see more of the English countryside."

He knew that such an act would be pure folly. It would put him in her company far too often for his peace of mind. "I would hate for him to interrupt his busy schedule only to entertain a few guests," Alasdair said, striving to keep his expression impassive. "Perhaps after the Season . . ." When he would be safely back in Scotland.

"That is a good idea," she said. "Katrine says you are planning to attend Catalani's concert next week. Have you heard her sing?"

"No."

"Are you fond of vocal music?" she asked.

"No," he said again.

Harry nearly stamped her foot in vexation. He was being deliberately provoking. She halted and turned toward him, anger in her dark blue eyes.

"Mr. MacKyle, I am endeavoring to make polite conversation. It is quite apparent that you have no desire to do so, but a gentleman would at least make some sort of effort to hide his disinterest."

"Perhaps I am no gentleman," he said with a mocking grin, half hoping she would accept that assessment and dismiss him.

She eyed him with a guarded expression. "No, I think you are," she said slowly. "But only when you wish to be."

"Or in company I find amenable," he said.

"Do you find my company so distasteful?" she asked.

"You can hardly expect a gentleman to answer such a question." He carefully took her hand and placed it on his arm.

"You seem quite inclined to speak your opinion when it suits you."

He laughed. "Then obviously it does not suit me at this time. I believe your cousin has had ample time to guide my sister through the maze. Shall we look for them?"

Harry nodded, too filled with anger and frustration to speak.

Alasdair remained coolly correct in all his conversation with Lady Harriet for the remainder of the visit. While Katrine stared delightedly at all she saw, he stood back, arms folded across his chest, with a look of bored indifference on his face. He knew Lady Harriet was provoked with him and he fully intended to foster her annoyance in any way he could.

But all the time he watched her surreptitiously, looking for some key to the puzzle of why he was so attracted to a woman he wished to loathe. He was afraid the answer lay within himself.

He had nearly slipped, out there on the walk, when she had talked so naively about Scotland's problems. He had wanted to grab her and shake her and tell her the damage that men like her father were doing to the people, to the land itself. To tell her about the beauty of Scotland and the plans he had to make Kintail a model estate.

But why should he care what she thought? It would not change who and what she was. An English lady. One who had no place in his life. One who was quickly driving him to distraction despite all his best efforts to ignore her.

After that awkward trip to Hampton Court, Harry resolved to keep away from the MacKyle household for a few days. Katrine could come to her. Harry did not relish an unexpected encounter with Alasdair MacKyle. They always ended up exchanging harsh words. It was not at all what she wanted from him, but she began to wonder if she could ever reach behind the wall he erected in her presence. Besides, it would do Tris good to stay away as well.

On this rainy spring morning, while she waited for Katrine's arrival, Harry reached for her newly purchased copy of *Waverley*. Perhaps she could pick up some insight into the strange character of the Scots from the book.

"Harry?" Tris poked his head through the morning room doorway. "Alone?" At her nod, he stepped into the room and closed the door. "Do you think I am impetuous and impractical?"

Harry did not look up from the book in her lap. "Sometimes," she replied absently.

He frowned. "Be honest. Do you not think I have grown more responsible over the last year?"

"Responsible for what?" she asked, glancing at her cousin.

"Well, you know, *things*. I escort you about town, do the pretty at parties, settle up promptly at Tatt's."

"Sounds shockingly dull," she said. "And most unlike you. Who is this paragon with whom you have yourself confused?"

"Dash it all, Harry, I am serious."

Harry set her book aside with a sigh and focused her attention on Tris. "What point are you trying to make, dear coz?"

"Well . . ."—he fumbled with the words—"marriage, for example. Am I ready to get married, do you think?"

"Married?" she asked skeptically. "Why ever would you—oh, no, Tris, do not even think about it."

"Think about what?"

"Katrine MacKyle."

"Why not? I know I do not have a title or any hopes to one, but it does not matter to her. I do not have a lot of money, but enough that we could live comfortably."

"Apart from the fact that you are far too young to even think about marriage, there is the small matter of her brother. He would never countenance such a thing."

"I am not that bad a catch," he protested, standing up.

"You are English," she said. "Anathema to a rabid Scotsman like MacKyle. Have you discussed this with Katrine?"

"Of course not," he said, pacing across the room. "I only just thought of the idea myself."

"Tris, you have known the girl for barely a month," Harry cautioned.

"I do not need four years to determine if my affections are engaged," he retorted. "I am sorry, Harry, but I just know she is the woman I wish to wed. Time will not alter the fact."

Harry smiled sadly at her cousin. "I fear big brother has other plans for her, Tris. I understand a marriage is all but arranged."

"She has not said a word about it," he stated defiantly.

"I believe she has little to say in the matter," Harry told him. "You know her brother. He may allow her some manner of choice in a husband, but not to the extent that he would accept an Englishman. It might taint the Scottish blood, you know."

"That is stupid."

"I quite agree," said Harry. "But I am not her brother."

"What am I to do?" he groaned.

"Is this not a bit premature when you do not even know the lady's feelings?" Harry asked. "She may not feel as strongly as you, Tris."

After seeing his bleak expression, she almost regretted her words. But Tris needed a severe dash of reality. She knew he was in the throes of his first severe infatuation, but it would do no good to tell him that now. He would have to discover it on his own. Hopefully, without making a cake of himself in the process.

Yet she was well on the way to making a fool of herself over a man who treated her with equal portions of disdain and detachment. What was wrong with her? Harry was not so desperate for male attention that she needed to chase after a man who did not want her. Why, she could have marriage proposals from half a dozen gallants if she only said the word. Lord Hanover would be on his knees in an instant if she indicated she wished it. Why was she expending all her energy and thoughts on that exasperating, dark-eyed Scotsman?

Because, in her heart of hearts, she suspected he was not so indifferent to her as he pretended. She remembered the way he had held her during the waltz at Lady Wentworth's, when for one brief moment he clasped her tightly in is arms. Or the strange, penetrating looks he gave her at Hampton Court when he thought she was not watching. She had sensed, from the moment that they laid eyes on each other in the park, that they were destined for something together.

Was it love? Or heartache?

By the following morning, Harry was thoroughly disgusted with her continuing obsession with Alasdair Mac-Kyle. She firmly resolved to put him out of her mind and divert her attention with some entertainment. A picnic would be just the thing. Tris and Katrine would surely like to go, and she would include Lord Hanover in the company. Harry felt a momentary sense of guilt that she had been ignoring Han recently while she tortured herself about Alasdair MacKyle's perplexing behavior. Today she would devote her full attention to Han.

The cook had prepared enough food for ten, and upon arriving in Richmond they contentedly stuffed themselves with all manner of delicacies.

"I shall explode if I eat anymore," Harry complained good-naturedly as she finished off her last bite of raspberry tart.

"That would be a sight to see," teased Lord Hanover.

"For that remark," Harry said, poking him in the ribs,

"you shall be consigned the task of walking me about to ensure that I do not."

"My ever-wagging tongue" he said with mock despair. But he helped Harry to her feet, tucked her arm in his, and headed in the direction of the rose garden.

"I say, it was deucedly good of Harry to take Han off for a while," Tris said as he lolled on the grass alongside Katrine.

"She left us here on purpose?" Katrine asked. "Is that not improper?"

"Why should it be improper?" Tris said. He darted an injured glance at Katrine. "You do not think I would do anything improper, do you? Devil take it, Katrine. I thought you knew me better than that."

"No, no," she protested. "I do not mean that at all. It is only if Alasdair discovered such a thing—"

"Which he is unlikely to do unless you run home and confess all." He stood up, brushing an invisible crumb from his trousers, and reached down a hand to assist Katrine to her feet. "Let us walk down to the pond."

Her hand wrapped snugly about his arm, Katrine walked along beside Tris. There was no need to feel uneasy—she would trust Tris with her life. It was only because Alasdair had become more and more pointed in his criticism of the amount of time she spent with Harry—and Tris. She feared Alasdair would use any excuse he could to cut the connection. If Harry was anyone other than Egerton's daughter, their friendship would have been severed long ago.

She stood alongside Tris as they each silently contemplated the pond before them.

"How glad I am that you like books," he said suddenly.

She turned and looked at him with a puzzled expression.

"If you had not been in Hatchards that day we might never have met," he exclaimed.

"Perhaps then I should be grateful you are clumsy," she teased.

"Do you think I am clumsy?" he asked earnestly.

"No," she said. "You are not clumsy at all. Merely easy to tease."

Tris sighed. "I know. Harry is forever twitting me."

"I promise not to anymore."

Tris smiled warmly and took her hand, bringing it to his lips. "Katrine, I—" Out of the corner of his eye he saw Harry and Lord Hanover heading toward them and he dropped Katrine's hands with a guilty start.

"It is time we returned if Katrine is to be home on time," Harry said, amused by her cousin's embarrassment. "We do not dare antagonize her brother. I would not put it past him to lock the poor girl in the attic on a diet of bread and water if she displeased him."

"Alasdair is *not* that bad," Katrine protested. "He wishes me to be happy. It is only that we disagree on what that is."

"Does he ever unbend and laugh?" Harry asked.

Katrine nodded. "I know he has not been happy in London, what with worrying about me and the bill and having to work with Lord Egerton and—oh!" She blushed in embarrassment. "I forget he is your father."

"Undoubtedly," said Harry with a laugh. "Do not look so stricken. I know it takes all the forbearance your brother can muster to endure London. I am certain he would be much happier running about the heather, spouting Gaelic, and sporting a skirt."

"Kilt," Katrine corrected. "And yes he would. But the restoration of the title means a lot to him, even if it keeps him from home. As an earl, he feels his voice would be heeded more. He cares so much about what is happening in Scotland."

"Let us hope, then, that he is successful," said Harry as she linked arms with Katrine for the walk to the waiting carriage.

Tris, Katrine, and Han chatted gaily on the drive back to town, but Harry did not feel like joining in. It was quite obvious that Tris and Katrine were madly in love with each other. Whether it was a temporary infatuation or a lasting regard, she did not know. But she did know that Alasdair MacKyle would not approve.

Moreover, their clear display of devotion reminded her again that her own heart was yet untouched. Would it ever be thus? The only man who sparked the slightest degree of interest in her was Alasdair MacKyle, and that certainly did not bode well. He was irritating, infuriating, exasperating, and annoying. Why could she not get him out of her mind?

She groaned silently. Here she was again, worrying about Alasdair. She darted a guilty glance at Han. When would she regain control of her senses?

At the beginning of the Season, Harry had worried that she would expire from boredom by June. That looked an unlikely prospect now. Alasdair MacKyle had removed boredom from everyone's life. The only question now was what would he replace it with? Heartache for Tris and Katrine? And what for herself?

8

Rather than I'd be lonely
    I'd give my heart and han'
With easy condescension
    To a gentle manly man.

William Ross,
The Highland Maid's Wish

"Is Katrine to be at Lady Uppingham's tonight?" Tris asked Harry as the Egerton town carriage departed Grosvenor Square.

"You do not know?" Harry asked her cousin with a teasing smile.

"When I spoke to her yesterday she was not certain of her brother's plans," he replied.

"I assure you, he has not confided in me," Harry said. "I have not even spoken with Mr. MacKyle since our outing to Hampton Court."

"Why is that, I wonder?"

Harry was glad the dim interior hid her dark look. "In case you have not noticed, coz, Mr. MacKyle and I seem to have a definite talent for rubbing each other the wrong way."

"Rather lowering, is it not, to have a man who will not eat out of your hand? I should be worried, if I were you."

"Thank goodness you are not," she replied with a twinge of acerbity.

"What do you think of him?" Tris asked. "In all honesty. You have spent as much time with him as with Hanover this Season. Are your affections being swayed?"

"Not in the slightest," Harry replied. "Alasdair MacKyle is a most provoking creature. Do not think I shall be able to put in a good word for you. I believe he would take great delight in going against anything I wished."

"So good of you to be optimistic," Tris said sarcastically. "I knew I could count on your help."

"Tris, I know you care for Katrine, but you must know it will not be easy to overcome her brother's objections. You should talk to Father about it. He and MacKyle seem to be thick as thieves these days, now that the bill is before the Lords."

"I had not thought of that," said Tris, brightening. "Do you think he would help?"

"I think he would, I only do not know how successful he will be," Harry replied.

"Has MacKyle said anything to you about me?" Tris asked.

Harry shook her head. "I am hardly the person he would confide in."

"Perhaps you could ask him," Tris said.

"Too afraid to approach him on your own?"

Tris gave an eager nod. "If I knew beforehand what his thoughts were . . . I might be able to make a better case."

"Better that you wait until he has the title in hand," she advised him. "He is more likely to be in a generous mood then."

"Maybe," said Tris. "But if the opportunity presents itself, would you?"

"I make no guarantee I will speak to Mr. MacKyle this evening," said Harry. In point of fact, she would consider the evening a complete disaster if she did not. But she was not going to tell Tris that. Let *him* wear his heart on his sleeve.

"Please?" he pleaded.

"I will try," she assured him. "More than that I cannot promise."

Tris sat back against the seat, satisfied.

He seemed to be more confident of her relationship with Alasdair than she was, Harry reflected. Each time they met, she never knew whether they would converse amiably or argue. Could he not once speak with her without erecting that wall of reserve between them?

It was with a mixture of dismay and elation that she noticed Alasdair and his sister were already at Lady Uppingham's. She did not know whether to seek him out, as she had at Lady Wentworth's rout, or to avoid him. Either choice had its pitfalls. Her reluctance had nothing to do with Tris's request.

It would have been better if Han had been here tonight. He could tease her out of the sullens. But he was at Newmarket, seeking to increase the vast fortune that was already his. A pity she was not mercenary, or she would marry him without a second thought.

But it was not money she wanted. It was that elusive thing "love." Why had it eluded her when it had snagged Tris in its grasp? She watched him standing among his friends, pretending to listen to the gossip while all the time he kept his eyes on Katrine as she danced.

Staring at Katrine was a popular activity tonight, Harry thought wryly, noting Alasdair on the opposite side of the floor watching his sister as well. He had not danced yet this evening. But Harry feared if she asked him again, he would refuse this time, and she did not want to give him such an opportunity. Let Alasdair MacKyle think she was supremely indifferent to his arrogant ways.

Alasdair leaned against the far wall of the ballroom, his arms folded across his chest. There was no doubt he needed to do something about Katrine and Tristan Winterbourne. The situation could not be allowed to continue. It was very clear they were growing entirely too fond of each other.

His intention was to watch Katrine with fierce protectiveness, but more often than not, his eyes strayed toward Lady Harriet Winterbourne. It seemed there was no escape from the woman. Despite his deliberate attempts to avoid her company, she still intruded on his world daily through the excited ramblings of Katrine. One would think the two were twins, the way they delighted in each other's company. Lady "Harry" was the chief topic of conversation for Katrine, to the extent that Alasdair had been tempted more than once to place a gag over her mouth. He did not want to hear any more of Lady Harry.

Now here she was across the room and he could barely take his eyes off her. He could not shake this fascination with Lady Harriet. He admired her as he had no other woman, appreciating her beauty and her brains. He could easily forget she was an English lady. And without that wall of contempt to protect him, he had no defense against her charms. Every encounter weakened his determination to resist the blond, blue-eyed temptress.

If he were not careful, he would soon find himself at her feet. Which was undoubtedly exactly where she wanted him. With an irritated shake of his head, Alasdair headed for the doors leading out into the garden. Perhaps some fresh air would restore his sanity. Mrs. Fraser was here to keep an eye on Katrine.

Harry watched with an curious eye as Alasdair slipped out onto the terrace. Her interest was aroused. When the dance ended she, too, slipped outdoors. The thought of finding him alone emboldened her. If she approached him now, would his guard be down again?

As her eyes adjusted to the dim light, she saw him on the far side of the terrace, his elbows propped on the stone wall, looking out over the darkened gardens. She stealthily crept up behind him.

"Are you admiring Lady Uppingham's gardens?" she asked. "Or escaping from the oppressive heat?"

Alasdair whirled to face her. "Neither," he replied, dismayed she had followed him.

"I myself found the heat bothersome," she said, waving her fan before her face in languid motions.

"Perhaps you will find the supper room to be cooler."

Harry brushed past him and rested her arm on the stone balustrade. "The company was also wearisome," she continued. "Did you not find it so?"

"I would not insult my hostess by saying such a thing."

"Even an English hostess?"

"Should you not be rejoining your chaperon, Lady Harriet?" he asked pointedly.

"I do not think I am in need of such close chaperonage," she said. "Perhaps you feel that you are?"

"In your presence?" He laughed uneasily. "Hardly."

"Then perhaps, since I can feel so safe in your company, you will escort me about the garden." Harry flashed him a winsome smile. "I do not wish to return inside quite yet."

Alasdair looked at her silently for a moment, as if weighing his options. Yet he already knew what he would do.

Ignoring his reservation, Alasdair guided her down the steps to the darkened garden. Her hand barely rested on his arm, yet it felt as if her gloved fingers were burning a brand into him. How could he allow her to disorder him so? He was not some young puppy, still wet behind the ears, to be set on edge by every attractive young female. Yet that was exactly how he felt in her presence.

"Are there gardens on your estate?" Harry asked, breaking the uneasy silence.

"The gardens are Katrine's province," he said.

"How do they compare with this one?" she asked.

"It is difficult to make a comparison in the dark, Lady Harriet."

"Oh?" she asked sweetly. "I thought you would have no trouble making a comparison between anything English and Scottish."

"Gardening is hardly a matter I concern myself with. It does not improve my tenants' lives."

"But surely you must admit that everyone needs some beauty in their lives," she said. "Do not your tenants grow flowers outside their cottages?"

Alasdair knew that it was so. But he did not wish to admit it to her.

"We have beautiful gardens at Highbury," she said. "I love to walk through them in the summer when everything is abloom."

As another whiff of her soft perfume drifted past his nose, Alasdair trembled with the effort of checking the desire he had fought against for so long. Here, alone with her in the darkened garden, the struggle no longer seemed important. What did it matter who she was or who her father was? She was only a woman he wanted very badly. Why should he not act upon his desires?

He had a very good idea that this was what Lady Harriet had planned all along. Well, he was only too glad to oblige her. Perhaps loosening the rein on his desire would give him some release from the insanity that gripped him in her presence.

He stopped suddenly, taking her by the arm and twirling her to face him. "I rather thought you preferred strolling through a night garden with a gentleman," he said, gently clasping her other arm.

"Only those I trust," she said with a hint of a smile.

"Very dangerous business," he said, pulling her closer and dropping his hands to her waist. "Very dangerous," he said before lowering his mouth onto hers.

He realized his folly the instant his lips touched her, but he was powerless to draw away. He had ached for this for so long, fighting his want, struggling against his attraction to this English witch. His pent-up desires boiled over.

His kisses deepened and he pulled her tightly against him. He could not hold her closely enough, could not still the burning longing in his body. He teased her lips apart with his tongue then boldly thrust into her mouth, groaning with unleashed delight when she responded ardently. He reveled in her touch as her hands roamed up his chest to wrap themselves behind his neck.

Some odd noise out of the night jolted him out of his heedless actions, and with sudden shock he thrust her away with such force she stumbled and would have fallen had he not caught her arm. *Mo Dhia*. What was he doing?

Alasdair took several deep breaths to calm himself. It was sheer madness, unbelievable folly. This was Egerton's daughter. For the space of a few moments he had willingly ignored who he was—who she was—and nearly created a disaster. He stared at Harry in growing horror.

"It seems you have less dislike for English ladies than you claim," Harry said, her voice shaky with passion and unease at his abrupt rejection.

"Liking has nothing to do with the matter," he said, furious at himself for losing control, and furious at her for causing it. He would make very certain it would not happen again. "Lust does not always come with liking."

He could not have caused her more physical pain if he had struck her. "Lust, sir?" She glared scornfully. "T'would seem more than mere lust was governing your actions tonight."

He laughed harshly. "If you mean to imply I hold a *tendre* for you, Lady Harriet, I most assuredly do not. I was merely taking advantage of what was being offered."

"Why, you—"

"I do not know what the practice is here in England, but in Scotland, if a maid asks a gentleman to escort her into a darkened garden, it means she has only one thing in mind."

"Your mind is so poisoned with hatred that you would cut off your nose to spite your face," she retorted. "Do not talk to me of *lust,* sir! I am certain such a base emotion is quite beneath your dignity."

"Are not all Scots savages?" he taunted. "We have little knowledge of the niceties of polite behavior."

"You are simply afraid to admit you find me attractive," she said.

"I never said I found you unattractive," he answered, a gleam leaping into his dark eyes as he reached out to trace a finger along the top of her bodice. "But liking and attraction are two different things."

She shivered at his touch, praying he would not see her weakness. "If I were a Scottish lass you would be on your knees with a declaration," she retorted.

"You certainly hold yourself in high regard, Lady Harriet. Have all the pretty words of the London lads turned your head for good? Is it so puffed up with your own consequence you are that you cannot conceive of there being a man who does not wish to be one of your playthings?"

"I do not deny what is there," she snapped. "As you do."

"I fear you are quite mistaken, my lady. I have no liking for you. If you were not a high-born lady, I perhaps would accept your invitation and take you here in the garden. But since you are—"

Harry slapped him.

"You are despicable," she said, before she turned and fled toward the house.

Alasdair stood in the darkened garden, absently listening to the faint strains of music drifting from the house. His harsh words would leave her in no doubt of his feelings. That was the way he wanted it. She would keep her distance now, and he would be safe from this temporary madness that held him in its grip. The foul London air had clogged his brain as it had clogged his lungs. Why else had he made such a foolish mistake? He did not want her—Egerton's daughter.

But want her he did. After that kiss, he could no longer deny his feelings, and Lady Harriet had been dangerously close to seeing the truth. He was drawn to her as he had been drawn to no other woman. His loss of control frightened him.

How could one define attraction? Lust was only a very small part of it. Other things drew him just as surely to Harriet. She had a quick mind, a facile tongue, and an unerring instinct for seeing right through the defensive facade he had built. After tonight he would be hard-pressed to maintain the charade. A glance would give him away. His only protection was to get away from her. Now. Before it was too late. He would wrap up his business as quickly as he could and return to Kintail.

It was much safer—for both of them.

9

Light my movement in returning,
Fleet my step this district spurning
For Highlands of true men sound-hearted
From Lowlands in full flight I'm parted.

William Ross,
The Bard Praises His Sweetheart

"Shall you be accompanying us to the theater tonight?"
Katrine asked her brother when she finally located him
in the library after luncheon. He had looked so angry
last night when they departed from the Uppingham rout
that she had dared not broach the subject to him then.

"Sit down, Katrine," he said wearily. "There is a matter I wish to discuss with you."

With a sinking sensation in the pit of her stomach,
Katrine took the chair nearest the window. Was he going
to restrict her social activities? Force her to stay at home?

"You look so dreadfully solemn," she said. "Someone
has not died, I hope?"

"Not yet," he muttered and took a deep breath. "I
am asking, Katrine, that you cut your connection with
the Winterbournes."

"Harry?" Katrine stared at him. "Why ever for?"

"It is not particularly Lady Harriet's companionship
that disturbs me—although it is upsetting enough." He
looked at her with concern. "It is Tristan Winterbourne
who has become far too particular in his attentions to
you."

Katrine felt a huge lump in her throat and she swallowed hard. This was worse than she could ever have
imagined. "You are putting far too much emphasis on a
mere friendship," she said, though she knew her voice

quavered in her distress. "Mr. Winterbourne has behaved with the greatest civility."

"If he is only a friend, then my decision will not cause
you much distress," he said evenly, watching her closely
to gauge her reaction.

Katrine lowered her eyes so he would not see the dismay in them. He knew, then. Or at least suspected. "Do
you wish me not to see Lady Harriet again either?"

"I think that would be best."

"What, then, am I to turn my back on the woman
who has been my greatest friend here in London, merely
because you do not like her?" she said angrily.

"I do not think Lady Harriet a suitable companion,"
he said. "She allows her cousin far too many familiarities
with you."

"While you would prefer, of course, that no man ever
spoke to me." She jumped to her feet. "You are hateful,
Alasdair MacKyle," she called over her shoulder as she
fled toward the door. "I wish you had never brought me
to London." The door slammed shut with a resounding
thud behind her.

Alasdair sighed. He had known his edict would be
painful to Katrine, but it had to be done. His damnable
fascination with Lady Harriet had led him to pay less
attention than he ought to the situation between Katrine
and Tristan Winterbourne, and he now feared it had
gone beyond what even he suspected. That connection
had to be severed now, or Katrine would only suffer
worse distress later.

And as for Lady Harriet . . . After last night he had
no doubt she would avoid him like the plague, but he
wished to do likewise. For the longer he stayed in London, the harder it would be to stay away from her. Last
night had been a nightmare. He must never let himself
lose control like that again. And in Lady Harriet's presence, he no longer had the strength to keep himself in
check. The only way he could accomplish that was not
to see her again. And that mean forbidding her presence
to Katrine as well.

Else both he and his sister would be driven mad when
they returned to Scotland.

* * *

Alasdair tried to distract his thoughts with work, but by the following day he was forced to confess he had accomplished little. The agricultural treatise he had bought last week lay open on his desk, but he had not read more than a page in the last hour.

"My lord?" Finlay stood in the doorway, an apprehensive look in his eyes. "There is a young lady here to see you."

"Who?" Alasdair asked crossly. Since his edict to Katrine yesterday, his sister had spoken nary a word to him and had taken her meals in her room. He understood her anger, but it did not make it any easier for him to bear

"Lady Harriet Winterbourne," Harry said as she pushed past Finlay into the room. "I am sure your master would like you to bring tea," she said to the man with a sweet smile.

"I am certain he would not," Alasdair retorted, torn between anger and pleasure at her presence. He stood. "What the devil is it that you are doing here?"

"Really, Mr. MacKyle, you should have more concern for the social amenities," Harriet said, untying the ribbons of her bonnet. She set the hat down on the desk and gestured to the chair beside it. "You do not mind if I take a seat?"

"Go ahead," he said in resignation. "Finlay, bring the tea."

After sitting down, Harry glanced around the room with curious interest. In rented quarters, it was unlikely it would show much of the current occupant's stamp. Indeed, she suspected that there was nothing in the room that even belonged to Alasdair MacKyle. It was too refined, too elegant, for this rough northerner. His home was probably adorned with animal skins and axes.

Alasdair took his own seat, glad the wide expanse of desk was between him and his nemesis. "May I ask the purpose of your call?"

"I assure you, it is not out of any wish for your company. I have called to speak with you about your sister,"

Harry said. "Your abominable treatment of her, to be precise."

"How is it that I have made Katrine suffer?" he asked, marveling once again at the lady's boldness.

"I received a letter from her, explaining that you have instructed her not to see or speak either to me or my cousin again," Harry said, barely able to repress her temper at the very thought. "Apart from sounding like something out of a badly written gothic novel, it is unconscionable of you to allow our disagreements to spill over onto your sister."

"I was not aware that our 'disagreements' had a thing to do with the matter," he said.

"Oh?" She raised her brows. "I find it highly coincidental that the edict came down from on high the day after the Uppingham ball."

Alasdair gripped the edge of the desk, fighting back the vivid memory of Harry clasped in his arms in the Uppinghams' garden. "I had already been thinking along such lines before then," he said evenly. "The events that transpired had nothing to do with my decision."

"And pigs have wings," she said derisively.

"If you wish to know, Lady Harriet, I am far more concerned with Katrine's relationship with your cousin than with you," he said. "But I do not feel it is possible to cut one connection without cutting the other."

"Now we have gone from farce to tragedy," she said. "Tris and Katrine are not children. You cannot order their lives around."

"Katrine is my sister and I am responsible for her," Alasdair said. "If I suspect she is becoming entangled in an unsuitable relationship, it is my duty to disentangle her."

"I would hardly call Tris unsuitable," she said.

"What would you call him?"

"Responsible. Determined. And he is very fond of Katrine."

"He shall be equally fond of another young lady once Katrine is out of his sight," Alasdair vowed.

"Simply because you have no heart does not mean others do not," she retorted. "Have you ever once stopped to consider Katrine's feelings?"

"Katrine is my sister; I am her guardian. I am guided by what is best for her."

"I pity the poor woman who ever consents to marry you," Harry said heatedly. "And the children you shall raise. They will chafe under you autocratic yoke."

Alasdair endured her taunts without reacting. To his regret, he had said worse things to her the other night. He only wished she would leave. "Was there anything else you wished to discuss, Lady Harriet?" he asked.

"You will not be happy until the entire world is as miserable as you," she said. "I pity you more than anything, Alasdair MacKyle. You would not recognize happiness if it reached out and grabbed you by the arm."

In her sheltered life, she knew nothing of the heavy weight of responsibility. In his frustration, he longed to reach out and shake her. But he knew if he touched her his anger would disappear and he would be lost to her charms. As he had been the other night. He remained in his chair, his hands clenching the arms.

"You would have benefited from a firm hand on the reins while you were growing up," he said. "Having both your father and cousin under your thumb, you will not be content until everyone bows to your demands. But I am afraid, Lady Harriet, that you have met someone who is quite impervious to your desires."

"Have I?" she asked.

She stood and for a moment Alasdair feared she would walk around the desk to prove the truth of her doubts. But she merely reached for her bonnet and he uttered an inaudible sigh of relief.

"Your problem, Mr. MacKyle, is that you are far too aware that you are *not* impervious to me. Rather than admit it, you retreat behind cold stares and disdainful words. It is only yourself whom you lie to."

By not a single sign did he reveal that she had cut to the truth of the matter. Alasdair did not move from his chair, but watched with a pose of studied indifference while she restored her bonnet to her head.

"For Katrine's sake, I ask you to reconsider," Harry said. "She is the one who will suffer most from your stubbornness."

"Forgive me if I do not show you out, Lady Harriet," Alasdair said. "Since you found your way here unaided, I am certain you can find your way to the door again."

Harry did not slam the door behind her.

Slumping against the carriage cushions, Harry wearily closed her eyes. It had been a futile attempt; she knew that before she started out. But she could not allow that infuriating man to ruin so many lives without offering up a protest.

She felt genuinely sorry for Tris and Katrine, who were so much in love. True, they were young, but she suspected that both knew their own hearts quite well. Tris, while rather fun-loving, had always had a streak of seriousness to him. And Katrine was more mature than the usual giddy girl at a come-out. This wrenching parting would bring misery to them both.

And Alasdair . . . She had never met a man who was so infuriatingly blind. He would deny to his grave that he felt anything for her, when she knew that he did. No manner of angry words could hide the spark that had flamed between them in the garden. He was too stubborn to admit it. And because of his intransigence, three other people would suffer.

Harry swore silently, damning whatever vengeful god had brought the MacKyles to London this Season. The year she had vowed to find a man to wed, whether or not her heart was involved. And in the bitterest of ironies, her heart was fully involved—with the one man who refused to admit he wanted her.

Katrine made a concerted effort to avoid her brother over the next days. Fortunately, he seemed equally eager to keep his distance, so they did not see or speak to each other. She took her meals alone.

She told Finlay not to allow any callers today. Katrine did not have the energy for making polite social conversation when her heart was breaking. Mrs. Fraser was out running errands; Katrine determined to remain at home and—

She stood up abruptly, pacing across the drawing room

with determined steps. Alasdair was not the only stubborn one in the family. He thought to rule her, but he would find she would not bend so easily to his will. She would find a way to see Tris again.

Katrine turned when she heard the door open and stood rooted in surprise at the sight of Tris, standing there with a look of pained longing on his face. "Tris, you should not be here!" she cried.

He stepped quickly to her side and took her hand in his. "I could not help myself," he said solemnly. "I made certain that your brother was not at home. But I had to see you one more time."

Katrine looked into his eyes and saw the ache in her own mirrored there. "Oh, Tris," she moaned. "Whatever are we to do?"

"I shall have to talk with your brother, of course," he said.

"It will not do any good," she protested. "Alasdair does not care a thing for my happiness. All he cares about is Scotland and things Scottish. He has condemned you out of hand because you are not."

"But surely he will be willing to entertain a formal offer for your hand," Tris said. "I have been with Egerton's man of business all morning. I know exactly how much money I shall have. There is a house in Norfolk and a farm in Dorset—do not cry, Katrine!" He fumbled for his handkerchief. "All will be well."

"It will not," she said tearfully. "Alasdair does not care about any of that. He hates you only because you are English."

"Then we shall just have to wait until you come of age," Tris said with a stubborn set to his chin.

"Tris, that is three whole years!" she exclaimed. "I could not bear it."

"Neither could I," he said. "But if it is the only way . . ."

"I could not ask you to wait so long," she said with a sad smile. "You will forget all about me after a few months."

"Never," he vowed. "I shall love you always, Katrine. And if I have to wait three years to make you my wife,

I will wait. Gladly. You are worth every minute of that long time."

"Oh, Tris," she sighed, leaning against him, feeling the comfort of his arms as he wrapped them around her.

"Unhand my sister at once!" an enraged Alasdair exclaimed from the doorway.

Tris and Katrine jumped apart.

"Alasdair, please," she begged as he crossed the room toward her and Tris, an angry glint in his eye.

"Go to your room, Katrine. Now."

"No," she said. "I shall not."

Alasdair glared at Tris. "What is the purpose of your visit here?"

Tris reddened. "I came to speak to your sister."

"Knowing I had forbidden her to see you?"

Tris nodded. "I wanted to talk with her before I spoke with you." He looked briefly at Katrine, then took a deep breath. "I should like to marry your sister, Mr. MacKyle."

"No," Alasdair said firmly. "And if that is all you have to say, Mr. Winterbourne, I think you can take yourself off now."

"Alasdair." Katrine turned pleading eyes on her brother. "Please talk with Tris. Listen to him."

"There is nothing to talk about. He proposes a marriage to which I am inalterably opposed, and I see no point in continuing the discussion." He looked steadily at Tris.

"I am going to marry Tris," Katrine cried. "Against your wishes if need be, but I will!"

"If you dare an elopement . . ." Alasdair's eyes filled with warning.

"I would never insult Katrine with such an action," Tris said evenly. "I am prepared to wait until your sister comes of age and can wed with or without your permission."

"You are here against my express wishes," Alasdair said. "Will you leave now or shall I call Finlay and have you forcibly removed?"

"That will not be necessary," Tris said stiffly. "Good day, sir." He stepped toward Katrine and took her hand.

"I shall wait," he promised as he squeezed her fingers with his. Bowing low, he left the room.

Katrine dared not speak. She did not want to dissolve into tears in front of Alasdair. Tris's declaration of faithfulness had strengthened her spirit.

She watched in uneasy silence as Alasdair stood in deep thought, a scowl upon his face. At last he turned his gaze to her, and she flinched at the fury in his eyes.

"I suggest you and Mrs. Fraser begin to pack," he said in clipped tones. "You are going home."

She had half expected such a declaration, but his words still chilled her. At least in London there was the slim chance she might see Tris at a party or in the park, even if she could not speak with him. And notes could be secretly exchanged. But now they were to be separated by the length of the country—and Alasdair would have control of the mail. Her knees weakened as the miserable prospect washed over her.

Still, she had her pride. She was a MacKyle. She would not give Alasdair the satisfaction of seeing her cry. Without a word she walked into the hall, quietly shutting the door behind her.

10

Edinburgh is beautiful
In many and many a way,
There's no town in this kingdom
But must humbly own its sway.

Duncan MacIntyre,
Song to Edinburgh

Highbury Hall, Kent

The Marquess of Egerton eyed his daughter with fatherly concern. She was so quiet of late, quite lacking her normal enthusiasm. Just look at her—reading after dinner instead of challenging him to a game of piquet. . . . It was more than the move from London to the country that bothered her. He suspected a different change of scenery would do her more good. Scotland, perhaps. Egerton hid his smile as he poured himself a glass of port and took the seat beside her.

"It has been a rather dull summer," he commented. "I had looked forward to your young friends livening up the house."

Harry looked up from her book. "I find the quiet refreshing, actually. The Season was far too busy. It is pleasant to have some peace at last."

"Nonsense," he said. "Makes me sleepy." He took a large swallow of port. "It reminds me too much of the years after your mother died."

Harry felt a pang of guilt. "I am sorry, Papa, I had not thought—"

He waved a dismissive hand. "It is not your fault, my dear. Sweet summer nights like this always make me a bit maudlin." He heaved a deep sigh. "Too many reminders . . ."

"Then we shall have to devise some entertainments to divert you," Harry said.

"I am not sure even entertainment could do the trick this time," he said wearily. "What I need is to get away for a while. I thought, perhaps, to go to Scotland for the king's visit. Should you like to accompany me?"

Scotland. The very thought struck both delight and terror in her heart.

It was unlikely she would see Alasdair MacKyle. For was not Kintail in the remote Highlands, far from Edinburgh? And no man was more unlikely to leave his home to see the king.

But if he *was* there . . . what would he think? That she had followed him north? She could not bear that—she did have her pride. Seeing him again might only intensify the hurt and longing she had struggled against for the last two months. Why take the chance?

Harry directed a smile at her father. "Afraid to travel on your own?"

"Exactly," he replied.

"I shall think on it," she said.

"It would do us both good," he told her. "It will give me the chance to confer with the factor and see what progress is being made on the lands. Who knows, I might even decide to go out and examine them myself." He smiled gently at her. "And I daresay I could authorize a few new gowns for the occasion."

Harry laughed. "Now, Papa, you know I have far too many already. Do not tempt me."

"If it brings a smile to your face, I will buy you a hundred gowns," he said, then drained his glass. "Perhaps we can take your cousin along, so you will have a more suitable escort than this old man."

Harry reached over and squeezed his hand. "You are quite suitable," she said.

"Talk with Tris," he suggested. "You will need to decide soon, so I can make suitable arrangements. I should like to go by boat, I think. 'Tis a long journey on indifferent roads else."

Harry nodded and determinedly returned her attention to her book. But she could not stop thinking about her father's suggestion; in fact, the prospect kept her awake for most of the night.

On the one hand, it would be interesting to travel to the Scottish capital. It would be crowded and noisy for the visit of the king, but it would also be filled with innumerous activities. There would be balls and concerts, she was certain. And the novelty of the setting would make them diverting. It would not be like returning to London, after all. Edinburgh was new and different.

And even if Alasdair MacKyle was there, it would not bother her overmuch. He would certainly ignore her. After their last conversation in London, she expected nothing more from him. He would stubbornly refuse to acknowledge his interest in her until the day she died.

Yet despite all her efforts, he still dominated her thoughts with a regularity that frightened her. After his departure, the final months of the London Season had passed by in a blur. Two long visits in the country had lifted her spirits slightly, but it was all too easy for the image of his handsome face to intrude on her mind at the least likely times.

Perhaps seeing him in Scotland would make it different, for both of them. He had hated London, had hated everything associated with it. In his homeland, would he be able to look at her without prejudice? He had the title now as well. Would it improve his attitude, make him less acerbic and more conciliatory? Make him more willing to admit the truth? Or would he continue to lie to himself as well as to her?

It was quite possible nothing would have changed. Yet it was a chance she would have to take. It was her only chance, after all. If this attempt failed, she would accept defeat and get on with her life. She would be free to accept the patient Lord Hanover.

This trip could be for the best. Seeing Alasdair MacKyle again might free her heart from the stranglehold he held on it. It was wasteful folly to yearn after a man who did not want her. After another encounter, she would be able to dismiss him from her thoughts. She would be free.

Harry knew that once more she was lying to herself.

Loch Kyle, Scotland

Alasdair's irritation mounted as he scanned the contents of the letter. "*Abair baothaireachd!* How dare they make a public spectacle of this!" With a disgusted shake of his head, he flung the letter down on his desk.

Katrine looked at her brother with curiosity. "What has you so upset now?"

He gesture toward the letter. "The king approved the petition. The attainder is reversed and the title will be restored."

"That is wonderful!" she exclaimed; then her expression grew puzzled. "But why is it that you are so angry?"

"Read this," he said, handing the letter to her.

Katrine quickly scanned the contents. "Edinburgh!" she exclaimed. "A special presentation by the king himself. Oh, Alasdair, how exciting!"

Her enthusiasm elicited a laugh from Alasdair. "It is a fine joke, is it not? The king restores the title his grandfather took from ours."

"Highly appropriate," Katrine said. "It will put the crowning touch to the king's visit, I am certain."

"I will be only too happy to oblige His Majesty," Alasdair said dryly.

He glanced at Katrine. After her brief flurry of excitement at his news, the perpetually sad expression she had worn ever since they'd left London returned. She would be hard pressed to believe him, of course, but he did have her best interests in mind. Tristan Winterbourne was a most unsuitable connection. She would realize that eventually.

Still, Alasdair felt a measure of sympathy for her. Infatuation, no matter how foolish, was not easily overcome. Particularly in the isolation of the Highlands. He should know. Despite all his efforts, he was still unable to free his mind of thoughts of Lady Harriet. That one kiss they had shared was burned into his memory.

Katrine needed diversion: people, activities, excitement. He regretted the results the last time he had tried to entertain her with London. But Edinburgh was far safer. And with everyone flocking there for the king's visit, it would be a perfect time to encourage Katrine to look over prospective suitors. She was bound to forget that English idiot with every suitable man in Scotland at her fingertips. He knew Katrine needed the excitements of town as he did not, and the events of the spring had not made her life here easier. He owed her this much.

"How should you like to go to Edinburgh with me?" he asked.

Katrine stared at him in disbelieving silence.

"If we can find rooms," he cautioned her. "I have already heard that the town is nearly full. I can find a room easily enough, but it may be more difficult with you and Mrs. Fraser."

"Oh, I do not care if I have to sleep in a tent," Katrine said breathlessly. "It would be so wonderful to go to Edinburgh now. There will be parties and dancing and—"

"If there are suitable lodgings available, you may go," he said.

"Shall I be presented to the king again?" she asked with an impish grin.

"Oh, Lord, I imagine you will be." He smiled one of his rare smiles. "As Lady Katrine MacKyle this time."

"I am not certain I shall be able to accustom myself to being in the company of such an exalted personage as the Earl of Kintail," she told him.

"And I shall forever forget to refer to you as Lady Katrine," he said in rejoinder. "A sad pair of aristocrats we shall be."

"I am very happy that you have the title back, Alasdair," Katrine said with sincerity. "I know how much it means to you."

"I think Grandfather would be pleased as well," Alasdair said, remembering the white-haired old man of his childhood. "Very pleased."

"When shall we go?" Katrine asked.

He consulted the letter. "The presentation is scheduled for the seventeenth of August," he said. "I imagine we shall have to arrive some days before that."

"Of course," said Katrine. "There must be time for shopping."

His eyes widened and he could not resist the impulse

to tease her. "Did you not buy enough in London to last a lifetime?" he asked.

Katrine grinned. "I am only funning, Alasdair. I will even shock and scandalize all society by wearing the same presentation gown. I know how much money you spent on me in London."

He watched her carefully but did not notice any hesitation as she spoke the city's name. Perhaps, after all, she was well on her way to recovery. This trip to Edinburgh had come at the right time. They could both put the London spring behind them.

"Well," sniffed Mrs. Fraser as she inspected the tiny set of rooms Alasdair had managed to find them in Edinburgh's Old Town, "I must admit I have seen better lodgings."

"There is no question I have," said Alasdair with a rueful grimace. "But this is the best that could be done on such short notice. And I was lucky to find this as it was—a last-minute cancellation. It is not grand, but it will do."

"Did you say we had an invitation to dine tonight?" Katrine asked as she peered out the window of the tiny front room. Below were the narrow, cobbled streets of the old section of the city. The clouded sky promised rain before long.

"At the MacKinnon's," he replied. "They were most desirous of seeing you again. Unless you are too tired from your journey."

"Of course not," Katrine protested. "I shall begin unpacking at once."

"Early dinner hours," he reminded her. "This is Edinburgh, not London. They will send the carriage, thank goodness. I do not think there is a carriage or mount available to rent in the entire city."

"I shall not mind walking here," Katrine said. "Francie Stewart wrote and said she will be here with her cousins. I cannot wait to see her again." She followed Mrs. Fraser to supervise the distribution of their baggage.

Alasdair could not quite recall which one of Katrine's school companions Francie was, but he was glad that his sister would have at least one friend in the city. Since he had discovered the full extent of his duties during the king's visit, he worried that Katrine would not find much enjoyment in her time here. He would be too busy with official matters to pay her close attention.

He took Katrine's place at the narrow window, taking in the uninspiring view with a quick glance. If only the royal yacht would sink on its way to Leith and release him from this folly. He sighed and turned back to the room. No such reprieve would be coming, he was certain. It was going to be a very long fortnight.

A fortnight that would not be any easier to endure now that he knew that Egerton was scheduled to play a major role. It was understandable that one of the largest landholders in Scotland would take an important part in the ceremonies for the king. His presence here was not a surprise. But had the man brought his daughter with him?

The thought filled Alasdair with apprehension. It was ironic how difficult he found it to keep Harry from his mind. That should not surprise him, however. He had been determined to ignore her from the moment they met, and had failed miserably at the task. He wanted to feel indifference, yet he felt need. And anger at himself for feeling anything at all.

Why had Lady Harriet touched him like no other woman had? He had tried so hard to dislike her, yet only found more things about her to like. She was not the brainless, simpering English lady he wanted her to be. Perhaps that was part of her allure—the unexpectedness of her nature. He could fight against the image, but was defenseless against the real woman.

Yet he could not forget that she was Egerton's daughter. He was grateful to the marquess for his help with the title restoration, but that did not excuse the way he dealt with the Keppoch lands. However much he was drawn to Lady Harriet, Alasdair knew he would never be able to forget that.

He shook his head ruefully. He told himself it was foolish to be concerned. It was highly unlikely Egerton would bring her on a journey of such length—or that she would even wish to travel north. She probably gave him no further thought. It was what he told her he wanted during their last conversation, was it not?

He only wished to be free of her. But it was quite evident that despite all his arguments and protestations, he was far more attracted to her than he wanted to admit. All his life he had been strong and determined, planning his course and obtaining his goals with unswerving tenacity. He owed his allegiance to Kintail, his family, and Scotland. And nowhere in that life was there room for the daughter of English privilege and wealth.

Why could she have not been some other man's daughter? If her father was anyone else, he might find himself able to look beyond her birth and title, might be able to picture her content and happy amidst the hills, water, and sky of Kintail.

But she was Egerton's daughter. Even as he tried to keep that idea firmly in mind, it was crowded out by a picture of a smiling Harry, whirling about the dance floor in his arms. The remembered feel of her as he held her captive on that dark night in the garden was vivid and painful, reanimating the fire that had raced through his body when their lips met.

He had never wanted a woman as he wanted Harry— and by some horrid quirk of fate, she was the one woman he could not want. Did not wish to want. And he did not know, if he saw her again, whether he could hold firm to that view.

Alasdair impatiently turned back to the room. Egerton would not bring Harry to Edinburgh. And Alasdair had no intention of ever returning to London. They would never meet again. It was for the best. As the memories faded, his peace of mind would return.

11

Oh, little do I love to trace
    Edina's streets and lanes,
Or breathe lip-love with courtly grace
    In palaces or fanes;

Archibald MacDonald,
Give Me the Forest Wide and High

Katrine picked her way carefully across the muddy street, Mrs. Fraser following close behind. Now that she had seen London, Edinburgh certainly suffered in comparison. The city's provincial nature became more and more apparent with each step.

Katrine marveled at the change in her outlook. Last year she had thought Edinburgh a grand place. Her carefully chaperoned outings from school had been eagerly awaited treats. After the isolation of Kintail, Edinburgh was all that was wonderful.

But now everything looked drab, dreary, and dirty. In the Old Town there was no grand avenue to compare to Regent Street, with its bright new shops filled with glittering wares. The Cannongate shops looked old and dingy, and had little to offer. Even the influx of London merchants for the royal visit was not much of an improvement. After seeing London, nothing else would ever look as good.

"Katrine?"

The voice brought her up and she whirled in surprise. "Harry?"

"It is you!" Harry exclaimed, reaching out to give Katrine an exuberant hug. "Whatever are you doing in town?"

Katrine laughed. "Undoubtedly, the same as you. We

are here to see the king." She looked anxiously at her friend. "Is Tris . . . ?"

Harry shook her head. "I asked him to come, but he did not wish it. We were not at all certain you would be here, and we knew your brother would be watching you closely. Tris thought it would only make things worse for both of you if he were here but unable to see you."

Katrine nodded, swallowing her disappointment.

Harry smiled encouragingly. "But I have a number of things for you from him—letters and presents and packages. I nearly had to pack an extra trunk to bring it all. I planned to ship it from Edinburgh so your brother would not suspect from whom it came. Are we not grand conspirators?"

"Oh, Harry, it is so wonderful to see you again," Katrine said. "I want to hear everything you have been doing."

"You really mean you want to know what Tris has done to occupy himself," Harry said, smiling at Katrine's flush of embarrassment. "I shall tell you all, however. Do come back to our lodgings for tea."

Katrine looked anxiously at Mrs. Fraser, who was busy chatting away with Harry's chaperon.

"Do not worry about your brother," Harry said. "There is little more he can do to you, after all."

"You are right," Katrine said emphatically. She linked arms with Harry and they strolled amiably toward the waiting carriage.

During the short drive, Harry sought to quell her excitement. Alasdair *was* here. A thrill of nervous excitement raced up her spine. When, exactly, would they meet again? And what would happen?

"What does your brother think of all the fuss?" Harry asked Katrine as they sat sipping their tea in the elegant Charlotte Square house rented by Lord Egerton.

"He is quite dismayed," Katrine said with a laugh. "He was almost willing to give up the title when he first heard that the king himself wished to present it in a public ceremony. I have rarely seen Alasdair more angry."

"Indeed," said Harry. "I imagine he was swallowed his ire and will be on his knees before his sovereign."

Katrine giggled. "In a kilt, no less."

"Oh?" Harry's eyes danced with amusement.

Katrine nodded. "It has been decreed that all Highland nobles must appear in full 'Scots' regalia—kilt, hose, bonnet, and dirk. Alasdair spent days muttering how his ancestors had never dressed up in anything so ridiculous. But he relented, of course. And I must admit he looks quite handsome in the outfit."

A sharp stab of disappointment smote Harry at the thought she might never see the sight. "Are you going to be presented to the king?" she asked quickly.

"I shall," said Katrine. Then, with another giggle, she continued, "And I am to wear the same dress I did in London. You and the king will be the only ones to know."

"I shall not tell a soul," Harry promised. "But have you thought of what you shall do if the king stands up and says, 'You wore that dress in London!'?"

"Melt into a puddle," Katrine said. "As if he would ever recall such a thing. I know how many ladies were presented that day. I doubt he could even remember a one."

"Do you think your brother would care to dine with us one evening?" Harry asked, trying not to let her eagerness show. "Papa has a dinner party planned."

"I am not certain what Alasdair shall say," Katrine said. "He has been behaving rather oddly of late."

"How so?"

Katrine's face reflected her perplexity. "Apart from his display of temper over the presentation, he has been unnaturally amiable. I own I was shocked when he asked me to come to Edinburgh. I had to beg him to take me to London."

"Ah, but Edinburgh is much safer for a Scottish lady," Harry said with biting sarcasm.

"True," Katrine said. She studied her hands for a long moment. "Harry, is Tris . . . that is . . . has he said . . . ?"

"Anything about you?" Harry finished for her. "Only that you are the one love of his life and he will wait for

you forever if he must—or at least the three years until
you come of age and can marry without your brother's
permission."

"Tris still says that?" Katrine asked.

Harry nearly winced at the hopeful glow in her friend's
eyes. She patted her hand in a comforting gesture. "I
own I was not certain how long Tris's devotion would
last," she confessed. "But it seems to grow stronger
every day, Katrine."

"I wish Tris had accompanied you," Katrine said,
blinking back her tears. "Even if I could only see him
across the room, it would be better than not seeing him
at all."

"And we could have contrived a meeting or two, I
know," said Harry with chagrin.

"We could have wed," Katrine said with barely dis-
guised bitterness. "I do not need Alasdair's permission
here."

"And we both know Tris would never countenance an
elopement—for that is what it would be if you wed without your brother's permission." Harry smiled sadly at
Katrine. "I know three years seems like an enormous
time, but it will be worth the wait if you start your life
together with a proper marriage."

"Do you think you would ever be willing to defy your
family and marry where your father did not approve?"
Katrine asked miserably.

Harry considered. She had never felt a grand passion
so consuming that such a course would be necessary. At
least, she realized with a pang, not until this fateful
spring. And she knew, beyond any doubt, that if Alasdair
had asked her to run off with him, she would have done
so without a second thought.

But her own ill-considered wishes would be of no comfort to Katrine.

"I think it is best to be cautious—for now. Your
brother may have a change of heart when he sees how
ceaseless your devotion is."

"The only reason Alasdair wished me to come to Edinburgh was to make a connection with some suitable
man," Katrine said, wiping away a tear with the corner

of her handkerchief. "He will never relent. I shall have to wed without his approval anyway, so why cannot it be now?"

Harry patted her shoulder gently. "I am sorry to have upset you, Katrine." She took the handkerchief and swabbed at the red cheeks. "Now dry your tears and let us find a more productive outlet for your love. I have my writing things here. I shall give you time to pen a letter to Tris, then we can take it to the post office."

Katrine smiled gratefully at Harry's suggestion. If she was very lucky there was a chance that she might receive his reply before she returned to Kintail and Alasdair's ruthless examination of the mail.

Harry tactfully retreated, leaving Katrine to pen her letter to Tris in private. In actual fact, she was grateful for the opportunity to be alone.

She tried to dampen her rising hopes with a dash of practicality. There was no reason to think that things would be any different between her and Alasdair here than they had been in London.

But if there was the slightest chance of a new start, she would take it.

Alasdair was surprised by the cheerful expression Katrine wore that afternoon when he found her in the small morning room. "I see the roses blooming on your cheeks," he said while he poured himself a glass of claret. "Did you have an enjoyable day?"

Katrine darted a warning glance at Mrs. Fraser. She wanted to tell Alasdair this in her own way.

"It was tolerably entertaining. I bought some new gloves, and Mrs. Fraser found a lovely brooch—a silver thistle. I have never seen town so full of people! It was quite astounding. I even ran across a good friend."

"Oh?" he said absently while he scanned the daily paper.

"Harry is here," Katrine said quietly.

Alasdair looked up suddenly, a guarded expression in his eyes. "By herself?"

"With her father," Katrine replied. She raised her chin

in defiance. "And you may rest assured, Alasdair, that Tris is not with them."

As quickly as a wave of relief washed over him at that news, a new emotion surged through his body. Harry. Here, in Edinburgh. He clenched his fists over the agonizing decision he must make. Dare he see her again? How could he possibly *not* see her again?

"Harry should like us to join them for dinner one night," Katrine said, her tone pleading. "She is acting as her father's hostess and says she would welcome the sight of familiar faces."

Alasdair was not certain that Harry would look upon his face with welcome. Amiable would be the last word to describe their last interview. She probably wished never to set eyes on him again.

But oh, he ached at the thought of seeing her. To stare into her dancing blue eyes; to touch the golden hair that had felt like silk beneath his fingers. His hands flexed convulsively. "We shall see," he said noncommittally, and refilled his glass with studied calmness.

Katrine let out her breath. She had half expected an immediate refusal. Anything less was tantamount to acceptance. "I thought I would take Harry about town tomorrow and show her some of the sights," Katrine said. If Alasdair was in a good mood, she would make the most of it. "That is, if you do not have any objections."

He drained his glass. "No," he said curtly. Katrine was safe enough with Harry.

It was himself he did not trust to be in her presence. For he did not know if he would turn his back on her or gather her up in his arms again, and he did not know which course was worse.

Following dinner, Alasdair took himself off to one of the interminable meetings in preparation for the king's visit. Perhaps the boring discussions would drive thoughts of Harry from his mind. For a little while.

Katrine returned from her jaunt with Harry about Edinburgh the next day with the promised invitation to dine. Alasdair had taken great pains to be out all day,

in case Katrine brought Harry to their rooms. He did
not wish to meet her unexpectedly.

He wanted to be absolutely certain about what he
would say to her when they next met. He could lie to
himself no longer—he was firmly caught in the spell
woven by Lady Harriet Winterbourne.

Admitting that fact did not tell him what to do about
it, however. The situation was far too complicated for a
simple solution. Perhaps it would be best to discover
what had brought her to Scotland. Was it mere curiosity—or something more?

Knowing he must see her again, Alasdair reached for
a pen. He would send his acceptance to Lord Egerton,
and meet with Harry. Perhaps he would discover that the
clear air of Scotland had the power to free him from her
spell.

Despite his determination, as he dressed for dinner
the following evening Alasdair viewed the coming dinner
party with trepidation. What rash impulse had allowed
him to accept Lord Egerton's invitation? He could have
pleaded another engagement, allowing Katrine to attend
on her own. He could have invited Egerton to join him
for dinner at Oman's later in the week. He could have
avoided Lady Harriet entirely.

Instead, he found himself pacing the width of the front
room while he waited for Katrine. His nerves were on
edge in anticipation of the upcoming meeting. Would she
be pleased or dismayed to see him?

"You are not wearing your kilt," Katrine said in dismay as she entered the room.

"We are going to dinner, not a masquerade," he said
sourly. "I have no intention of being on display for Egerton's guests."

"Harry will be disappointed," Katrine said as she gathered up her reticule and gloves. "She said she was quite
desirous of seeing you in a kilt."

Alasdair's eyes widened as he recalled that overly
warm conversation with Harry. Did she still remember it
as clearly as he did? He shook his head. It did not matter. Tonight he would prove to both of them that London

was far in the past. Things would be different here in Scotland.

Other carriages were pulling up to the door of the Charlotte Square mansion when Alasdair and Katrine arrived. Alasdair was relieved to discover that it would be a large dinner party. A small, cozy gathering would have been more difficult to endure. This way, by the time he had chatted politely with all the guests, there would be no time to say more than a word to Harry. They would not be forced into intimate conversation.

"Kintail." Egerton greeted Alasdair as he and Katrine entered the drawing room. "I see you have your lovely sister with you." He took her hand, bowing elegantly. "Lady Katrine. Harry was delighted to find you here."

"So was I," Katrine said. "I hope you had a pleasant journey."

While Egerton and Katrine chatted, Alasdair glanced about the room. He was not looking for Harry, he told himself firmly. Yet when he spotted her at the far end of the chamber, his chest gave a painful lurch.

As if sensing his gaze, Harry turned in his direction. Her blue eyes widened as she caught sight of him, then her mouth curved into a welcoming smile.

Alasdair, his composure shaken by just how enticing he found that smile, nodded briefly. He was lost, he realized with a sinking sensation. One quick smile and he was lost.

"Well, Kintail, are you pleased to have the title back?" Egerton beamed like a proud father.

Alasdair reluctantly dragged his eyes from Harry and turned his attention back to the marquess. "Pleased and grateful for all your assistance," he said. Though he hated to admit it, he knew that Egerton's support had greatly facilitated the matter.

"Glad I was able to be of service," Egerton said. "Here, let me introduce you to some of the other guests."

Alasdair had met a few of them in London, but most were unknown to him. English all, with holdings in Scotland. Not the company he would have chosen, but Edinburgh was filled with strange visitors these days.

A light hand on his arm caused him to turn, and he found himself looking into Harry's deep blue eyes.

"Hello, Alasdair," she said.

He took a deep breath to steady himself. "Lady Harriet." He nodded politely.

"Oh, we are to be formal, are we?" She smiled. "Very well, *Lord* Kintail. I trust you are as excited about the impending visit as the rest of Edinburgh seems to be."

"Undoubtedly," he said tersely. She knew full well he felt no such thing.

"I congratulate you on the restoration of the title," she said.

"Thank you."

Harry gestured about the room. "Have you met the other guests?" she asked. "I think some faces will be known to you."

"Your father took that task upon himself," he replied, wondering why he found words so difficult.

"I had not realized you would be the only Scots lord here," she continued, "else I would have added some other names to the list. To make you more comfortable."

He smiled faintly. "It is little different from London."

Alasdair was grateful that the announcement of dinner brought their stumbling conversation to a halt. But his gratitude faded when he found himself seated beside her.

"I thought you might prefer at least one familiar dinner partner," she said easily as he took his seat beside her.

"How thoughtful of you," he said with growing dread. This evening was not going at all as he had planned. He had intended to convince himself it was mere infatuation he felt for Harry. Instead, only a few moments in her presence were enough to convince him that it was far more than infatuation. And now he was to sit next to her all through dinner. . . .

He glanced around the table to find Katrine looking at him with an apprehensive expression. He smiled reassuringly. He knew how to conduct himself. He was an earl, after all.

The woman on his left, Lady Yarmouth, seemed much more interested in her other dinner partner, so Alasdair was forced to converse with Harry more than he wished.

"The salmon was delicious," she said after the fish course was removed. "Has the fishing been good this summer on your estate?"

"Exceptional," he replied.

"And the harvests?"

He frowned. "Not so good," he admitted. "The weather was poor."

She looked at him with teasing eyes. "You mean the new Earl of Kintail cannot control the weather on his lands?"

He laughed for the first time that evening. "No, I fear that is beyond my power."

Harry glanced across the table at Katrine. "Does Katrine enjoy being a 'Lady'?"

"My sister is not one to have her head turned by titles" he said.

"I did not think she would," Harry said. "Still, it does improve her status. I imagine you are busy entertaining offers for her hand."

Alasdair turned and glared at her with an exasperated look in his dark eyes. "She is not betrothed, if that is what you wish to know, Lady Harriet." He took a sip of wine. "But I fully expect that she will be surrounded by suitors before our visit to Edinburgh is over."

"Scottish suitors, no doubt," Harry retorted.

Alasdair refused to be goaded into an argument with her this night. "Of course," he said. He nodded at her plate. "How do you find the stewed pigeons?"

Harry sighed. "Quite delicious," she replied. It was obvious Alasdair MacKyle was determined to be a properly behaved dinner partner. Somehow, she rather enjoyed it more when they were involved in their customary verbal fisticuffs.

She made no attempt to engage him in any but the most ordinary topics for the remainder of the meal. Harry greeted the dismissal of the ladies to the drawing room with a great deal of relief. Alasdair's polite disinter-

est during dinner was worse than his scathing denuncia-
tions. For it meant that he did not care at all. Had her
journey to Scotland been in vain? She sat down with the
other ladies, a small frown creasing her brow.

12

'Tis the great town of *Dhun-eideinn*
Wherein I'd gladly stay
A wide and hospitable place,
'T'was pleasant every way;

Duncan MacIntyre,
Song to Edinburgh

"I declare, I find Scotland most intriguing," Lady Yarmouth said as the ladies sipped their tea.

"But so primitive," added Lady Blackmore. "Of course, it is to be expected. The Scots are hardly a civilized people. Have you not found it so, Lady Harriet?"

"On the contrary," said Harry. "I find the Scots to be friendly and amiable. And most civilized."

"But just look at this city," Lady Yarmouth protested. "Not that Charlotte Square is not a lovely part, my dear, but the Old Town! I declare I was appalled."

"Perhaps this visit will do the Scots a world of good," interjected Lady Norton. "They will have the opportunity to be exposed to a higher class of people."

"Meaning us English?" Harry asked, irritated by their arrogance. "Do you honestly think the Scots need us to show them the way?"

"Well, certainly," Lady Blackmore said. "After all, what have they accomplished on their own? The men are all bloodthirsty savages, highly suited for the army but little else. And for culture . . . all those atrocious bagpipes! They need a little civilizing influence."

"I suppose you never read *Marmion* or *The Lay of the Last Minstrel*," said Harry acidly. "Walter *Scott* is most appropriately named. And Lady Norton, did not Mr. Adam design your very own saloon? He was, I fear, a Scotsman by birth."

In the heat of argument, Harry did not notice that the men had begun to rejoin them. Alasdair's eyes widened in surprise as he listened to Harry's spirited defense of his country. He would have expected her to agree with the other ladies. Was she saying all this for the sake of argument, or did she truly believe it?

"Well, certainly, there are some exceptions," Lady Norton acknowledged with an embarrassed smile. "But the ordinary people! It is all one can do even to believe they are speaking the King's English. And those Highlanders do not speak English at all."

"The people in France speak French, and we do not think any less of them," Harry said with a falsely sweet smile.

"Yes, but France is quite unlike Scotland." Lady Norton sniffed.

"Yes, it is fortunate, since the Scots were so helpful in our fight against Napoleon," Harry said acidly. At least Lady Norton had the sense to look abashed.

"There is that lovely song by Burns," Lady Yarmouth admitted. "Something about roses, is it not?"

"Indeed," agreed Lady Blackmore, and the conversation drifted to musical topics.

"I had not thought you such a patron of Scottish culture," Alasdair whispered softly in Harry's ear when she stepped away from the group.

Harry eyed him with a challenginge stare. "There is quite a lot you do not know about me, Lord Kintail."

"So it seems," he said, studying her with bemused curiosity. "Tell me, Lady Harriet, what is it that I should know about you?"

That I am in love with you, she wished to blurt out. Instead, she managed to reply in a calm voice, "That I have a care for things more elevated than fashion or the latest gossip. That I enjoy literature, and music, although I must confess I do not care for your Scottish pipes."

"One must be born to it, I fear," he said with a wry smile.

"It cannot become an acquired taste?" she asked.

His smile widened. "Perhaps—after years of exposure.

Shall I arrange to have a piper sent back to England with you? To begin your training?"

"I shall think on it," she replied saucily.

Before Alasdair could respond, Egerton advanced upon them. "You promised to entertain us tonight, my dear," he said to Harry. "A song or two?"

"I will be pleased, Papa," she said. Glancing quickly at Alasdair, she asked, "Will you allow Katrine to sing a song as well? I know she has a pleasing voice."

Alasdair hesitated, not wishing to draw undue attention to his sister, but then relaxed. This was no different from the gathering they had been to on their first night in Edinburgh, where Katrine had also been asked to sing. He nodded his acquiescence.

"Thank you for your kind offer," she said to Alasdair as she turned to join Katrine.

Alasdair noted Egerton was looking at him with a curious gaze. "Bagpipes," he explained sheepishly. "I told Lady Harriet that if she brought a piper back to England, she might grow accustomed to their sound"

"They do make a deuced racket, don't they?" Egerton observed. "Still, all a part of the Scottish atmosphere."

"Quite so," said Alasdair with a hidden smile.

Footmen quickly placed chairs in an arrangement facing the piano. Alasdair took one of the distant seats. He was curious to hear Harry sing. Egerton would not have asked her to if she did not do it well. And she had mentioned her fondness for music. Why had he never learned that before?

Because he had not wanted to know such things about her. All that time in London, he never attempted to learn about her, blinded as he was with his condemnation of her family and country. For all he knew, she wrote poetry and composed symphonic music between her social obligations. He had not bothered to ask.

Yet there had been safety in his lack of knowledge. For each new thing he discovered about Lady Harriet only raised his estimation of her. Having now caught a glimpse of her complex nature, he was eager to discover more.

Katrine gave him a wavery smile as she stepped forward to sing first. He listened with brotherly approval as she sang several Scottish songs—in honor of the occasion, she explained—but he frowned openly when she sang "Loch Lomand." Was she thinking of that feckless Englishman while she sang? His good humor was not restored when she followed it with a mournful Gaelic tune that he knew no one else in the room understood. Which was fortunate, as it was the tale of a young lady seduced and abandoned by a faithless lover. He saw Katrine's impish smile as she glanced his way and he frowned more deeply to indicate his displeasure. He would take her to task later.

He stiffened to rapt attention when Lady Harriet stepped forward. Indeed, she sang well. Her voice was competent, pleasing. He found himself wishing to hear her sing some of his favorite tunes. It took no effort at all to imagine her seated at the pianoforte in the music room at Kintail, the warm glow of candles softly lighting her features. Then he shook himself into awareness. A most foolish thought. Lady Harriet had no place in Kintail. He leaned back against the chair and listened politely.

He was not terribly surprised when she began to sing Burns's "My Love is Like a Red, Red Rose." The song was popular everywhere. But a song of undying love was an odd one for a young, unmarried miss to sing, he reflected.

Yet her voice was soothing and he found himself being drawn into the words, wondering about the strength of a love that would last to the end of time, even if thousands of miles separated the lovers. Could such a thing be possible?

He felt a pang of disappointment when she stopped singing. He enthusiastically began to join in the applause; then his hands froze in midair. What in God's name was wrong with him? He realized with shocking clarity that he was no more free of her spell here than he had been in London.

God help him.

He stood up and walked quickly over to Katrine. It was late enough that they could depart without drawing undue attention. He whispered his desire to leave in her ear and told her to make her good-byes.

"Thank you for allowing Katrine to sing," Harry said, coming up to intercept him. "She sounded lovely. Someday you shall have to explain the words of that last song. It sounded dreadfully sad."

"It is," he said, nervous in her presence again. Then a faint smile flitted over his face. "I see you were not telling tales when you said you had an appreciation for Scottish music. Robbie Burns should be honored."

"Perhaps I can persuade Katrine to teach me some other songs," Harry said. "If I can wrap my tongue around your strange language."

"I wish you luck, Lady Harriet," he said with another smile, then bowed low. "It is time for us to depart. I thank you for your hospitality."

She tried to hide her disappointment at his words. She thought things had changed between them this night, and she wanted to reassure herself that her instincts had not been wrong. She forced a bright smile. "I thank you and your sister for coming tonight, Lord Kintail."

He hesitated, as if wishing to say something more, but then he nodded and turned toward her father. Harry released an imperceptible sigh. She must not get her hopes up. He might merely have been polite, for once.

But oh, how she hoped that she had opened a little chink into that rigid exterior.

After seeing Katrine back to their rooms, Alasdair took himself back down the stairs. He needed time to think—and to walk.

He was not certain what he was going to do about Harriet Winterbourne. He had gone to her house tonight prepared to discover that it had all been foolish infatuation. But one glance at her had told him that was a wishful dream—he had enjoyed every minute spent in her company. Indeed, he had found that amiable conversation with Lady Harriet could be a pleasing affair.

And that was not at all what he had intended when he decided to see her again. He had been determined to prove to himself once and for all that she was most unsuitable. Instead, he found himself drawn to her even more than he had been in London.

The absurdity of his position struck him. He, who had despised the English for as long as he could remember as the defilers and despoilers of his beloved Scotland, was now looking with charity at a woman from that country. And it was more than charity, he countered. It was desire.

But what was it he desired of Harry? Pure physical need could easily be taken care of by any number of ladies. He already knew, to his peril, how much he wanted her in that way. That punishing kiss in the night in London was emblazoned on his mind and body forever.

Yet it was more than that. He almost believed, however foolishly, that he could talk with her, explain his plans for Kintail and his people, and she would understand. He found himself wanting to show her the Highlands, the lochs and the glens and the burns. To see if she would find in them the beauty and peace that he did.

But it was a ridiculous thought. An English lady, accustomed to the entertainments of London and the grand country houses of the aristocracy, would find Kintail a rather uninspiring place. She was a city lady, after all, who took delight in the theater, concerts, and entertainments only the city could provide. A woman like Lady Harriet would not find pleasure in climbing to the top of Ben Duich, sailing across the loch in his small boat, or fishing for salmon in the river. She would perish of boredom in less than a fortnight. There would be no daily visits from neighbors, no fancy dinners or card parties in the evening. She would be totally unsuited to such a life. She would be as out of place there as he had been in London. There would be no purpose in taking her to Kintail.

Unless it was to convince himself, once and for all, that she had no part in his life. And he feared it might take something that drastic.

Yet perhaps not. Once the initial thrill of seeing her again faded, he might be able to restore his objectivity. With the upcoming festivities, there would be ample opportunity to spend time with Harry. Familiarity might ease the shock to his senses that her presence elicited.

He hoped so.

Harry set out the next morning to visit Katrine and to continue their explorations of Edinburgh. She found the narrow, ancient streets of the Old Town fascinating, but she grew daunted by the long length of stairs that led to the MacKyles' rented room.

"I do declare, that climb left me breathless," Harry said as Katrine greeted her in the morning room. "How many stairs are there?"

Katrine laughed. "It is the bane of Edinburgh, these multilevel houses. I am only glad Alasdair was able to find us accommodations on the lower floors. You should try climbing to the very top!"

"I hope this hill you plan on leading me up is not as steep," Harry said.

"Much more gentle," Katrine promised. "Although the climb up Nelson's Tower may be more of a challenge."

"Lead on," Harry said with mock horror.

They both froze when Alasdair walked into the room. "Good morning, ladies."

He looked straight at Katrine. "I thought I might intrude on your expedition," he said with a self-conscious smile. He would make use of the opportunity to learn more about Lady Harriet.

Harry regarded his announcement with bemusement. Despite his amiability of the previous evening, she did not actually think he wished to spend time in her company. He had behaved with such intolerable rudeness in London. Was he only waiting for a propitious time to insult her again?

"That . . . that would be wonderful, Alasdair," stammered Katrine.

"Good," he said. He turned toward Harry. "Do you mind, Lady Harriet?"

"I should like your escort, Lord Kintail," Harry replied truthfully

He allowed his gaze to linger on her, noticing how well the dark pink hue of her gown accentuated her blond locks. Then he hastily turned toward Katrine, afraid Harry would read more than she ought in his expression.

"Mrs. Fraser can remain here, if she likes. I think I can provide sufficient protection for you two young ladies."

"Bring your broadsword along, just in case," Katrine teased. "Harry, you should see the amount of weaponry he is required to carry for the ceremonials. Rather like a small army."

"Ah, yes, Katrine said you were to be wearing the kilt," Harry said with an arch look at Alasdair. She saw from the glint in his eyes that he remembered their conversation on that topic quite well. "I do look forward to seeing you in all your Highland regalia."

"Damned Scott," said Alasdair. "This is looking more and more like a stage play of one of his novels."

"Like *Rob Roy Macgregor*?" Harry asked in an amused tone. "You know how the king loves that sort of thing. It will only increase his interest in Scotland. Which could be of benefit for all."

Alasdair had to concede that was true. He looked pointedly at Katrine. "Is it ready to depart you are?"

"I only need my bonnet," she said, and darted from the room.

Alasdair stood awkwardly, not certain what he should say to Harry. If he should say anything at all. He waited, hoping she would set the tone for their future relations. But the ensuing silence was even worse.

"Edinburgh is a very picturesque city," she said with feigned brightness, strangely ill at ease in his presence. This new, amiable Alasdair puzzled her.

He laughed. "Dirty and cramped and foreign, you mean," he said with a grin. "Even Katrine admits it is not so grand after seeing London."

"But the setting is lovely. The Palace of Holyrood looks very romantic, and the castle on the hill is breathtaking. I look forward to seeing it from Nelson's Tower. How fortunate for the people here that they have so many grand viewing places."

"I am ready," said Katrine, returning to the room with her bonnet on and a shawl trailing from her arm. "Mrs.

Fraser says she will quite enjoy *not* going to Calton Hill, so you will be forced to entertain us, Alasdair."

"I will do my best," he said laconically, holding open the door for them.

Alasdair sat in the carriage facing Harry and his sister, wishing that Harry was seated beside him so he would not have to look at her. Yet that might be an even worse situation, for the swaying of the carriage as it lurched over the rough cobbles would surely cause their bodies to touch. And he did not think he could bear that.

He was relieved when they finally arrived at the foot of Calton Hill. They were not the only ones who planned to enjoy the view; a long line of carriages waited. He drew in a deep breath. It was all to the good. What he most dreaded was being left alone with Harry again.

He assisted both ladies from the carriage, then extended an arm to each. "I shall be the most envied man in Edinburgh with two such lovely ladies at my side," he said as they started out on the gentle walk.

Katrine giggled. "Until they find I am your sister."

"What are they building here?" Harry asked as they walked past an accumulation of carts, tools, and stones on the side of the hill.

"A monument to the war dead," Alasdair said. "A glorious replica of the Parthenon in Athens."

"A rather unusual structure for a Scottish hillside," Harry observed.

"A pity you were not on the committee," said Alasdair dryly. "They might have listened to you."

Upon arriving at their goal, Alasdair paid the three shillings for admittance, and they climbed the winding staircase to the top of Nelson's Tower.

"What a beautiful view," Harry said as the panorama of the city lay beneath her gaze. "You can even see the Forth."

"The view from Arthur's Seat is even better," Katrine said as she leaned over the parapet wall to watch the people below.

"This is magnificent enough," Harry said. She

turned to Alasdair. "I must admit that Scotland is far lovelier than I had imagined."

"You have not yet seen the Highlands," he blurted, then looked chagrined. She might take his words as an invitation. He did not want to think about Harry at Kintail.

"True," she said. "Papa has talked about visiting some of his properties. Do you think I would enjoy such a trip?"

Alasdair felt dismay. Her father's land would bring her far too close to Kintail. It would be too tempting to invite her to visit. Seeing her like this, in the constraints of the city, was difficult enough.

"I think," he said slowly, "that you would find the Highlands very remote and wild. Not at all like the English countryside."

"Alasdair," said Katrine, interrupting their conversation, "may we descend? I should very much like an ice."

"If that pleases Lady Harriet," he said, relieved to have the subject changed.

"An ice sounds very welcome," she said, and they descended the steps of the tower.

The cooling ices were a welcome treat in the unseasonably warm day. Refreshed, they returned to the waiting carriage. After leaving Calton Hill, they journeyed to the Botanical Gardens, which Harry pronounced as being very fine. Alasdair took great delight in pointing out many of the native Scottish plants to her.

He fell silent on the drive back to their rented rooms, hating for the day to end. After the initial awkwardness, he had relaxed and allowed himself to enjoy Harry's company. It had been laughably easy task, in fact. Yet he wondered if the feeling was as ephemeral as the clouds that drifted lazily overhead. Would more time in Lady Harriet's presence reestablish the unavoidable conflicts that flared between them? He was reluctant to find out.

"Will you be marching in the procession when the king arrives?" Harry asked.

"I fear so," he said.

"Perhaps Katrine would like to join me that day," Harry said. "We have several friends who have accommodations along the route. We can watch from the windows in comfort.''

"A most welcome plan," he said. "Else I fear Katrine would climb to the top of one of those abominable viewing stands that are springing up all over. T'will be a miracle if many of them do not collapse."

"It is amusing to see more enthusiasm here than there was in London for the coronation," said Harry.

"Novelty always draws onlookers," said Alasdair. "You have only to see how much attention the Laplanders have drawn to see that."

Harry refused to react to his veiled taunt. She was not overly fond of the king either. And if she did think that the overwhelming enthusiasm of the Scots was an indication of their provincialism, well, she had learned to keep her own counsel on matters where she and Alasdair MacKyle differed.

When they reached their destination, Alasdair stepped down from the carriage, then assisted Katrine to the pavement.

"Thank you for your escort today, my lord," Harry said with a demure smile.

"It was my pleasure, Lady Harriet," he replied with surprised honesty.

Harriet was too bemused at this display of affability to do more than nod in agreement.

It must be the Scottish air, she decided as the coach wended its way back toward Charlotte Square. Alasdair could not have undergone such a radical transformation of his personality in two short months. It made her very glad she had decided to visit Edinburgh with her father.

She wondered if their relationship would have started better had they met for the first time here instead of London. Would he have been less critical of her and all things English? Or was he merely hiding that hatred and bitterness behind a false facade of amiability?

The journey to Edinburgh had looked like a golden opportunity to convince herself that Alasdair MacKyle meant little to her. But his totally unexpected friendliness threw her plans into disarray. Once again she began to hope. She and her father would be in Scotland for over a fortnight, at least. Was that not time enough to see if this arrogant Scottish lord had truly thawed? Time enough to see if she could rouse a more tender emotion in his breast?

Harry smiled with determination. She would begin her campaign anew. The king had not yet arrived. She would have at least a fortnight to weave her spell.

13

The tartan plaid I'd rather wear,
Wound round and on my shoulder laid,
Than any coat however grand
That e'er in Saxon land was made.

Alexander
Macdonald,
The Proud Plaid

After two days of wet and stormy weather, the king finally arrived on Wednesday, and on the following day a massive processional marched from the harbor at Leith to the Palace of Holyrood. Katrine joined Harry in watching from the windows of one of the houses along the route. To Harry's consternation, Alasdair had managed to absent himself from the entire event. She did want to see him in a kilt!

"Will you escort us to see the illuminations tonight?" Katrine asked Alasdair on Friday morning.

"Us?"

Katrine smiled pleadingly. "Harry was mindful of seeing them. Lord Egerton is to dine with the king tonight."

He sighed, as if it were an onerous request. "I imagine I can force myself to such a task," he said with feigned reluctance, though his heart danced at the chance to see Harry again. They had not spoken since the excursion to Calton Hill. Tomorrow would be taken up with the blasted Levee, and who knew what other official events he would be required to attend before the formal presentation of the title the following week. This would be his best chance to see her for days.

He and Katrine took a hackney to the Charlotte Square house. An illuminated saltire was prominently displayed—a rather presumptuous choice for an Englishman, Alasdair thought wryly.

When Harry joined them in the drawing room Alasdair suddenly wondered at the wisdom of this outing. All manner of people would be in the streets tonight. He did not anticipate any trouble—the streets of Edinburgh were remarkably safe when compared to London's—but the boisterous revelers might make it highly unsuitable for young ladies. Would Harry's English sensibilities be shaken? "We will have to walk everywhere," he reminded her. "Is it certain you are to go out tonight?"

"I would not miss this for anything," she said. "Surely you do not think I will quail in the face of a little exercise, Lord Kintail?"

He accepted her insistence. "Then, ladies, let us proceed." He extended an arm to each. "We shall see what Edinburgh has in store for us this night."

They walked from Charlotte Square to St. Andrew Square and back again, along Queen Street, George Street, and Princes Street. Ornaments of varying complexity decorated the houses and commercial establishments: crowns, thistles, cherubs, obelisks, and stars were executed on color transparencies, then lit from behind. The streets were more crowded than Alasdair had ever seen them, even in the middle of day on the busiest shopping avenues. It seemed as if the entire town had come out tonight to look and wonder.

The massive bonfire lit at the king's arrival still burned on Arthur's Seat, and now that the weather had cleared, the glow lit the sky. Baskets of burning coal illuminated the battlements of the castle, and cannons fired noisily into the night. Rockets, shot off all about the town, streaked into the dark sky. At ten, the guns on Calton Hill and Salisbury Craigs joined the battery at Leith and the ships in the firth in thunderous salutes.

It was a gaudy, ostentatious display. And everyone in the crowded streets loved it.

The crowds were thickest along Princes Street, and it took the three some time to make their way down the broad avenue. Harry insisted on walking to Canongate,

to view more of the commercial displays in the Old
Town.

"Isn't this marvelous fun?" she observed with enthusiasm. "Why, I do not think the coronation was half as
exciting."

"Yes," Alasdair admitted, amused by her childlike delight. He was surprised that such a worldly lady would
be so open in her enjoyment.

"Oh, look!" exclaimed Katrine as another rocket
arched into the sky. "We should learn how to make rockets, Alasdair, so we could shoot them off over the loch.
Would it not be beautiful?"

"It would scare every living creature within fifty
miles," he said tersely.

"Spoilsport," she said with a fond look.

Alasdair smiled at Harry. "Should you like to have
rockets to shoot off at your house, Lady Harriet?"

"I think I shall content myself with a piper for entertainment," she replied with a teasing smile. "Although
he may frighten every living creature within fifty miles
as well."

Alasdair laughed. "Not at all the thing to say to a
Scotsman, Lady Harriet."

"A true Scotsman would be wearing his kilt on such a
night," she countered, glancing around at several men
garbed in that manner.

"Perhaps I thought the night was a trifle—ah—cold for
such attire," he said with a grin.

"Yes," she said with a bold smile, "I can see how it
could be chilling."

"Harry, see this," squealed Katrine, grabbing her arm
and dragging her down the street better to view the front
of a house, which displayed a representation of the king,
with two sea horses at his feet. "Why ever would one
put sea horses with the king?"

"What should it be instead?" Harry asked. "Lions?"

"Elephants," suggested Alasdair. "More befitting the
size of the office."

"Or the man." Harry looked at Alasdair and they both
burst out laughing.

"Dear me, such treasonous thoughts from one of the

king's subjects," Alasdair said with a warning shake of his finger. He took Harry's arm and tucked it under his own. "I shall have to watch you closely, Lady Harriet, to make certain you do not make any more indiscreet remarks. Else you may find yourself clapped in the Tower."

"Somehow, Lord Kintail," she said dryly, "I find it hard to picture you as the person to caution me against indiscreet remarks."

"And when have you known me to be indiscreet?" he asked with a mocking smile.

"I should like to see your face at the Levee tomorrow, when you step before the king."

"No one will find anything amiss in my behavior," he replied.

Harry laughed. "But oh, if they could only hear the thoughts inside your head."

"Alasdair! Harry!" Katrine called to them. "Do hurry. Come see the sailors."

A crowd had gathered around a group of men from the Royal Yacht who were displaying their prowess in dancing the hornpipe. When one dancer retired in exhaustion, another was ready to take his place.

Harry stood and watched, acutely conscious of Alasdair beside her, feeling the strength of the arm beneath her hand. It was a magical night and not simply because of the fantastical lighted pictures.

She was so glad she had decided to come to Scotland with her father. She held a glimmer of hope that something could come of this after all. Something that might last a lifetime.

It was with great reluctance that Alasdair finally took Harry home, and Katrine as well. Sitting in the tiny study, a glass of whisky in his hand, Alasdair reflected on the evening. Despite the rarity of the illuminations, and the enormity of the huge crowd, it had been a rather ordinary evening. Too ordinary. He and Harry had laughed and chatted about nothing in particular—and everything as well. No one thing stood out from their conversation, and that was what bothered him the most. It had been like any evening spent with a good friend.

Yet he had been with Harry. And it was much like that day at Calton Hill, except that he had been too nervous then to appreciate it. But now they had been together twice in perfect harmony and amiability. What did that portend?

Why were they able to deal so well together now, when they had been so at odds in London? Because his attitude toward her had changed. Instead of looking for the worst in her, he now looked for those facets of her personality that he liked or found intriguing.

Was she, like he, finding that they were good companions, that he was someone whose company she genuinely enjoyed and whose presence made even the most mundane things seem more interesting? He could not quite believe it. Had he really misread her so badly in London? Or was his current favorable opinion of her only a mad delusion, fostered by the novelty and excitement of the king's visit?

The desire he felt for her was no delusion. It was real and growing. And he did not know how he was going to deal with it.

Perhaps sanity would return once he was home at Kintail. He hoped so. It must. He could not, would not, fall in love with Harry. It was sheer madness. She had no place in his life—the life of the Highlands. She might endure it for a week, or a month, but the newness would soon pale and she would yearn for the excitements of the city. He did not want a wife who lived apart from him, and he would not live his life in a city. Friends they could be, on the rare occasions when they would meet after this visit. But lovers, never. It was not possible.

Katrine looked thoughtfully at her brother, who sat reading the Wednesday *Evening Courant* with a marked lack of attention. They were both exhausted from all the festivities for the king's visit. Alasdair had, of course, found the Levee as boring as he anticipated, while for Katrine even the excitement of dressing in all her finery for the Drawing Room on Monday paled during the interminable wait for that brief moment in the monarch's presence. Only the thought of the Peers' Ball in two days, and the Caledonian Hunt Ball on the following Monday, gave any inspiration. The thought of returning to Kintail loomed pleasantly for once. Particularly if she could get her brother to agree to her plan.

"Alasdair?" She began timidly.

He did not look up from the paper. "Yes?"

"I have a favor I should like to ask."

"Do you need a new bonnet? Or another pair of gloves?" He lifted his head and eyed her with an amused glance. "Are the temptations of the city becoming too much?"

"I have quite enough bonnets and gloves," she said. "It is something different. I should like to invite Harry to Kintail." There. She had said it.

Alastair took great pains to carefully fold the newspaper and set it on the chair beside him while his sister's words roared in his ears. Harry to Kintail. He dreaded the idea, and wanted it as well. "Do you really think she would care to come?" he asked carefully.

"I think she would," Katrine replied. "She is always saying how much she wishes she could see the Highlands, after hearing so much about them. And she is a good sailor—the journey would not upset her."

"Her father may not feel Kintail is an appropriate house to host the visit of an unmarried young lady," he said. There were a million reasons why Harry could not—should not—go to Kintail. And the biggest one was because he wanted her to.

"Mrs. Fraser will be there," Katrine pointed out. "I am certain she would be acceptable to Lord Egerton."

"And how will she return home when the visit is over?" he asked, eagerly looking for obstacles to throw in Katrine's path.

"Send Finlay and Dougall to escort her," Katrine suggested.

"I doubt Egerton will approve," Alasdair said slowly. In truth, his biggest fear was that Egerton *would* approve.

"You can at least ask. Please?"

Alasdair looked at her pleading face. He was almost persuaded. Almost. "I shall think on it," he said slowly.

Yet he did not mention it either to Harry at the Peers' Ball or to Egerton after the Civic Banquet on Saturday, when the king at last graciously restored the title of Earl of Kintail to the family of MacKyle. He kept putting it off, telling himself that Harry undoubtedly had no desire to go to Kintail, or that Egerton would never allow her to visit in the home of a bachelor. But he knew he was only avoiding the issue because he was afraid to have her come to Kintail.

Still, it might be a good thing. They would both see how unsuited she was to life in the Highlands, and they could say farewell as friends who knew that friendship was all there ever would be between them.

He clung with desperate hope to the belief that she would hate the Highlands, would hate the isolation of Kintail and the foreignness of the Gaelic people. For if she did not, he was lost. He would have no reason, no need, to push her away again. That thought frightened him most of all.

The Caldedonian Hunt Ball was the grand climax to a near-fortnight of celebration in Edinburgh. The portico of the Assembly Rooms was illuminated with the newly installed gas lamps, which threw their bright glow on each coach that pulled up to the front.

Harry, following her father up the circling stairs to the ballroom, was relieved to note that the crowd was not so large as it had been for the Peers' Ball. Yet, as on that occasion, the rooms were awash in a sea of plaid. It would be easier to spot Alasdair if he were in formal court dress, she noted with amusement. Although Katrine had assured her that Alasdair had appeared at any number of functions in the required Highland dress, Harry had yet to see the sight.

As they stepped into the ballroom, she was once again grateful that Katrine had taught her some of the steps of the Scottish dances, for it was obvious that Neil Gow's band was in an informal mood this night. Accepting the invitation of a young Scot, she managed a creditable performance through the opening bars of the reel, but quickly became lost during the more intricate footwork. Her partner, a jovial member of some clan, took no offense at her lack of skill.

The arrival of the king did little to slow down the tempo of the dancing. Harry looked about her in vain for Alasdair and Katrine, worrying that they would not be here after all. She had nearly given in to despair when she saw them in the doorway. Katrine was in a lovely white gown, with a shawl of tartan draped across her shoulders.

But Harry's gaze was riveted on Alasdair. She had seen any number of men in the ever-present garb of the Highlands. But none had taken her breath away quite like this. Although tight pantaloons or court breeches showed the shape of a man's legs quite clearly, they did not look at all the same with that area of bare skin between kilt and stocking.

He looked every inch a Highlander from the top of his cockaded bonnet to the tips of his shoes. The tight-fitting tartan jacket emphasized the broadness of his shoulders, and as he led Katrine across the room toward her, the gentle sway of his kilt could only be described as spellbinding. She trembled with anticipation as he drew nearer.

"Good evening, Lady Harriet," he said, his dark eyes studying her intently.

Harry was afraid he could somehow read her thoughts. "Good evening," she replied, lowering her lashes. She opened her eyes again and smiled impishly. "I see you are wearing the kilt tonight. But where are your pink tights?"

Katrine giggled. Alasdair grinned. "I am afraid that is a fashion item only the king can wear," he said in mocking tones.

"And they will soon be all the rage in London, I predict," she teased.

"It is well I will be back in Kintail, then," said Alasdair. "It is a sight I have no wish to see again."

The thought that he would soon leave for his beloved Highlands distressed Harry. They were only beginning to deal together well; she needed more time. But the king's visit was nearly over and her father would take her back to England.

She looked up and saw Alasdair watching her closely.

"My I have this dance, Lady Harriet?"

She nodded and he guided her out onto the floor. It was another reel, and although she stumbled over the more difficult parts, Alasdair praised her skill.

When the dance ended, Alasdair led her toward the refreshment room, where he procured them each a glass of champagne. They walked to the tall, curtained windows overlooking George Street. Carriages lined the far side, waiting to begin their homeward journey, while more vehicles pulled up to the door to disgorge or collect passengers. The curious mob that had plagued the Peers' Ball had not gathered this night.

"Do you think the city will ever recover from this orgy of entertainment?" Harry asked lightly, sipping her drink.

"I find it difficult to picture Edinburgh in the grip of this madness for long," he said. "By fall the city will be back to its normal, unpretentious occupations."

"And leave revelry and sin to London?" she teased.

"Quite so," he replied with a smile.

They stood quietly for several moments, looking down on the street scene outside. Alasdair knew if he was ever to invite her to Kintail, this would be the time. Yet he hesitated, afraid of the results of such a visit.

"Has your father decided to visit his Scottish holdings?" Alasdair asked at last.

Harry shook her head. "He was satisfied with the reports from the factor. And I think he is as exhausted as we all are from this celebration."

Alasdair took a deep breath. "Katrine would be pleased if you would visit with her at Kintail."

Harry turned and looked at him with a bland expression that did not hint of the agitation inside her. "And do you wish it also?"

"It would be a pity if you traveled all this way and only saw Edinburgh," he said evasively. "There is much more to Scotland."

An answer that neatly avoided her question, Harry reflected. But that very act of avoidance told her much. Her heart raced with excitement.

"I shall speak with your father, of course, if you wish to accept our invitation," he continued. "He will want to ensure that you will be adequately taken care of during your visit and your return."

"Yes, he will wish to be consulted," Harry said, hardly daring to breathe. He had said "our invitation," a slip of the tongue that sent her heart racing. He joined with Katrine in asking her to Kintail.

With any other man, such an action would be a very strong indication of interest. But as she was beginning to learn, one could never compare Alasdair Mackyle with other men. He did things in his own manner. He could be acting out of mere politeness and a wish to please his sister.

Yet by his own words he never did anything he did not wish to do—except perhaps participating in the extravaganza of the king's visit. So although she could not be certain of his motives, she could at least feel confident that he was sincere in inviting her to visit his home.

She took another sip of her champagne, trying to appear calm and collected, even though her insides were in a joyous tangle. "I should very much like to see your and Katrine's home," she said. "I would like the opportunity to judge for myself if it is as marvelous as you pretend."

He smiled. "I pretend nothing," he said. "As I think you will agree when you see the Highlands."

"I look forward to that."

"I shall call tomorrow and speak with your father," he said. "If he is amenable, you and Katrine can leave on Friday. The Scots are fearsome strict about the Sabbath."

"You are not coming with us?" she sked with dismay.

He shook his head. "I am leaving for Kintail on Wednesday. On horseback. It is a quicker trip, but not suited for ladies. You and Katrine shall travel by boat."

"From Edinburgh?"

"There is the canal boat to Glasgow, and from there the steamer to Loch Kyle."

"How long does the journey take?"

He shrugged. "It depends on how many stops the steamer has to make. Less than a week, at any event. I will send Finlay along as well as Mrs. Fraser to make certain all goes well."

"I am sorry you will not be joining us," she said with a bold glance.

He looked at her for a moment, the expression in his dark eyes inscrutable. "I will be there to greet you when you arrive at Kintail," he said.

As he led her back to the dance floor, Harry could barely keep a broad smile from forming on her lips. But it would not do for Alasdair to see exactly how pleased she was by this turn of events. There would be time and enough for that once she reached his home. A thrill of excitement raced up her spine at the very thought. Where once she had thought she had no hope, now everything looked possible. Once again she cast blessings down on her father's head for having brought her with him on this trip.

She had no doubt he would approve of her visit. Harry sensed that her father had a liking for Alasdair. She was less certain of what Alasdair thought of her father, but that did not matter.

September looked to be a promising month.

14

Sae flaxen were her ringlets,
    Her eyebrows of a darker hue,
Bewitchingly o'er arching.
    Twa laughing e'en o' lovely blue;

    Robert Burns,
    Sae Flaxen Were Her Ringlets

Harry's first view of Kintail House came as the steamer rounded the point and headed into the small bay. Amidst the trees along the shore, she caught a glimpse of gray stone and the flash of sunlight on glass. They were almost there. Soon she would see Alasdair again.

"Thank goodness we are here at last," Katrine said. "I do not think I could endure another hour on this boat."

As the vessel drew closer to the shore, the outlines of the house became clearer to Harry: the many-gabled roof, the tall tower at the left that surely commanded a sweeping view of the loch. It was much more impressive than she had anticipated.

She glanced around eagerly. Everything in Scotland looked greener than elsewhere—the trees, the bushes, and the grass that clung to the rocky soil and steep hills. Even the sea was green. No wonder London had seemed anathema to Alasdair—all buildings and paving and stone. Scotland, in contrast, was wild, untamed, natural. The tall, rugged hills that ran down to the water's shore made their small boat seem inconesquential.

Several people were gathered on the beach, and when the steamer drew within hailing distance, the spine-tingling notes of a bagpipe swirled across the water. Harry searched eagerly for a glimpse of Alasdair. A wide smile crossed her face when she espied him.

She turned to Katrine. "Do you always welcome the boat in such a grand manner?"

"I believe Alasdair is putting on a show," said Katrine, hiding a grin. No bagpipe had ever greeted her before.

The steamer pulled close to shore, the engines idling while a small boat was put into the water to transport the passengers and their baggage to land. Alasdair stood on the beach, his arms folded across his chest. Harry squinted against the light in a vain attempt to read the expression on his face. Would he display any pleasure at her arrival?

She waited impatiently while the trunks were taken ashore, her eagerness growing as the small boat returned to the steamer. Following Katrine's lead, she climbed carefully into the boat and with a farewell wave to the captain, they headed toward the waiting men.

Alasdair splashed into the water when the boat neared, catching the bow and turning the small craft sideways to the beach. Harry wondered how she was expected to reach land without dampening her skirts, but before she could voice her concern Alasdair was beside her, reaching out his hand.

"Stand up carefully," he commanded, taking firm hold of her hand.

Harry did as he asked and before she could take a breath she was caught up in his arms. He tromped through the shallow water and deposited her on the rocky beach.

With her feet firmly on the ground, Harry struggled to catch her breath. Alasdair had already returned to the water to retrieve Katrine and she was glad she had this moment to compose herself. The sensation of being held in his arms had been most disconcerting. She watched while he set Katrine on her feet.

"*Fàilte do'n Ghaidhealtachd,*" Alasdair said, walking toward Harry with a broad smile. "Welcome, to Kintail, Lady Harriet."

"Thank you, my lord," she said with a smile that equaled his.

"Should you like to ride up to the house in the cart?" he asked, gesturing at the baggage-laden vehicle.

She threw him an amused glance. "I think I am capable of walking such a small distance."

"Very well. Come along."

Like that day at Hampton Court, his stride was so rapid that she nearly had to run to keep up with him. She bit back a plea that he slow down. She would show him that she was not a weak city miss.

By the time they reached the top of the narrow drive, she was breathing hard and she knew her cheeks were flushed. But she halted beside Alasdair with a triumphant smile, then turned to look more carefully at the house.

"Elizabethan?" she asked at last.

He laughed. "Elizabeth was not queen here, you forget," he said. "Try James. Over there"—he pointed to a tall clump of trees—"is where the original castle stood. It's crumbled into ruins now. But the new house was designed to keep some of the original features—hence the tower."

"For spotting enemies?" she teased.

"For spotting the boat," he said laconically.

If Harry had entertained any doubts that they were in the wild Highlands, they vanished instantly when she set foot in the entry hall. She stared around her in mixed wonder and amusement at the profusion of stags' heads and weaponry mounted on the walls.

"Shot them all yourself, did you?" she asked.

Alasdair grinned. "No, I wrestled them to the ground with my bare hands."

Harry turned in a circle, taking in the wicked-looking weapons arrayed between the heads. "Is this your private armory?" she asked.

"No, that is stored in the cellar. These are only a few family relics," he said.

"And I suppose they were all carried into battle?" She raised a quizzing brow.

"Every one," he averred.

"Against the English?"

"Only a few," he said. "We Scots are more likely to fight each other. But this one"—he pointed to a hefty-looking sword over the mantel—"was carried by my grandfather at Culloden. It spitted a few Sassenach soldiers."

Harry shivered at the bloodthirsty image. It reminded her of the oft-expressed opinion that Scots were little better than savages. Alasdair was certainly no savage, but it showed her again how very different were the Scots Highlanders from the English. Were the differences too large to overcome?

Alasdair noted her confused expression. "Come, I shall show you into the drawing room," he said, taking her elbow. "You will find that more to your liking."

Harry noted appreciatively that the drawing room would not have been out of place in many a fashionable London mansion. She looked with admiration at the fine carpets and elegant appointments. It was totally incongruous with the wildness of the entry hall—and totally in keeping with the conflicting nature of Alasdair MacKyle.

"The great hall is a test," he said as he gently prodded her through the door. "If guests do not run in fright, we allow them to see the rest of the house."

"Which is, I assume, as refined as this room?" She traced her finger along the design on the delicate rosewood sofa table.

"Most of it," he said. "We have not furnished the dungeons in quite so grand a manner."

Before she could reply, a tiny, wizened woman dressed head to toe in black came through the door, bearing an enormous silver tea tray, which she set down upon a side table.

"Tapadh leat, a Mhairi," Alasdair said. With a quick, deferential bob, the woman disappeared.

Katrine, who had taken the walk from the beach at a more leisurely pace, strolled into the drawing room. "I hope all those old, moldy stags' heads did not give you a fright," she said to Harry. "I forgot to warn you about them. I keep suggesting to Alasdair that it would do much to improve the appearance of the entry if he had them removed, but you know how stubborn he can be."

"They are certainly dramatic," Harry said with a perfectly straight face.

"Tea?" Alasdair asked, ignoring the jibes.

She nodded and took a seat on the sofa while Katrine poured. The china, Harry observed, looked to be Sevres.

In fact, she decided as she looked about the room more closely, the furnishings were quite obviously Continental rather than British. It was not uncommon in any English home, but she rather suspected that in this house it was done deliberately. One more statement of Scottish independence.

Alasdair's steward appeared at the door, a worried expression on his face.

"What is it, Dougall?" Alasdair asked.

"The new fence," he said apologetically.

Alasdair grimaced, knowing Dougall would not come to him unless it was necessary. "I will be with you shortly." Dougall nodded and departed.

Harry smiled as she watched Alasdair sip his tea with obvious impatience. He clearly wished to attend to his duties, yet he was taking time to make her feel welcome. She set her teacup down.

"Katrine, could you show me to my room?" she asked. "I would not mind resting. All this fresh Highland air makes me sleepy at the oddest times."

"Of course," Katrine said as they rose.

Harry extended her hand to Alasdair. "I look forward to seeing more of your house."

"This afternoon I shall take you on a tour," he said.

"Even the dungeons and the armory?" she said smilingly.

"We shall start with those very places," he promised with a laugh.

"We do not have a dungeon here," Katrine reassured Harry as she led her out into the hall. "What has Alasdair been telling you?"

Harry laughed. "I know he was roasting me shamelessly," she said. "I own this house is much different than I expected."

"You imagined a stone cottage?" Katrine teased.

"Not exactly. The entry hall was very much in keeping with what I expected. The drawing room was the surprise."

"That is the civilizing influence of women," Katrine

said. "I am certain that if Alasdair was left to his own he would have his ridiculous animals and swords all over the house."

Harry laughed. She had fought the same battles with her father.

The room Katrine led Harry to was furnished as elegantly as the drawing room. A tartan canopied and curtained bed dominated one wall facing the fireplace, which was inlaid with blue and white tiles. Harry crossed to examine the view from the two tall windows. She was uncertain which side of the house they were on and smiled with delight when she found herself looking out on the sparkling waters of the loch.

"The view is lovely," she said. "I can see how your brother cannot bear to be away for long."

" 'Tis easier to endure as a guest," Katrine said. "It grows wearisome in the midst of winter when the sun has not shone for weeks and the wind roars down the chimneys."

"London in the grip of a fog so thick you can barely see your hand in front of your face is not pleasant either," Harry countered.

"I am sure that is true," Katrine said, absently toying with the vase on the mantel. "But in London you are at least surrounded with friends and entertainment. Kintail in the winter with only Alasdair and Mrs. Fraser for company can grow wearing."

Harry did not think she could ever grow tired of Alasdair's company. But he was not, after all, her brother. Would she grow equally tired of Tris if cooped up with him for months? She supposed it was highly likely.

"I am sorry to sound so complaining," Katrine said. "It is only coming back to Kintail—and knowing how far I am from Tris again."

"I will do all I can while I am here to convince your brother to change his mind," Harry promised.

"Harry?" Katrine firmly set the vase on the mantel and turned her gaze on her friend.

"Yes?"

"Is it in love with Alasdair that you are?"

Harry paused, her hand on the curtain. "I think so,"

she said at last. She smiled a little sadly at Katrine. "We are a sorry lot, are we not? You are forbidden to marry the man you love, and the man I love . . . well, there is little chance he will ever express such a tender emotion for me."

"I have never known Alasdair to invite a lady to the house," Katrine said.

"Ah, but I am here as *your* guest," Harry said. "That absolves him of any intent."

"I think Alasdair is the most pigheaded, idiotic man I have ever known," Katrine exclaimed. "You would make him a wonderful wife."

"I am not so certain of that," Harry said. "After all, I am much too accustomed to the excitement of town, a lavish wardrobe, and a life of luxury to be content in the wilds of the Highlands. Plus, I am English."

"Alasdair is stupid," Katrine avowed. "As if being English should have anything to do with it. He will not look at either you or Tris with an open mind. Sometimes I can almost hate him!"

Harry put a soothing arm around Katrine's shoulder. "Alasdair is who he is," she said. "We can hope that over time he will soften his attitude. But we cannot force him into anything. He will do what he wishes."

"How can you be so calm about it?" Katrine asked. "You should be as miserable as I."

"Perhaps because I am two-and-twenty," Harry said. "You become much more willing to accept life as it is, rather than rushing out to change it to suit you."

"I could never be happy with anyone but Tris," said Katrine.

"Perhaps that is your Scottish stubbornness," Harry answered. "You are much like your brother in that. Now," she said, taking Katrine's hands, "show me where my things should go. We can talk more about your pigheaded brother later."

Alasdair listened impatiently while Dougall explained the problem with the fence. It was unlike him to be inattentive, but he could not wait to return to Harry. It seemed as if he had been waiting a year for her arrival, only to be dragged away the minute she came. Alasdair sighed. He told Dougall to tear out the new section, remix the mortar, and start over. A poorly constructed fence was of no use.

Several other minor matters needed to be dealt with before he was finally able to return to the house. And Harry.

A smile lit his face when he found his sister and Harry in the drawing room. "Should you like to see the rest of the house?" he asked.

Harry nodded eagerly.

He led her through the entire house. Although it was no doubt smaller than her home, Alasdair felt no shame. He knew it was one of the most elegantly furnished residences in all of Scotland. His mother had seen to that. He was glad, for he wanted Harry to like it.

He could not keep the pride from his voice when he showed her some of the family heirlooms. It pleased him that Harry took interest in the collection of Pictish silverwork gathered from the estate grounds over the centuries. He thought more of those items than all the expensive French porcelain and Flemish paintings collected by his ancestors.

He was more than pleased when she gave an exclamation of delight upon entering his tower study.

"This is wonderful," she exclaimed, walking over to the window. "Do you ever grow tired of the view?" she asked as she gazed out onto the water.

"Never," he said, coming to stand beside her. "A sea view can never grow wearisome—it changes from minute to minute. And the land changes with every season."

"Do you have snow in the winter?"

"Not often. We are warmed by the sea. It falls deeply along the tops of the hills and inland. But only rarely at the edge of the loch."

"How ironic," she said, "when I can remember walking on the hard-frozen Thames."

"There are gardens in the Highlands where palm trees grow," he said by way of explanation.

"How far does the loch continue?" Harry asked.

"It is another ten miles to the end," he said. "Although it narrows considerably just beyond the point. Should you like to see? We can take the boat one day. And catch dinner while we are at it."

"I should like that," she said.

"Even the fishing?" he asked with a ghost of a smile.

"I cannot say that I have ever fished," Harry admitted.

"Then you must while you are here," he said. "You can regale your friends this winter with tales of battling the famed Scottish salmon."

"Are they difficult to catch?" she asked.

Alasdair laughed aloud. "I had one jump in the boat once."

Harry eyed him doubtfully. "I find that rather difficult to believe, Alasdair."

" 'Tis true," he said, holding up his hands in a defensive gesture.

"Do you sail often?" she asked.

He nodded. "Not as often as I should like now. When I was growing up my mother always feared I would be taken off by the silkies, I spent so much time on the water."

"Silkies?"

"The ocean fairies," he explained.

"Do you honestly expect me to believe that your mother—or you—believed in fairies?" she asked.

"Scotland is not England," he said with a slow smile, unable to resist the impulse to tease her. "It is a very uncivilized place. There are areas where no man has dared set foot for hundreds of years. Why, only last year we had a witch in the district."

"And I suppose you burned her at the stake?" she asked sarcastically.

"No. It turned out she was not a witch at all." He shrugged. "She drowned."

"Drowned?" Harry stared in horror. "You drowned her?"

"Well, it is the easiest way to tell if a person is a witch," he said casually. "Witches float."

"You drowned some poor innocent woman on the ridiculous charge of being a witch?" She glared at him, appalled, until she saw the devilment dancing in his eyes. "You are hoaxing me!"

He grinned. " '*S cinnteach.*"

Harry eyed him suspiciously. "Was that a 'yes'?"

He took her hand and placed it on his arm, turning her steps toward the tower stairs. "Let me tell you about the *each uisge*. The water horses. They live in the loch. If you look very carefully, just as the sun is rising, you can sometimes see them playing in the water."

Harry listened to his most amusing story. She did not believe a word of it, and did not think he did either. "Next you will be telling me there is a sea monster out there as well. I am rapidly losing my desire to sail with you."

"No monsters in our loch," he said. "They seem to have a fondness for the inland lochs instead."

"Do you always tease your guests so?" she asked with exasperation.

"I am not teasing you," he insisted. "*A'mhorag* inhabits Loch Morag, *Nisseag* is in Loch Ness, and *Seilag* swims the water of Loch Shiel."

She shook her head at his stubborn determination to be provoking, and turned to the painting that hung over the fireplace. "An ancestor?"

"My grandfather," he said.

Harry stepped closer to the portrait, studying it intently. "You look much like. him," she said.

He felt deep pleasure that she had noticed. "All Scotsmen look alike in a kilt," he said lightly.

"Hardly," she retorted.

"Come along," he said, drawing her down the stairs. "We have barely enough time to visit the old castle before the light fades."

Harry followed him down the curving tower stairs. She blinked as they entered the bright, sun-lit yard, then hastened her steps to keep pace with the impatient Alasdair.

"When was the castle built?" she asked.

He shrugged. "Many years ago."

"That could mean during the Roman occupation or the reign of Henry the Eighth."

He smiled. "The Romans never came this far north. I

believe—or at least family legend states—that the first castle was built before Robert the Bruce. It was modified, of course, over the years."

They emerged from the trees into a grassy field. The hulking shell of the old tower dominated the ruins. Only one tall section of wall remained in any size, and greenery dripped from its top. The remaining walls lay in crumpled piles.

"There is so little left," Harry said with amazement.

"It was abandoned over two hundred years ago," Alasdair explained. "A lot of it has been pulled down over the years to prevent adventuresome youths from getting hurt. There is a goodly part of castle stone in use all around the estate. No sense in letting it go to waste."

"Is it safe to explore?"

He nodded. "Follow me."

He walked around the left side of the ruin, leading her to a wide gap in what was left of one crumbled wall. In places the interior courtyard was still flat and clear of debris, while elsewhere large piles of stones marked the remains of the old buildings. Tall grass grew everywhere.

Alasdair took her hand and carefully guided her around the piles of stone. He stopped at the base of the ruined tower and gave her a challenging look. "Should you like to see a *real* dungeon?" he asked.

"Oh, yes," said Harry eagerly.

He took her hand again and led her down the stone steps at the side of the tower.

"Will it be dark?" she asked apprehensively as she cautiously followed him down.

"There is enough light to see."

They walked down a long stone corridor, the arched ceiling low over their heads. Every ten feet or so there was a gap in the wall or a hole in the ceiling that opened the corridor to the light outside. Yet the stone floor under their feet was still smooth and even. Harry reached out and stroked one of the ancient rock walls.

"Did this passage go under the entire castle?" she asked.

Alasdair nodded. "It was used primarily as a store room." He halted suddenly and pointed to a dark spot before his feet. "There is your dungeon, Lady Harriet. The *toll-dubh*."

She peered around his shoulder, shuddering at the sight of the dark hole. "How deep is it?"

"Fifteen feet or so," he said in an offhand manner.

"Have you ever been down it?"

He nodded. "Dougall and I made an adventure of that one day." He laughed at the memory. "My father was none too pleased at the time."

He turned and saw the concerned expression on Harry's face. "Afraid I shall put you down it, Lady Harriet?"

She flushed, but backed away until she was pressed up against the wall. "I should hope not! Or do you still take English prisoners?"

"It depends," he said, taking her hand in his. Even in the dim light he saw the wariness in her eyes. He rubbed his thumb along her palm. "On how much danger they pose."

Harry uttered a nervous laugh. "I hardly think I pose any danger to you, Lord Kintail."

"Alasdair," he said, while he still traced absentminded patterns on her hand. "And I think you pose a very great danger, Harriet *na sùilean gorma*."

"What does that mean?"

He leaned closer, drawn by her spell. "Harriet-of-the-blue-eyes." Alasdair searched those eyes, looking for the answer as to why she had so bewitched him. Reaching out a hand, he touched an errant curl that lay upon her shoulder. "Harry," he whispered, the memory of that long-ago kiss burning in his brain.

The sharp intensity of his longing acted like a bucket of cold water on Alasdair, and he hastily dropped her hand. *Mo Dhia.* In another moment he would have kissed her again. He took a step back from her, eyeing her with sudden apprehension. "The light is fading fast," he said hoarsely. "We must get out before it becomes too dark to see." Without waiting for her response, he grabbed her arm and drew her down the corridor.

15

O will you leave your father's court,
    An' go along wi me?
I'll carry you unto fair Scotland,
    And make you a lady free.

Willie o'Douglas Dale

Harry kept Alasdair under close observation during dinner, and later as they sat in the drawing room.

Why exactly was she here? She knew her reasons, of course, but what of Alasdair's? Did he really want her here? Earlier, she sensed he did. The amiability he had displayed in Edinburgh was in full evidence. He played the role of the perfect host.

Until that moment at the castle. She knew he wanted to kiss her, but then he had drawn back as if scalded. As if he was afraid of her.

Why on earth would Alasdair MacKyle be afraid of her? Harry smiled to herself. It was not as if she were a dangerous person. Unless . . . unless he cared for her more than he was willing to admit.

A highly possible reason, she thought. It explained a great deal of his strange attitude toward her. And certainly accounted for his odd withdrawal earlier. But by inviting her to Kintail, was he indicating a willingness to acknowledge his feelings? Would he admit, in time, that he did care for her?

The thought made her spirits soar.

Alasdair was uncertain exactly where or when things between him and Harry changed. He had been so certain that she would quickly grow bored with the rural pleasures of Kintail. Yet as the days wore on, she jumped into each new adventure with an enthusiasm that surprised him. Whether it was sailing his small boat on the loch, or fishing for salmon in the river, she greeted every activity with delight.

Perhaps it was the day they went fishing, when they returned wet, muddy, and triumphant with their catch. Katrine had not gone fishing with him in years, and he remembered only too well how she had complained constantly when she went. Harry delighted in this activity she had never tried, squealing in pleasure when she hooked a salmon and insisting on netting it herself even if she dragged her skirts in the water.

He knew now that he had misjudged her from the very first. She might be a diamond in the city, but she was equally at home and comfortable in the country. And he began to believe that Lady Harriet would be content to live at Kintail.

From that moment on, he watched her with the eyes of a hawk, evaluating, judging, measuring. She spoke kindly with the servants, endeavoring to learn a few words of Gaelic, which pleased them inordinately. Harry helped Katrine with her duties around the house, laughing that she had not learned nearly so many accomplishments because of the army of servants her father retained. Alasdair even caught her mending—*mending*— their linen. Egerton would probably suffer apoplexy if he heard of it.

And Harry totally ignored the need for a chaperon on their outings. He worried at first, when she was perfectly willing to accompany him alone, for he had promised Egerton that he would take good care of her. But Harry only laughed when he brought up the subject, insisting that a chaperon was only a sop to society's strictures and her father would never worry about such a thing. He trusted Lord Kintail implicitly. Alasdair wondered how long he would remain worthy of that trust.

For every minute he spent in Harry's company only increased his desire for her. As each new day revealed some new facet of her personality, he found himself spinning dreams of what might be. Harry sitting at the table, entertaining their guests. Harry caught up in the frivolities of Hogmany. Harry, her body wrapped around his

in the massive four-poster bed that had been his parents',
and his grandparents' before that.

But every time he thought about the possibilities, reality came crashing down around him. She was English.
The life in the Highlands was as foreign to her as the
city had been to him. Yes, she was enjoying her visit.
But would she be content to live here, without the amenities of city life?

Could he overcome that? He did not know. But he
wanted to find out. Because he began to think that he
was desperately in love with Lady Harriet Winterbourne.

"Shall we go riding today?" Alasdair asked one morning at breakfast.

"Certainly," replied Harry. She glanced down at her
light jaconet muslin dress. "Perhaps I should change."

"A good idea," Alasdair said. He turned to his sister
with an inquiring look.

"I have no desire to go riding with you today," she
said.

He shrugged. "As you wish. I will meet you in the hall
when you are ready, Harry."

"Do not let Alasdair lead you too far today," Katrine
warned Harry. "Once he gets out in the hills he loses all
sense of time and place."

"While I shall be simply lost," said Harry with a self-
deprecating smile. She stood up. "I must hurry."

"I will find you a plaid to take," Katrine said, rising
herself. "The weather can become chill this time of
year."

"Particularly when your brother has been provoked,"
Harry said, and they laughed. Yet Harry remembered
the look in his eyes when he had nearly kissed her at the
castle. He had been provoked then too. But in a different
manner.

Harry restrained the urge to laugh when she joined
Alasdair in the entry hall. He was clad in plaid trousers,
and his boots were unpolished and scratched. She rather
thought they were more practical than what one saw in
the country at home. He would not have any qualms
about tramping across a field in those.

He nodded approvingly at the length of plaid she carried over her arm. "A good item to take," he said as he led her to the door. " 'Tis the best thing you can have in case of a sudden shower."

Harry had hoped to discover the location of the Kintail stables, but the saddled horses were waiting for them when they stepped outside.

"Did you conjure them up from the earth?" she asked. "Or are they the *each uisge*?"

"Actually, they came from the far side of the orchard," he said. "We will pass near the stables on our ride."

Alasdair helped her to mount and, after warning her the horse did not understand a word of English, motioned for her to follow. In a short moment they were among the trees. Although the stand of fir looked thick from the shore, it formed only a thin line on this side of the house, and soon they were on the fringes of the Kintail orchards.

"Apples?" she asked as she looked at the nearest tree.

He nodded. "And pears. Another advantage of the ocean warmth."

When they reached the far end of the trees, he pointed to the collection of buildings that comprised the stables. A small stone-fenced pasture lay between them and the stables, and in it were two of the strangest animals Harry had ever seen.

"Those do not look like the deer in your hall," she said at last. "Are they some special Scottish breed?"

Alasdair laughed. "Those are reindeer, my ignorant one."

"I did not know there were reindeer in Scotland," she said defensively.

"Only two," he replied. "Mine."

"Dare I ask why you have two reindeer?"

He shrugged. "They were for sale this spring in London. I thought I should like to see how well they adapt to the Scottish countryside."

"What does one do with a reindeer?" she asked as they continued on their way.

"They might make passable eating," he said. "I understand that is what the Laplanders consume."

"Out of choice or necessity?" she asked. "Reindeer meat might taste dreadful."

"That we shall find out when the time comes," he said. "First we need more than two."

"Do you have any other interesting animals about?" she asked. She would not be surprised to find he had an elephant hidden in one of the glens. He probably thought they were good eating too.

"Deer, cattle, and sheep," he said.

"You have sheep?" she asked in surprise.

"Why should I not?"

"But you hate sheep."

"I do not hate sheep," he explained. "I only hate depriving people of their livelihoods in the name of sheep. They are useful creatures. Meat to eat, wool for clothing. Whence did you think the yarn for that plaid you carry came?"

Harry was slightly confused. Once again, she had misunderstood.

"Do your people tend your sheep?" she asked.

He nodded. "We do not raise a great amount. There is not enough land. We feed ourselves and sell some meat and the wool. This year the prices are bad and we may only find a market for the wool."

The rough pathway they had been following began to ascend the side of sloping hill. Harry turned and looked behind her. Kintail House loomed out of the treetops, and the orchard lay spread out below them. To her left were tilled fields, their bounty harvested already.

"What grows on your land?" she asked.

"Everything," he said. "Oats, barley, rye. Potatoes."

"And do you market all of it?"

"If there is enough," he said. "The tenants keep their share, we keep what we need for the house and sell what is left. This year there was not much to sell."

"If you raise only a few sheep, and sell so little grain, where do you get enough money to live on?" she asked.

He grinned. "Various places."

She looked at him suspiciously. "Legal ones?"

Alasdair laughed. "Spoken like a true Englishwoman. English law is not Scots law, my lady."

"You are actually involved in illegal things?" she asked, aghast. "Smuggling?"

"There is little of that nowadays. We produce a little *uisge-beatha* that has found favor in some circles."

"*Uisge-beatha?*"

"Whiskey."

"You have an illegal still?" she asked incredulously.

"Everyone in the Highlands has an illegal still," he explained. He reined in his horse and turned to her. "Since the government banned distilleries that produce less than two hundred gallons, we all operate on the wrong side of the law."

"An earl involved in illegal distilling?" She gave him a skeptical look, thinking he teased her again. "I cannot believe it."

"It is no worse than a king who drinks it," he said. "I understand that he developed quite a taste for Glen Livet while in Edinburgh."

"You sound as bad as the 'gentlemen' who inhabit the southern coasts," she protested. "They think of smuggling as an honorable profession."

"As is whiskey production," he pointed out.

"May I see the still?" she asked.

He shook his head. "Not today."

Harry frowned but did not protest. Alasdair urged his horse forward again and they soon came to the crest of the small hill, and started down the opposite side into a deep glen.

"Is this still your land?" she asked, looking about the heather-covered hills.

He nodded and pointed. "To the top of that ridge," he said, his voice tightening.

They rode on in comparative silence. Alasdair pointed to a swooping osprey, and identified the rowan and hawthorne trees that dotted the glens. They stopped to let the horses drink from the stream at the bottom of the small vale, then forded the water and started up the far slope.

Harry was surprised when the track they followed did

not continue up the hill, but traversed its slope. "Are we not going to the top?"

"We will eventually," he said mysteriously. "But there is something I wish you to see first."

The horses ambled along the meandering path for half an hour. The land grew wooded, but with alder this time instead of the tall firs that surrounded Kintail House. At last, beside another stream, Alasdair called a halt.

"We shall have to continue on foot," he said, dismounting and tying his horse to a tree. He helped Harry down and secured her horse, then without a word scooped her up in his arms and splashed across the shallow stream bed.

She was back on her feet before she could blink. It was the first time he had done more than touch her hand since that day at the castle. Harry took a deep breath to steady herself.

"It is not far," he said, holding out his hand.

Harry followed beside him as they climbed the grassy slope. A strange noise, which had been barely discernable where they left the horses, grew louder and louder until it roared in her ears. "Is it the wind?" she asked.

"You will see," he said with an eager smile.

The path wound its way between scrubby bushes, the ground underfoot growing increasingly rocky. Harry almost stumbled once, but Alasdair's strong hand kept her upright.

They reached the crest of the hill and continued down the far side, where the trail became a zigzag track and the roar grew almost deafening. Alasdair stopped suddenly and turned toward her. "Keep close and hold tightly to my hand," he warned. "It is a narrow ledge." He stepped forward, then halted. "You are not averse to heights, are you?"

"No," she said, taking his proferred hand. She crept along behind him carefully, as they climbed out on to a rocky ledge.

Harry's mouth opened with an 'Oh' of surprise at the sight. A tall column of water poured down before them, crashing to the rocks below, then spilling over the next ledge in a froth of white.

"It is magnificent," she said in awed wonder.

"The Falls of Lochalsh," he explained with a trace of pride. "There is another fall below, but we cannot see it from here."

Harry stood quietly, impressed by the power and sound of the rushing water, enjoying the damp breeze on her face. A rainbow danced in the mist above the water. She stole a quick glance at Alasdair, who stared down at the frothy pool with a pensive look. Then his gaze lifted and he regarded her with a curious expression on his face.

They stared at each other silently for a long moment, then Alasdair turned abruptly. "We must go," he said, motioning for her to move.

He said nothing as they retraced their steps to the horses. Harry sensed this place was special for him, and was pleased that he had shown it to her. Yet his silence confused her. Was he angry with her? Had he expected a more awed reaction?

After remounting, they backtracked to the first stream they had crossed, then followed along it single-file for a pace. Gradually the stream bed widened, and they rode side by side again.

Alasdair quickly resumed his light bantering with her, and Harry thought that she had been mistaken in feeling that brief chill of his displeasure. She had only imagined it. Alasdair was no longer the rude, arrogant man she had known in London. She understood that now. It was only when he withdrew from her in this puzzling manner that she grew uncertain, not knowing the cause of his silence. But she did not ask. Things were going far too smoothly between them. She did not wish to open any cracks that were not there.

Alasdair busied himself about the estate for the rest of the day. He should not have taken Harry to the falls. It was his special place, where he always went when he wished to be completely alone. But he had wanted her to see it, to see the gleam of awe and wonder in her eyes as she viewed the roaring cataract.

And she had reacted in just such a way. Then why did he regret his impulse? Because it demonstrated once again that she *did* fit in at Kintail. She shared his appreciation for natural beauty, and enjoyed riding over the countryside. She even enjoyed fishing.

Lady Harriet had the uncanny knack of turning all his expectations topsy-turvy. Rather than demonstrating how ill-suited she was to live in the Highlands, she reveled in it. Instead of convincing him that she would be a most unsuitable companion, she was well on the way to showing him that he could not live without her. And he was in no way certain whether that would bring him joy or despair.

He tried to keep his roiling emotions firmly in check during dinner. He concentrated on light amiability, complimenting both Katrine and Harry on their gowns, and assuring Harry he would be more than happy to introduce her to the reindeer on the morrow. But when dinner ended, he pleaded the need to speak with Dougall and promised to join them later in the drawing room. It was a cowardly escape, but he was not certain he would be able to speak comfortably with Harry this night. His thoughts were a confused jumble, and he would not be able to participate in the light banter of the drawing room. He needed time to think.

He walked to the beach, picking his way down the familiar trail with ease even in the darkening night. He picked up a handful of pebbles and tossed them one by one into the water, listening to the satisfying splash as each one hit.

Harry. Today at the falls, he had fought against the urge to pull her into his arms and kiss her until they were both breathless. Never had he felt so out of control in the presence of a woman. What was he to do? Marry her and damn the consequences? Send her home on the next boat before they made a disastrous mistake?

If there were only some way he could see into the future, to know if they would be happy. For once he wished that he possessed the sight. It would be easier to make decisions about such monumental things.

But the sight was no guarantor of reality, either. It did not always show what would be, but what could be. He would be left with as many doubts as before.

Could Harry be happy at Kintail?

He glanced up to the sky, as if seeking the answer in the stars, and a smile spread over his face. All his doubts dropped away, and he knew he had to share this with Harry. Dropping the remaining pebbles, he ran as quickly as he dared to the house.

"Grab your cloaks," he gasped as he raced into the drawing room. "We have the lights in the sky tonight."

"What lights?" Harry asked.

"The northern lights. *Na fir-chlis.* The aurora borealis," he explained hastily between breaths. "You must come see."

"I have seen them enough times," Katrine said, turning back to her book.

"Harry?" he asked, reaching out his hand in an imploring gesture.

"I should love to," she said, and grabbed a plaid shawl from a chair.

The warm plaid she wrapped herself in was adequate protection from the cool September night. Alasdair took a lamp from the hall to light their way down the path to the beach. But before they reached the rocky shore, he turned off onto a narrower trail leading through the trees.

"Do the lights occur often?" she asked.

"Probably more often than we know," he said, "for you can only see them on a clear night. They are best seen from the point," he explained. "But we will not go so far."

In a minute they reached the edge of the trees, which ended in a tumbled fall of boulders.

"Look," Alasdair said, pointing to the sky.

Harry looked up to the hills behind Kintail, and sucked in her breath at the sight.

Dancing patterns of light seemed to leap from the hilltops, arcing high into the sky, fading briefly before a new burst of light and color rose up to replace them. The whole sky was alive with color: white, blue, red, and green mingling in ever-shifting patterns. It was much like watching the play of light on a moving sea, except here it was the light that was moving, not the sky behind it.

Alasdair carefully guided her down the jumble of boulders to the beach, where he spread out a plaid on the sand. "Sit down," he said, taking her hand and drawing her down to the blanket. He propped himself against a rock. "Lean into my shoulder," he suggested, putting his arm around her. "You will be more comfortable. If we are lucky, they will last for a while."

Harry did as he said, unable to tear her eyes away from the spectacle in the sky.

They sat in total silence, listening to the lap of water on the shore providing rhythmic accompaniment to the dancing lights in the sky. Harry watched intently, but it was never quite the same. At times, one single flame of color would lunge toward the sky, growing and building, then fading before her eyes. At other times, the entire horizon would be awash with color that spread over the dark background like an application of watercolor from an artist's brush. Once, when it grew black for a moment, she thought it was over, but then a faint flickering to the right signaled a new burst of activity.

Even when it became apparent that the display had finally reached its end, Harry said nothing. Words were too inadequate to even describe what she had seen. It was like much of Scotland—wild and colorful, beautiful and frightening at the same time. Like Alasdair. He belonged to this country.

She shivered.

"Cold?" he asked gently, drawing the plaid closer around her shoulders.

Harry shook her head. "I am still in awe," she said. "That was the most beautiful thing I have ever seen."

"It does not often last that long," he said. "We were lucky tonight."

Harry was only sorry it had ended at all. She could have sat here watching contentedly forever. She looked out toward the inky blackness that was the loch, hearing the rippling waves rushing and receding. The lamp still burned brightly on the sand where Alasdair had set it, sending wild shadows leaping against the waves.

She was indescribably content, sitting here next to him. She felt they had reached a new accommodation with each other. They were comfortable together. But would he ever look upon her with the devotion that she desired?

As if in answer to her unspoken question, his arm tightened around her shoulder.

"We should return to the house," he said, the reluctance in his voice clear.

"On such a magnificent night?" she said softly. "T'would be a shame."

Indecision tore at Alasdair. Despite the spectacular attraction in the sky, his attention had been focused totally on Harry. Sitting in such close proximity, his arm wrapped around her and her head resting comfortably against his shoulder—it felt *too* good. There was no room for doubts tonight. Harry was too beautiful, too perfect.

Brushing back an errant wisp of hair from her forehead, Alasdair allowed his fingers to trail across her cheek. "Harry," he whispered softly, then lowered his mouth onto hers.

It was so unlike that kiss in London. There, it had been fueled by anger at his desire for her. He had meant it as a punishment. This time it was a caress, a yearning, a declaration that however confused he had once been about his feelings for her, they had suddenly grown clearer.

He slipped his arm about her waist while his other hand sought to wrap itself in her tumbling tresses. And with a deep sigh of joy, he felt her hands inching up to circle his neck.

"Mo ghraidh," he breathed, drawing her closer, wrapping her in his arms. His lips danced over hers, testing their sweetness, seeking, demanding; his pulses raced at her answering response, a passion that seemed akin to his own. He groaned in sheer delight as he gathered her even closer to him.

Harry's heart was pounding so hard that the sound nearly deafened her. But above it she was still able to hear the strange words he murmured, and even though she did not understand them she knew he spoke of love and desire. It was all she had ever dreamed of from the moment she first laid eyes on him in London. Alasdair, holding her in his arms and kissing her with an intensity that drew her breath away.

"Harry, Harry," he whispered over and over again as his kisses softened, and his grip loosened. His lips trailed gently over her face, planting soft kisses wherever they touched.

At last he drew back. She could barely see his face in the dim light from the lamp, but it was bright enough to see the look of amazement and desire on his face.

Harry reached up and cradled his face in her hands. "How does one say 'I love you' in Gaelic?"

"Tha gradh agam ort," he said softly.

"Tha gradh agam ort," she repeated. *"Tha gradh agam ort,* Alasdair MacKyle."

He squeezed her tightly, crushing her against his broad chest. *"M' eudail,"* he whispered in her ear.

Harry lost all sense of time. If Alasdair had not drawn her to her feet, enveloping her in soft folds of plaid, she might have sat with him until the dawn. In the warmth of his arms, she had not felt the chill Scottish night. Alasdair helped her scramble up the rocks, then lay his arm across her shoulders as he guided her toward the house.

The entry hall was in deep shadow when they entered. Suddenly shy, Harry turned to speak with Alasdair, but before she could utter a word he drew her into his arms for one more lingering kiss.

A hesitant cough broke the silence. Alasdair lifted his head and spotted Finlay on the far side of the chamber. "We are not robbers," Alasdair said with a dismissive wave of his hand. He looked back at Harry. "It is late, *mo ghraidh,"* he said softly. "We will talk of this in the morning."

She nodded, overwhelmed by all that had happened, and what it meant for them both. The servant Màiri appeared as if invisibly summoned, candle in hand, and Harry followed her up the stairs. She turned once to look back, seeing Alasdair watching her with a perplexed expression on his face. She blew him an airy kiss and even in the faint light she saw his smile.

Harry quickly prepared for bed. After blowing out the candle at her bedside, she pulled the covers over herself. But sleep was the last thing on her mind.

It had happened. The very thing she had longed and hoped for since March. *Alasdair loved her.* The thought brought a smile to her lips. She had done the right thing by coming to Kintail; all was working out as she had hoped.

She could hardly wait until the dawn. *We will talk in the morning,* he had said. About their future? Their life together? She snuggled down further under the covers, ignoring the creeping lassitude that stole over her limbs. Alasdair, she thought over and over, until she drifted into sleep.

16

Think'st thou that this love can stand
Whilst thou still dost say me nay?

Andrew Marvel,
Ametus and Thestylis Making Hay Ropes

After he awoke the next morning, Alasdair lay in bed, still awed by his feelings for Harry. Yet as much as he loved her, and knew she loved him, it was not enough.

He had to know—she had to know—if she could live in the Highlands, if she could transfer her loyalty to Scotland. It was the only way their love could survive.

There was one more thing she needed to see, one more place she had to visit before he would know. One more test before he could be certain. He uttered up a fervent prayer that she would pass it.

After dressing hastily, he grabbed a few oatcakes from the kitchen and fled the house before either Katrine or Harry stirred. He made his way down to the beach and stood silently, watching the waves lap against the rocks. Harry had come to Scotland to see the country. Today they would view her father's land. He firmly shoved all memories of last night from his mind. He could not think about them now. Not until he knew.

When he returned to the house, Katrine and Harry were finishing their breakfast.

Harry looked up brightly when he entered.

"I thought to show you your father's land today," he said abruptly. "That is, if you still wish to see it."

"I would love to," Harry replied.

"We will need to take the horses," he said.

"I can be ready shortly," Harry said. "Is it terribly far?".

A pained expression crossed Alasdair's face. "No, it is

169

not far." He rose from the table. "I have a few things to attend to. Send word with Dougall when you are ready." He left the room with hasty steps.

Harry turned to Katrine. "Why do I have the feeling that was more of a command than a request?"

Katrine shrugged nervously. "You know Alasdair. He is very much accustomed to having his own way."

The path Harry and Alasdair followed on horseback meandered close to the water and was crisscrossed with several streams. Alasdair was quiet. After last night Harry was not certain what to expect from him, but silence was not it. Once again, she sensed he was withdrawing from her. Did he regret having kissed her? Had her declaration of love displeased him?

They had ridden for nearly an hour when Alasdair turned away from the water and headed toward the low inland hills. Harry gave up trying to draw him into conversation. She would wait for him to break the silence.

She followed him over the top of a low rise, and gazed down into a small, tranquil valley where a flashing stream cut a crooked path through the middle.

Alasdair turned in the saddle and gave her a penetrating look. "This is your father's land," he said.

She urged her horse forward until it stood next to his, looking down at the peaceful green of the Scottish countryside. He gestured at the far side of the stream, where a ruined stone hut stood, the roof gone and weeds and grass growing around it in profusion, inside and out.

"Three years ago, five people lived there," Alasdair said in a flat voice.

"Sheep?" she asked, although she knew what the answer would be.

He nodded.

"Do you know where the people are now?" she asked.

He shrugged. "Glasgow, maybe. Or Upper Canada." His voice lowered. "Or dead."

Harry shut her eyes. She knew that Alasdair felt strongly about the introduction of sheep and the displacement of the small farmers. But times were changing, and progress had to come to the Highlands sometime. Else it would remain forever a poor and impoverished place, the butt of jokes from Edinburgh to London. Could he not see that?

"And have none of your own people gone to the cities, or North America?" she asked.

"A few," he admitted. "But it was by choice, not necessity." He shifted in the saddle and looked at her. "You do not understand a Highlander, Harry. We are only half-men when we are away from the Highlands, as I was in London, like a fish out of water. It is in our blood forever. My grandfather spent fifty years away from Scotland, and his dying breath was his wish to come home."

"Did he?" she asked.

He nodded. "He is buried in Kintail, where he should have lived his entire life." He looked at her in an imploring manner. "You cannot understand the helplessness of people who are torn away from all they have ever known, with no hope of ever returning. I ache for every person I have to send to Glasgow or Upper Canada." His voice grew bitter. "But I cannot help them all."

"Different men have different ideas of what is best for the Highlands," she said, trying to reconcile the two conflicting views. "Remaining in your home, only to starve, is cold comfort."

"No one need starve if things were managed properly," he said. "Scotland is no lush farmland, but it can produce enough to support the crofters and the fishers, if one makes the attempt. Sheep are only easier—and cheaper."

"Is it not the right of a landlord to make the best economic use of his land?" Harry asked.

"Not if the profits are only going to line his pockets," he said.

Harry bit her lip, unwilling to argue with him. "What would you do if you had the land?" she asked, trying to draw him out.

"Bring the people back," he said. "Farm the land that is good. Raise animals where it is not. Experiment, and try things that have not been done before. Use the land wisely, not arbitrarily."

"And profits be damned?" she asked softly.

"Use profits for improvements," he replied. "And expansion. Not for fancy clothes and fine furnishings."

Harry sat silently. What more was there to say? His way was right—for him. But she found it unfair that he condemned all those who disagreed with him. Like her father. "Perhaps there is more than one way to use the land," she suggested. "Certainly, not every inch is good for farming."

"What would you have us do?" he asked sarcastically. "Build factories to manufacture trinkets for the wealthy?"

"Factories would provide jobs."

"Highlanders are not meant for the factory," he insisted stubbornly. "We are tied to the land."

"You cannot stop progress, Alasdair," she said gently.

"And who says that sheep and factories are progress?" he asked bitterly.

"It is the way of the world."

"Then I wish to have nothing to do with the world." He glared at her.

She felt Alasdair's scrutiny and knew he was weighing her. And she knew that she would not pass the test. In a rush she realized how futile all her longings had been, how futile this trip had been. He would never accept her; there would always be this barrier between them. Last night had been a dreadful mistake. She raised her head, a challenging look in her eyes. She was the daughter of the Marquess of Egerton, and nothing was ever going to change that.

"You are undoubtedly hungry," he said suddenly. "There is a good place to stop up ahead." Without waiting for her reply he turned his horse and followed a new path that ascended the hill.

Harry thought any food would taste like sawdust to her right now. She guided her horse behind his. It was quite clear that nothing had changed between them. The amiability of the last days had been an aberration. And oh, how deeply she wished it could be otherwise.

Harry was near despair when they returned to the house, although she thought she hid her feelings well.

She thanked Alasdair warmly for escorting her, then slipped up to her room to change from her riding clothes and think.

She had wanted so badly to show him that she could fit into his life. Yet nothing she did would ever erase who she was—the daughter of an English landowner. And after today, she knew he would never be able to look beyond that.

Yet he had kissed her last night. Kissed her and held her in his arms and whispered Gaelic endearments in her ear. He wanted her.

And with a dawning horror, she realized that mere want was not enough for him. No desire was so great that it could cut through his hatred for the English. Desire her he did, but that did not mean he wished to wed her. She had misunderstood everything.

With a sad smile, she gathered up her shawl and went in search of Katrine. Harry did not wish to be alone with her thoughts any longer.

"Did you have an enjoyable ride?" Katrine asked when Harry walked into the drawing room.

"No," Harry said.

Katrine looked up from her sewing with a pained expression. "Alasdair has been trying to buy that land for years from your father, you know."

Harry stared at her. "Indeed?" No wonder it had upset him so.

Katrine nodded. "That whole valley—Keppoch—used to belong to us. But my great-grandfather was forced to sell the land after the '45. Alasdair wants it back almost as much as he did the title."

"It is called Keppoch?" Harry asked, a puzzled expression on her face.

"Yes."

"Then it is mine," Harry said, sinking down into a chair. "Or at least, it shall be when I marry. Papa set aside some of the Scottish land for me when I was born. But I never dreamed it was the piece adjoining your estate."

"Or that Alasdair would want it so much," Katrine

pointed out. "At least your problem is solved—tell that to Alasdair and he will marry you in a trice."

"Oh, Katrine." Harry sighed disconsolately. "That is virtually blackmail."

"A time-honored Scottish custom," replied Katrine.

"And one no self-respecting Englishwoman would ever use to snare a husband," Harry said. "What a ghastly thought! I would never wish to taunt him with such a thing."

"It is too bad Tris does not have the land," Katrine said with a trace of sadness. "I might be allowed to marry him after all."

"What a wonderful idea!" Harry exclaimed. "I am certain we could arrange that. Papa would not object. He can trade some of the land in England that belongs to Tris."

Katrine looked unconvinced. "I was joking," she said. "I do not think Alasdair will ever relent on the matter of Tris."

"I will write Papa and see if he is amenable," said Harry, ignoring the other girl's doubts. It was far too late for her happiness. But perhaps she could turn this disaster into happiness for someone. There was no piece of land on earth she wanted less than Keppoch.

"The mail boat was here early this morning," Katrine said. "There is a letter for you."

"From Papa," said Harry eagerly as she broke the seal. She scanned the first page quickly, then laughed as she glanced at the rest of the letter. "I stand corrected. It is from Tris. For you."

Katrine turned toward her, her face a mixture of eagerness and apprehension.

Harry smiled and thrust the papers into her hands. "Alasdair is not here. Read it."

"Oh, thank you," breathed Katrine, and she sank down in the nearest chair, clutching the letter to her chest. She shut her eyes for a brief moment, then quickly turned to the first page.

Harry watched her with a fond eye. How clever of Tris to take advantage of her presence here to smuggle a letter to Katrine. Right under Alasdair's nose. At least one good thing had come of her visit.

After escorting Harry to the house, Alasdair walked the horses back to the stable. Already he regretted having taken her to the old crofter's hut today. He had been fueled with anger and fear, wanting to show her what the actions of her father meant on a human level. It had bothered her, he knew from her reaction. But was that not all to the good? He had tried to tell her how things could be done differently—the dreams he had for his own property and people. But she would not listen. She nattered on about progress, as if it were progress to tear people off their land. Harry did not understand the Highlands; it was ridiculous to think she ever could. A love for the Highland people was as foreign to her as their language.

He unsaddled the two horses himself, rubbing each down with a soft cloth of wool and then brushing their coats till they shone. He only wished he could have found a more difficult task. For all the time he worked, thoughts of Harry danced through his mind. He had asked her to Kintail to prove to himself that she had no place here. And in the end he had succeeded only too well.

Weary at last from his exertions, he walked back through the orchard to the house. He would have to speak with Katrine, and broach the topic of Harry's departure. Learning his sister was in the drawing room, Alasdair strode through the doorway, frowning when he saw Harry there as well. "I hear the boat stopped this morning. Did it bring anything of importance?"

Harry darted a glance at Katrine and cringed at the guilty flush that crept up the girl's cheeks. She wanted to shout out a warning, but dared not draw her attention.

"Some letters," Katrine murmured, frantically fumbling with the pages in her lap. "The ones for you are on the table."

Alasdair walked to the table near the sofa, scooped up the mail, and sat down across from Harry. "You will think we Scots are severely lacking in manners, to read our mail before you," he said with a pointed look at Katrine. "Did I not hear you received a letter of your own, Harry?"

"A short note from my father," she lied, nervously watching as Katrine attempted to fold up the letter from Tris.

"While it looks as though Katrine received a book" he said. "Francie Stewart again? Or a note from one of your new Edinburgh beaus?"

Katrine flushed scarlet. She jumped from her chair, scattering the sheets of paper at her feet.

Harry was on her knees in an instant, but Alasdair was faster, stooping next to Katrine while he collected the papers. He reached out to hand them to her, but then he glanced down at the papers in his hands and his expression darkened. He glared at his sister. "Were you not forbidden to receive letters from this man?" he demanded harshly.

Katrine's eyes filled with tears. She nodded.

Alasdair crumpled the pages in his hand. "Go to your room, Katrine."

Harry stepped forward. "That is my letter," she said calmly, holding out her hand. "I should like it, please."

Alasdair looked from her to Katrine and back again. "I kindly ask you not to interfere in family matters."

"Tris is part of *my* family," Harry said. "Or have you forgotten?"

"This has nothing to do with you," he said. "It is between Katrine and myself."

"Tris is my cousin."

"That does not make him a suitable husband for my sister," he said.

"Because he is English?"

"Harry, let us not argue about this," he insisted.

A cold chill swept over her as she studied the implacable look on his face. From the corner of her eye, she saw Katrine slip out of the room. Tris and Katrine were the issue here, but the problem ran deeper than that. It ran back to the land, and that ruined crofter's hut. To her father.

She took a deep breath. "If Tris is so unsuitable for

your sister, how can you bring yourself to spend time in my company?" she demanded. *Or kiss me*, she thought. "I am as English as he."

"It is not the same," he said with a dismissive wave of his hand.

"How does it differ?" she asked.

He impatiently brushed back a lock of hair from his forehead. "Everything is different. Katrine is *banaghaidheal*. A Highlander. An Englishman would take Katrine away from here, the country of her birth. That I cannot allow."

Harry's expression remained impassive, but her mind was filled with dread. She forced herself to press on. She had to know. Now. There was no point in letting this drag on.

She had been so uncertain about his feelings until last night. The magical day at the waterfall, and that wonderful night on the beach, when he had kissed her and held her in his arms, made her think that he did love her. Yet his cold behavior today told her something very different. If only she could think clearly. But Alasdair was staring intently at her and she did not know where to start. Or what to say.

She looked at him with sorrow in her eyes. "Then how can you bring yourself to make love to an Englishwoman?" she asked. "Or were all your actions last night lies?"

"A darkened beach, a lovely lady at my side . . . I am only a man, Harry. Not a saint. You cannot think I would not take advantage of such a situation."

Harry felt tears spring to her eyes and she furiously blinked them back. "I told you I loved you, Alasdair. I meant it."

He shifted uneasily, not meeting her eyes. "Love can be a fleeting thing," he said.

"Why, Alasdair?"

"Because it was not meant to be," he said, fighting against the pain of his knowledge. "You know that as well as I. We come from two very different worlds."

"And yours, of course, is the only right one," she said with an angry toss of her head. "That is why you took me to Keppoch, to make certain I understood that. Well,

I do. More than you think. And it will give me great pleasure to ensure you will never get Keppoch back."

"That land is a matter between your father and I," he said. "Do not interefere here, Harry."

"Oh? You do not know Keppoch is part of my dowry?"

He stared at her with a look of blank amazement on his face. "It is?"

She smiled bitterly. "And it will go with me to the man I marry," she said harshly. "And he will certainly not be a MacKyle." With head high, she walked regally out of the room.

Alasdair watched her depart with impassive eyes until the door closed behind her. It was done then, he thought. Yet he was gripped by a sense of loss that went far deeper than Keppoch. A loss that went to the very core of his soul.

17

Farewell, hours that late did measure
Sunshine days of joy and pleasure;
Hail, thou gloomy night of sorrow,
Cheerless night that knows no morrow!

Robert Burns,
Raving Winds Around Her Blowing

Later that evening, Harry returned to the now-empty drawing room, staring at the crumbled pages of Tris's letter scattered on the floor. In a few short minutes all had ended.

These last weeks had been an illusion after all, she reflected sadly, built on her false hopes that she could win his heart. Now, she doubted if he even had one. For he had certainly treated her as if he thought she did not. If only . . .

Harry stopped herself. One could not roll back time, no matter how much one wished it. The damage was done. There was no point in carrying this farce any further. Pride forbade it. If, by some miracle, he realized he wanted her, he would have to come to her. He must lay his heart at her feet and then—and only then—would she deign to pick it up. She was a Winterbourne, after all. And a Winterbourne did not beg or plead.

With great sadness for what might have been, she retrieved the pages of Tris's letter and walked to her room.

She must have fallen asleep, for she jolted with a start at a sharp tap on her door.

"Harry?" Katrine asked. "Are you there?"

"Yes," Harry replied, sitting up on the bed. She brushed back her tangled hair.

Katrine slipped into the room. "What happened after I left?" she asked breathlessly. "Is Alasdair still angry?"

She gave Katrine a sorrowful glance. "How long until the boat returns?"

"You are not leaving?"

Harry nodded. "I must. Things have been damaged beyond all repair."

"Let me talk to him," Katrine urged. "I am the one he is angry with. Do not let his anger spill over onto you."

"It is too late for that," Harry said bitterly. "I was foolish to think he would ever accept my presence here. The sooner I can return to England, the better."

"The boat can stop on its return trip to Glasgow," Katrine admitted. "Although it may be a few days." A few days in which this breach with Alasdair could be repaired, she fervently hoped.

"I will be packed and ready," Harry said. "Tell Dougall to raise the flag."

Alasdair, however, refused to cooperate with Katrine's plans. When he had not returned to the house by dinner, she grew concerned. Finlay told her he had gone off into the hills, giving no indication of when he would return.

"It is for the best," Harry said when Katrine relayed the news to her. "I do not think his presence here would make any difference, Katrine. I fear some things were not meant to be."

"But what will you do?" Katrine asked in sympathy.

"The Little Season has yet to start," Harry said with forced insouciance. "I am certain London will prove quite diverting."

"I wish you would stay," said Katrine. "It will be so intolerably lonely with you gone."

"I will write often," Harry promised her. "And I shall send as much news of Tris as I dare. Perhaps we can devise another way to smuggle you a letter. I can send you a bonnet—with a letter hidden in the lining. Or a box of comfits with the paper cleverly concealed in the lid."

Katrine smiled at Harry's attempts to rally her spirits. "I shall miss you dreadfully."

"And I will miss you," Harry said.

It only took two days before the steamer passed Loch

Kyle on its return journey to Glasgow. Alasdair was still gone. Harry wondered, with pained amusement, if he would stay away forever if she did not leave. But she would be gone in a few minutes and then he could come out from the hills and be comfortable in his own home again.

She gathered up her cloak and bonnet. Katrine walked with her to the beach, where Mrs. Fraser and Dougall awaited them. They would both accompany Harry to her father's estate.

Harry looked out over the sparkling water with sadness. Would Alasdair ever be able to look back upon this time with anything but painful memories? She knew she would not, but all along she had suspected Alasdair's heart was not as involved as hers. She imagined the dull ache in her chest would be with her for the rest of her life.

When the small rowboat arrived at shore, Harry turned to Katrine and embraced her. "I shall miss you," she said, tears misting in her eyes.

"Gur sealladh Dia ort," replied Katrine. "Give all my love to Tris."

Harry bit her lip to keep back the tears. "Tell your brother . . . thank him for his hospitality. Kintail is a beautiful place."

She gave Katrine another swift hug, then allowed Dougall to carry her to the boat. Mrs. Fraser was seated beside her, Dougall hopped in, and they were rowed to the steamer. Harry waved farewell to Katrine on the shore.

Once aboard the boat, she quickly retreated to her small cabin. She could not bear remaining on deck and watching Kintail disappear from view. It would remind her too much of what might have been, and what she had lost.

Alasdair stood silently on the hill, watching as the steamer passed down the loch. He had no doubt why it had stopped, and who was aboard for the southward journey.

It was best this way, he thought. There were some

things that were too great to overcome, and the differences between Harry and himself were one of them. It had been a mad folly on his part ever to think that he could bring an English lady to Kintail. The conflict between their natures, and their histories, would always come between them. And it would come out at the bad times, as it had the other day. In between those times, it would be a festering wound, covered up but still always there. And ultimately it would destroy any feelings they had for each other.

His rational mind told him this was for the best. But as he watched the boat carrying Harry disappear from view, his heart told him another tale.

Upon their arrival in Glasgow, Harry posted a letter to her father, knowing the mail would arrive long before she did. Throughout the journey Dougall took charge of all the arrangements, providing for her comfort and convenience. Mrs. Fraser was an amiable companion, and if it had not been for the fact that every mile took her farther and farther from Scotland and Alasdair, Harry might even have enjoyed the journey. But not until the post chaise pulled into the drive at Highbury did she experience the smallest twinge of pleasure. She was home at last.

She was rather relieved to find that her father was not at home. She did not have the strength to face him yet. He would see too much in her eyes. In a day or two, after she had rested from the journey, she would be able to hide her pain better.

Tris, however, was there, and he came dashing into her room before she had even removed her gloves.

"You are back!" he exclaimed.

"Obviously," she replied.

"What happened?" he asked. "How is Katrine? Did she get my letter?"

"Patience," she said, as she tossed her gloves on the table and untied her bonnet.

"Well?" he demanded scant moments later.

"Katrine is well, she sends you her love, and she did receive the letter."

She almost laughed at the fatuous grin that spread over her cousin's face.

"Has her brother showed any change of heart?" he asked nervously.

Harry's face clouded. She shook her head. "It is worse than ever, I fear. We were not careful, and he found her reading your letter. There was a terrible row—one of the reasons I am home." She sat down on the bed. "I fear I can offer you no hope until Katrine is of an age to marry without his consent."

The sad slump of his shoulders only made her own pain worse. She forced herself to smile. "But I have several things for you from Katrine," she said brightly. "Enough letters to fill a mail bag, and some presents from Edinburgh. I even brought you something myself."

"How did you find Scotland?"

"Edinburgh was an interesting place—when the weather was good. The whole town was positively giddy with excitement. 'Tis a pity George does not receive such enthusiasm at home."

"And Katrine's home?"

"Kintail is lovely," she said, and her face softened. "Rolling hills and rugged mountains. And everything is green. We had the most exceptional weather, Katrine said, for it only rained a few times."

Tris looked glum. "I wish I could see it."

"Perhaps you will someday," she said. "Some of Father's land adjoins it, you know." She thought to tell him of her plan but then hesitated. Better to speak with her father first.

There was a light tap on the door and two footmen brought in her trunk. Harry saw the eagerness in Tris's face. She quickly opened the trunk and drew out the things Katrine had sent.

"Here are your letters," she said, handing them to him. "And your packages." She smiled at the excitement with which he took them from her. "Now be off with you," she said with a laugh. "I shall see you at dinner."

Tris did not need any encouragement to take his treasure trove to the privacy of his room.

Once he was gone, Harry sat down on the bed again.

It felt good to be home. Comforting. Secure. Yet it did little to lessen the pain.

She would recover eventually, she knew. As she had told Katrine, she was too practical to wear the willow for one who did not want her. But it would not be as easy as she had once thought. It would take much time and effort to accomplish. Fortunately, she would have a great deal of that coming.

Alasdair remained away from the house for a full week. After Harry left, he went deeper into the hills. There were ample provisions in the small hut he used as a base for hunting. From there he could make daily forays into the steep hills and ravines, returning exhausted at dark to eat a simple meal and fall asleep before the smoldering peat fire.

If he hoped that this repeated physical torture would somehow exorcise Harry from his mind, he was mistaken, for she dominated all his waking thoughts, and invaded his dreams with a regularity that disconcerted him.

It was that, finally, which drove him back to the house. If he was going to be miserable, he might as well be miserable in comfort.

He said little to Katrine, although he ached to know what Harry had told her before she left. But he could not bring himself to ask. And Katrine said little to him as well.

He said nothing when the letter arrived, franked by Lord Egerton. Yet he burned with curiosity to know what it said. At least it meant Harry had reached home safely. There had been little doubt of that, with Dougall in charge, but it was a comfort to have the confirmation.

Katrine broke the ice at dinner that night.

"I had a letter from Harry," she said after the first remove.

"I trust she had a pleasant journey home?"

"Yes, she said Dougall was most efficient. She says if he ever wishes to take up residence in England, her father would be more than pleased to have him."

Alastair snorted in derision. "As if Dougall would ever think of leaving Scotland," he said.

"Lord Egerton sends you his thanks for entertaining Harry and sending her back with such care," Katrine continued. "He also extended an invitation to us both to visit them in Kent whenever we find it convenient."

Alasdair did not respond. Who wished it? Egerton? Tris? Harry? He did not feel the urge to accommodate any of them. "I do not find that a likely prospect," he said curtly.

"Alasdair?"

"What?"

"I am sorry that you and Harry fought," Katrine said. She had read the pain between the lines of Harry's letter. "I feel it is my fault."

"It is no one's fault," he said, idly playing with his wineglass. "It is quite obvious we are not suited to one another. We both came to realize that in the end."

Katrine doubted that very much, but she kept her counsel. She was the last person from whom Alasdair would ever take advice.

September became fall, and fall drifted toward winter, and soon the early storms were pounding the loch at Kintail. The rain beat down on the roof and the wind howled around the chimneys and windows, creating to what Katrine seemed a suitably mournful atmosphere. It matched her mood perfectly.

For no matter how many letters she received from Harry—and with the weather so bad, sometimes it was weeks before the boat made an appearance—it became more and more difficult to elevate her sagging spirits. Almost three long years stretched ahead of her before she could legally wed Tris, and those three years looked endless. Alasdair would keep her captive at Kintail for the entire time, she knew, while Tris was free to come and go as he pleased. He would be able to meet other ladies, and perhaps find one who would not be so much trouble. One whose family would not object to a marriage.

It was difficult to keep up her faith when they had

been apart for so long. Even the letters that came, secreted in books that Harry sent her, made her more despondent. They reminded her only how much she missed him, and how long it would be until she could see him again.

Alasdair watched her grow paler and more listless as the winter dragged on. He knew what ailed her. And knew he had it in his power to make things better. But at what price to himself?

He was almost ready to consent to the blasted marriage in order to make Katrine happy. But how could he enture the idea of tightening the ties to the Winterbournes? It was bad enough now, knowing he would never have to see Harry again if he did not wish it. But if Katrine wed Tris, there would be cause for the families to join together. And he did not think he could bear that.

In fact, he did not think he could bear much of anything. There were times when he thought he was slowly being driven mad, that Harry had put on him some witch's curse to sap his strength and his will and his mind. For he could not rid his thoughts of her. And worse, the contents of his thoughts were driving him mad as well.

For they were telling him that it was his own damnable pride and folly that kept them apart. What did it matter who her father was? Keppoch had been out of Mackyle hands long before he was born. He did not need it. But he needed her.

Oh, how he needed her. It was like the old saying that you did not realize what you had until it was gone. And he was beginning to realize that he and Harry could have had something, if only he had allowed it. But he had poisoned things from the first, so when the slightest conflict arose, their fragile alliance easily broke. It was entirely his own fault. But he did not know how to go about rectifying the matter. He feared the damage had been too severe.

Sitting in his tower study, listening to the windswept rain lashing against the windows, he realized what a mess he had made of his life, and Katrine's. He remembered his grandfather, who had spent fifty years of his life atoning for his youthful folly. Was he destined to pay the same price?

Alasdair sighed. It was too late for him, he feared. But it was not too late for Katrine. If she still wanted her damnable Englishman, let her have him. He had the growing fear that she would never be happy again unless he consented to their marriage, and he knew he had been a fool, thinking he could dictate her happiness. People made their own, and as her brother, he could only guide and advise, not order. If Tristan Winterbourne was necessary for Katrine, she could have him.

With a wry smile, Alastair drew out a sheet of paper and dipped his quill in the inkwell.

Dear Mr. Winterbourne,
If you still are of the same mind regarding my sister, you are welcome to come to Kintail and discuss the matter with her. I shall not stand in your way.

He studied the words he had written carefully, a slight frown on his face. Then he scrawled his signature at the bottom, and lightly sanded the letter. It would leave on the next boat.

18

Wherefore should I be sad
  'Bout a maid me despises
Although caught in her love-noose
  By Cupid's surprises?

William Ross,
A Lament

As soon as Alasdair received news the boat was approaching, he hastened down to the shore. It was possible there would be a letter of reply from Tristan by this time. He did not want Katrine to know of his plans, and if it meant he would have to meet every boat that arrived—and at this time of year, their schedules were highly erratic—he would do so.

Alasdair realized there was more than a letter arriving as he caught a glimpse of the blond man standing at the bow. One question was answered. Two people, at least, would be happy.

He watched as the rowboat was lowered. Tristan clambered in beside the crew member, and even from a distance Alasdair could read the eagerness in his movements. As the boat neared shore, one of the Highlanders darted into the water, catching the bow of the tiny boat and pulling it up onto the rocks. Tris stepped out eagerly, grabbing his valise and splashing through the foamy surf to the beach. He stopped before Alasdair.

"I was expecting a letter of reply," Alasdair said, hiding his amusement.

"I thought . . . I thought it would be quicker if I came myself," Tris said apprehensively.

Alasdair smiled and stuck out his hand. "Welcome to Kintail."

"Thank you," Tris stammered.

"I have not said a word of this to Katrine," Alasdair explained as they walked up the trail to the house. "In the event that you had changed your mind."

"I would never—" Tris began in protest, then stopped. "I assure you, Lord Kintail, that my devotion and esteem for your sister have never wavered since we were parted."

"You may save the flowery words for my sister," Alasdair said dryly. "She will appreciate them more than I."

"Dare I ask," said Tris, "why you have reconsidered?"

"I want my sister to be happy," Alasdair said bluntly. "And she seems to think you are the indispensable item to that goal."

"I will endeavor to make her as happy as I possibly can," Tris said.

"I am certain you will," said Alasdair wearily as they entered the great hall. He noted Tris's faint smile as he examined the decorated walls—had Harry warned him of them? Alasdair felt a deep stab of longing at the thought of her, but swiftly quelled it. There was no point in lingering on that subject. "I would offer to show you to your room, but I imagine you would rather see my sister first."

"Yes, please, if I may," said Tris.

Alasdair barked an order in Gaelic to a waiting servant, then motioned for Tris to follow him. "Katrine will join us in the drawing room."

Alasdair watched Tris attempting to quell his anxiety as they both waited for Katrine. The sight brought a faint smile to his face.

"Alasdair, Màiri said you wanted—Oh!" Katrine's eyes widened in surprise at the sight of Tris.

Tris jumped to his feet. "Hello, Katrine," he said.

She glanced nervously at her brother.

"Mr. Winterbourne is here at my invitation," Alasdair said, watching the joy light her face. She took a hesitant step toward Tris.

Suddenly the whole scene became too painful to watch, and Alasdair strode toward the door. "I will leave you to explain matters, Mr. Winterbourne," he said.

"Tris?" Katrine's expression was a mixture of joy and puzzlement.

Tris stepped toward her and took her hands in his. "Your brother has given me permission to speak to you," he said softly, smiling at her.

"But why. . . ?"

Tris looked at her in surprise. "I thought you would know. He sent me a letter, telling me I could come to Kintail and ask you for your hand. That is," he said, looking down suddenly, "if you still wish to marry me."

"Oh, Tris," sighed Katrine. "Of course I do."

His smile widened as he took her in his arms. "I do not know what caused your brother to change his mind, but I do not care. We have each other now, and that is all that matters."

Alasdair went straight to the beach. He was tempted to take the boat out, but the sky looked ominous and white foam already licked the wave tops. Killing himself would accomplish nothing.

One look at Katrine's ecstatic face had been enough to convince him he had done the right thing. At last. He regretted his folly at having kept her and Tristan apart. At the time, it had as much to do with his confused feelings about Harry as it had with his concern for Katrine. And if his feelings regarding Harry were as jumbled as ever, at least he could undo the wrong he had done Katrine.

He would miss her when she settled in England, as he knew she would do. Oh, they would come to visit—in the summer, of course, when there was a more likely chance of decent weather. In a few years there would be nieces and nephews. With a pang, he wondered what they would think of their uncle's unusual home, where the people spoke a foreign language and wore strange clothes.

And with a worse pang, he realized that he, too, would have to do something about begetting children of his own. For what was the point of restoring the earldom, if there was no son to pass the title to? He was the last Kintail, and although the holdings would pass on to Katrine and her children, the title would die. A rather pointless outcome to his grandfather's dream.

But to have children, he would have to find a wife. And he had watched the woman he truly wanted sail out of his life without making the effort to stop her. Yet the thought of any other seemed incomprehensible.

When the chilling wind finally drove him back into the house, he found Tris and Katrine still in the drawing room, talking excitedly about wedding plans.

"When is this monumental event to take place?" Alasdair asked.

Katrine darted a glance at Tris. "I—*we* would prefer to have the ceremony in England."

Alasdair covered his dismay well. "It may be difficult for some of our friends to attend," he noted.

"Not by late spring," said Katrine. "And I think it is easier to ask our friends to travel south than it is to ask Tris's to come north."

"And how is it that we are to host a proper wedding in England?" he asked.

"Oh, that shall not be difficult at all." Katrine's face brightened. "Lord Egerton already told Tris we may wed from Highbury. It would be very simple." She grinned. "And the cost to you would be less."

"If you object severely, we could change our plans," Tris offered.

"No," said Alasdair in resignation. "If you wish to marry in England, that is fine with me. It will save the disruption of a wedding in the midst of the spring planting. We can hold a celebration here when you visit."

"Thank you," said Katrine. "We thought mid-May would be a good time. We need not go south until a few weeks before."

"As you wish," said Alasdair.

Katrine was surprised at her brother's acquiescent attitude. But after the shock of his turnabout on Tris, she was beginning to think Alasdair was full of surprises.

During the ensuing conversation, Katrine noted how carefully Alasdair avoided the topic of Harry. Tris brought a long letter form her to Katrine, but she did not speak of it to Alasdair. Were they irrevocably parted?

Katrine hoped not. She would make one more grand attempt to reunite the two. It was not merely convenience that motivated her desire to have the wedding in England. It would be too easy for Harry to beg off from a trip to Scotland. But with the wedding at her own house, she could not absent herself. She and Alasdair would have one last chance to work out their differences.

Over the next fortnight, Alasdair found himself pleasantly surprised by Tristan Winterbourne. Despite his youth, he was a sensible lad. He expressed a sincere interest in Alasdair's agricultural endeavors, explaining how he hoped to make his own small property a showpiece. In fact, the only thing Alasdair found to hold against him was his Englishness, and ties to the Egerton family.

He said nothing to Katrine, but the thought of accompanying her to England again did not sit well. A family wedding on the Egerton estate meant Harry would be there. And he suspected neither of them looked forward to that. The situation would be awkward in the extreme. For a brief moment he wondered whether Katrine had intended such a thing when she decided on a wedding in England, but then he shook his head. His sister could not be so duplicitous. It was as she said—it was more convenient for Tris and his family. *Her* new family.

Tris remained in Scotland for over a fortnight, but when the boat next arrived, he reluctantly took his leave. There was much to do before the wedding, and there was no way of telling how long he would have to wait for the next steamer. Katrine bade him a tearful farewell.

Alasdair was relieved to have him gone. He brought too many reminders of Harry with him.

Harry sat frowning over the latest *Lady's Magazine* when Tris unexpectedly strode into the drawing room at Grosvenor Square.

"Tris!" she exclaimed. "You are back! What happened?"

"You are looking at a betrothed man," he said with a huge grin.

"Katrine!" Harry squealed. "Oh, Tris, how wonderful." She danced across the room and enveloped him in an exuberant hug. "How? When?"

Tris disengaged her hands from behind his neck. "Let me sit first. I have been traveling for an age."

Harry rang for tea while Tris composed himself.

"It is as the letter said," he explained. "Kintail no longer has any objections to our marriage."

"It is unbelievable," Harry said with a bewildered shake of her head. "Did he say why?"

Tris shrugged. "He wants Katrine to be happy."

"And is she?" Harry asked with a smile.

"Radiantly," replied Tris. "And she will be here in less than a month. We are to wed from Highbury."

A sudden shock swept over Harry. Alasdair would be there, of course. It was all too soon; she was not ready to see him again.

"How did you find Scotland?" she asked with forced brightness.

"Amazing," he said. "I nearly laughed when I saw the entry hall—it was as gruesome as you described it. But Kintail runs an impressive estate. I was tempted to remain—shearing was almost ready to start. But he assures me I can return for it next year."

Harry chewed on her lip. Dare she ask Tris if anything had been said about her? No. He would not have noticed. She doubted whether even Katrine would have noticed; she was probably too excited by Tris's presence even to think straight.

"I have some things for you from Katrine," Tris said. "She particularly wished me to give you the two jars of honey."

Harry smiled faintly. "It was my favorite thing," she said.

Along with the honey came a long letter. Katrine had not totally lost her senses, and was able to give Harry a coherent picture of Tris's visit. And she pointedly mentioned that Harry's name had not been mentioned by Alasdair once the entire time. She could not vouch for when he and Tris were alone, for they spent a great deal of time roaming the hills about the estate, but she thought Tris would have mentioned it to her.

Harry sadly folded the sheets of the letter. It had been her last hope, that somehow this wild change of heart regarding Katrine and Tris would have extended to her as well. A rather foolish hope, as it now turned out.

But at least she finally knew. Knew that she was not destined for great love. A sad smile flitted across her face. Perhaps Tris would be the only one of this generation to win that prize. Maybe the prize would pass to one of her children. As for herself . . .

Walking over to her desk, she drew out a piece of paper, took her quill in hand, and began to write.

> Lord Hanover,
> *I would be most desirous of your calling upon me tomorrow to discuss a matter of great importance to us both. I shall be pleased to receive you at ten. Harry*

She carefully sanded the sheet, then folded it quickly and rang for a footman before she could change her mind.

Alasdair sat at his desk. It was late, and a branch of candles illuminated the room. Only a few more things to arrange and he could leave Kintail without too much worry.

Most of Katrine's things had already been packed and sent south. Although, from the pile he had seen in her room this afternoon, it looked as if another shipment would have to be sent ahead before their departure next week.

Next week. In a fortnight he would be in London again. Would Harry be there as well?

He had been fooling himself all through the long winter, he knew. He did not think of her any less now in the first week of April than he had in September. He had been utterly unsuccessful in freeing himself from her hold. Because he loved her. And needed her.

The pain of their separation was a never-ending ache, not made any easier to bear by the knowledge it was all his fault. He had deliberately driven her away, simply because he was afraid to want a woman so.

Now he was on his way to London, and he prayed he would be given one more chance to woo and win her. There was one last step he could take to prove his love. Keppoch was not the only thing that lay between them, but it was the most visible, and removing it would go a long way to healing their breach. He could only hope that it would be enough. Or had his damnable pride already ruined everything?

At least this way he would know.

He stared at the blank sheet of paper on his desk. How best to word this letter? Egerton might suspect his motives, of course, so he needed to do this carefully. He did not want awkward questions asked of either him or Harry.

But what excuse could he give for his strange request? Egerton would likely think him mad, interfering in a family matter such as this. The tenuous connection through Tris did not justify such an action.

Yet he had to do it. It was the only way he could win Harry back.

My Dear Lord Egerton,
I am writing to you again on the matter of the land in Keppoch. It has come to my attention that this land forms part of the dowry of Lady Harriet. You may find this a strange request, but I am desirous that this situation be changed. I ask you to exchange the Keppoch land for some other equally valuable property in either Scotland or England. I believe Lady Harriet would be amenable to such a trade.

19

My bonnie maiden
Of the curled yellow hair,
The smiling blue eyes
And the snowy hands fair;

William Ross,
Praise of the Highland Maiden

Alasdair struggled against his impatience as the post chaise rattled over the London streets. By the time he and Katrine were settled into the hotel, it would be too late to make any calls today. Yet now that he was here, he wished he could see Harry immediately.

What would she say when he told her about the letter? Would she believe him finally, when he said that the land was not important? That nothing was more important than her and her love?

Of course she would. Soon they would be able to look back on their argument as a silly misunderstanding, and could pick up the pieces of their relationship. He smiled faintly. There would be time tomorrow.

Katrine dispatched a note to Tris the moment they arrived at the hotel, inviting him to join them for dinner. To Katrine's delight and Alasdair's despair, he arrived long before the appointed time.

"I could not wait," he said apologetically to Alasdair, unable to keep his eyes off Katrine even for a moment.

"The impatience of youth," Alasdair replied dryly. "You will have to wait to dine."

"I do not mind," he said. He took Katrine's hand and led her to the chair near the window.

Alasdair turned away. Their happiness was painful for him to watch. Not tonight. Tomorrow would be better, when he had settled things with Harry.

"Oh Tris, it is lovely," Alasdair heard his sister's exclamation and realized with a touch of chagrin that he had not even thought about gilding his offer to Harry with a ring. What would she like? Some family heirloom? Or something modern and stylish? He would have to ask her.

"Look, Alasdair, is it not lovely?"

Katrine danced across the room, waving her hand under his nose. He took her hand and pretended to carefully scrutinize the ring on her finger. "Very nice," he pronounced it. He cast a quick glance at Tris, catching him in a self-satisfied grin. The lad would do all right, Alasdair thought. He gave Katrine a soft kiss on the cheek and turned to his guest. "Would you like a glass of claret?"

The three chatted amiably while waiting for dinner. Katrine was full of questions to Tris about their new home, while Alasdair wished to make certain all the settlement papers were in order. At the appointed time they descended to the dining room, where they were ushered into a private dining salon. Despite the opulence, Alasdair found it a rather dismal meal. Tris and Katrine lost interest in conversation, too busy looking at each other with sugary expressions. And Alasdair was too eager to see Harry again to pay much attention to his food. All in all, they were poor customers for the talents of the hotel's *chef de cuisine*.

Not until the table was cleared for dessert did Tris and Katrine finally begin to realize there was another person in their company.

"Thank you for the fine dinner," said Tris apologetically. "I should like you to be my guests at the opera tomorrow night. Mozart's *Figaro*."

"Will Harry be coming?" Katrine asked eagerly. "I cannot wait to see her."

Tris shrugged. "I am not certain what her plans are. She has been so busy since her betrothal."

Katrine turned to look at him, a puzzled expression on her face. "What betrothal?"

"She did not write and tell you?" Tris was incredulous. "Harry is going to marry Lord Hanover."

Alasdair reached with deliberate casualness for his wineglass. Carefully, he lifted it to his lips and took a sip. It was a rather odd sensation, he thought, to watch yourself go through the motions of normal behavior when in fact nothing was normal at all.

Harry betrothed. The words were like a knife cutting a deep wound into his heart. And he had only himself to blame. He was the one who had driven her away. Forever now, it seemed.

He almost laughed. He had come to London to make everything right between them, while at the same time she was planning her wedding. All the time he had been weaving fantasies about their life together, she was spinning ones about another man. The irony of it was rich.

And the worst thing was that he would have to see her—perhaps as early as tomorrow—and would be forced to present his warm congratulations on her upcoming nuptials when he felt more like dying inside. And not by one word or gesture could he ever let her know what he was feeling. She would never know how much he wanted her. For she obviously did not want him.

He was actually glad Katrine was going to live in England, for it meant she would not be at Kintail to see his pain and hurt. By the time she and Tris came to visit, he would have exorcised his feelings. No one would ever know.

Somehow he managed to get through the remainder of their meal without a slip. Although it was unlikely Tris and Katrine would have noticed anyway, for their concentration was devoted to each other. Still, he was glad when Tris finally took his leave, and Katrine prepared for bed. It meant he could be alone in his room.

He paced the floor, trying to quell the dreadful churning in his stomach. The first thing to do was rehearse what he would say to her when they next met. Best wishes on her upcoming marriage, of course. A few polite phrases on how he was pleased to see Katrine marry into her family.

Would she cross-question him on his change of heart about Tris and Katrine? God, he hoped not. For that matter had been so tied up with his complicated feelings about Harry that he did not know if he could explain it any other way. And had it not been that very subject that had precipitated their last argument? Maybe for that reason she would leave the topic alone. He prayed it would be so.

The three weeks before Katrine's wedding loomed large in his mind. He had looked forward to spending them in Harry's company. Now they stretched before him like an endless trial. One that he would have to endure until Katrine was safely wed. Then he could flee home to Kintail and spend his days contemplating what a mess he had made of things.

Katrine hastened to Harry early the next morning. She was bursting with questions. It did not bother her one bit that she caught Harry at breakfast. There was so much she needed to know.

"Katrine!" Harry greeted, rising from her seat. They embraced, and then Katrine was persuaded to take a cup of tea while Harry finished her morning repast.

"You saw Tris last night?" Harry asked with a mischievous spark in her eyes. "I understand he had a little present for you."

Katrine nodded and held out her hand so Harry could admire the ring. "But what is it he says—you are to marry Lord Hanover? Whyever did you not tell me?"

Harry kept her gaze lowered. "There was so little time," she dissembled. "It was not decided at all until after Tris returned from Scotland. I wanted to wait and tell you myself."

"I had thought . . ." Katrine began, but then clamped her mouth shut.

"That Alasdair and I would resolve our differences?" Harry laughed scornfully. "That will never be."

"But I assumed Lord Hanover was only a friend," Katrine protested.

"Han and I rub along well, and that is of great importance when one is looking at a life together," Harry told her. "He is perhaps not quite as effusive in his praise of me as Tris is of you—" she smiled—"but he will do well. We are very much alike, you know."

Katrine did not know any such thing at all, but she refrained from saying so.

"Have you decided on a dress yet?" Harry asked, firmly changing the subject. "Are we to go shopping today?"

Katrine nodded. "I found a plate I like, at last. We need to take it to the dressmaker. And Alasdair has given me an enormous sum of money with which to replenish my wardrobe."

"Opening up the coffers at last? Whatever is the world coming to?"

Katrine giggled. "I think he is only relieved that Tris will have to buy my clothes from now on."

"And a wonderful job he will do of it, I am certain," Harry said. She stood up again. "Allow me to change and we can be off at once. Shall I see if Tris is still home?"

Katrine blushed, and nodded.

Tris duly appeared in the morning room, and it was quite another hour before Harry and Katrine finally left the house. Their first stop was Harry's dressmaker, whom Katrine wished to sew her dress.

"Have you decided on your own wedding dress yet?" Katrine asked Harry while she stood for measurements.

Harry shook her head. "We need to get you and Tris securely wed before I can even begin to think of that," she said. "We have not even decided on a date."

"I do not know how you can stand to wait," Katrine said. "This last month had been interminable. And there are still three more weeks!"

A wistful smile flitted across Harry's face. If she were as in love as Katrine, she would find the wait interminable also. But while she was content with the plans she had made, she was under no illusion that she held a grand passion for Han. As she had told Katrine, they would suit. And suitability looked more important to her now than a grand passion. There was too much heartache involved with grand passions. She and Han would have a smooth life together. That was what she wanted.

So why did the thought make her so miserable?

"Which of these two laces do you like best?" Katrine's voice broke into Harry's thoughts.

She looked halfheartedly at the samples, finding it difficult to summon up much enthusiasm even for Katrine's wedding plans. "The first, I think. I like the edging on it."

"So do I," said Katrine. "Oh, Harry, is it not exciting?"

Harry nodded absently. Then, fearing Katrine would notice her despondent attitude, she forced herself to brighten. She would not dampen Katrine's happiness with her own wretchedness.

The dress decisions were made at last and they proceeded to the Burlington Arcade, where Katrine spent more time gazing in the windows at all the wondrous items than actually purchasing anything. She did finally settle on a new pair of gloves and a ribbon for the gown she was to wear to the opera that night.

Harry endured it all with growing detachment. Katrine's high spirits were not contagious—in fact, the very opposite. She found herself growing more and more morose as the day wore on. She could not help contrasting Katrine's enthusiasm for her upcoming marriage with her ambivalent feelings about her own.

Still, she did not think she was making a mistake in marrying Han. She had to marry someone. The life of an eccentric spinster was not for her. Under the circumstances, Han was the best choice.

But even at the most unexpected times, memories of Alasdair would sweep over her. The passage of time had not dimmed her recollections at all. It did not help in the least to be in Katrine's company, for a look or a turn of phrase would readily bring her brother to mind.

Harry dreaded the thought of going to the opera tonight and seeing him—especially when she was in Han's company. She toyed with the idea of pleading fatigue or a headache in order to escape the ordeal. But she would only be delaying the inevitable. She could not put off seeing Alasdair until the day of Katrine's wedding. At some point she would run out of excuses. Better she got it over with now. At least then she would not look to each and every social event with dread.

A determined look crossed her face. She *would* see him tonight. And hopefully put the past to rest, once and for all. It was something she must do, for both Han's sake and hers. Even if it was the most difficult challenge of her life.

Alasdair racked his brain to think of some plausible excuse to avoid attending the opera. But to abandon his sister on the night she was introduced to the *ton* as Tris's betrothed would engender comment. And his main goal was to have everything appear as normal as possible. No one, not even Harry, would have an inkling of the way he really felt.

At least they were not accompanying each other to the opera. When they met, it would be in a public atmosphere. Alasdair was grateful for that one small thing. It would make everything a little less awkward. Although not less painful.

He had come to London with such hopes, only to have them dashed by cruel reality. And he could only blame himself for the extinction of his dreams. He was the one who had driven her away. He had thought there would be time to rectify his mistake. But his stubborn pride had held him back for too long, and now it was too late. Harry was lost to him forever.

Once this night was over it would be better, he knew. He would be able to paste on his false smile and greet her like an old family friend. He would be able to endure all the routs and assemblies that led up to Katrine's wedding, and he would make it through the wedding festivities as well. Then he could go home and suffer in peace.

By the time he reached the theater with Tris and Katrine, Alasdair's nerves were stretched taut. He could only hope that Harry had not yet arrived, so he could compose himself into some semblance of control before they met. But that was not to be, he found, when they reached the Winterbourne box. Harry and Lord Hanover were already there.

Lord Hanover rose as they entered, greeting Tris and

Katrine, then turning to Alasdair. During his last visit to London, Alasdair had spent some time with him, but not enough to think they were more than acquaintances. But he was greeted as if he were a long-lost friend.

"Kintail, it is good to see you again."

Alasdair nodded. "And you." He finally dared to look at Harry. "You are looking well, Lady Harriet. May I offer you both my congratulations."

"Thank you," she replied in a barely audible whisper.

"Must be something in the air this spring," Lord Hanover joked. "First Tris, now Harry." He laughed. "We need to find you a wife as well, Kintail."

Alasdair smiled blandly, looking away from Harry. It was going to be a dreadfully long evening. He strove to remain calm as he took his seat next to her. Whoever had decided that he should sit there? As he stared toward the stage he grew acutely aware of her presence beside him. He smelled the spicy-sweet scent of her perfume, heard the rustle of her gown as she shifted slightly in her chair.

He breathed a sigh of relief when the musicians struck up the opening notes. Now he would not be expected to converse until the break between acts. And he could easily make his escape from the box then. He could even, if he so wished it, return to the hotel. Harry would be a quite acceptable chaperon for Katrine.

Yet he knew he could not behave in such a cowardly manner. It would cause undue attention, the very thing that he did not want. Better that he remain and suffer.

For that was what he was doing. Suffering. No one could have developed a more exquisite torture if years had been spent in the planning. To sit so close to her, knowing that he had lost her forever, was almost more than he could bear.

He sat rigidly throughout the performance, his eyes fixed upon the performers on the stage. But if questioned, he would have been unable to say a word about what they were singing or saying. He centered all his concentration on ignoring Harry.

Harry found tonight to be the most miserable evening of her entire life. Why ever had she allowed Tris and

Han to persuade her into such a mad act? She should have waited, and chosen a more private place for their first meeting. One where all eyes were not upon them. One where no one would notice if her voice faltered, or how she struggled to retain her composure.

But here, with Han beside her, she felt acutely conscious of every traitorous thought, every wayward desire. She was sitting between the man she was to marry and the man she foolishly loved, and every moment was an agony of torture. She wished she could run to the carriage and flee toward home, where she could give way to her despair behind the closed doors of her room. There, she could wail and moan and throw things until she collapsed into an exhausted heap, all emotion spent.

But sitting here, struggling with each breath to keep herself firmly in check, Harry felt as if she were fighting a grim battle to survive, and the final outcome was in doubt. Every breath was a long, painful inhale, and she had to consciously remind herself to expel each breath or she would forget. All her faculties concentrated on trying to drown out her awareness of the man seated to her right. And she was failing miserably.

She took a sidelong glance at him, admiring his handsome profile. Recognition of that admiration forced her to quickly avert her eyes. He sat so rigidly beside her; she could feel the tension in him. It was much as it had been during his first visit to London, when her very presence was an anathema to him. He probably hated her as much now as he had then. That trip to Scotland had ruined everything for them.

Thank goodness there was a definite time limit to his trip this time. She had no doubts he would depart for Scotland the day following Katrine's wedding—if he did not follow the newly married couple down the drive. He would only be here for less than a month. Then she would be able to regain control of herself.

20

I am shorn of all pleasure
Being so far from thee this year,
Of black dule I've a seizure
I my lost love deplore.

William Ross,
The Braies of Glen Broom

Alasdair brought Katrine to Highbury a week before the
wedding so she could attend to the last-minute preparations. They came in a post chaise laden with Katrine's
new purchases, the wedding dress safely tucked away in
its dressmaker's box.

Harry watched from the library window as the coach
pulled up in front of the house. She steeled herself for
the upcoming ordeal. A week in the close company of
Alasdair MacKyle would be a particularly cruel form of
torture.

Turning back to the room, she smiled brightly at Han,
who sat reading *The Times*. "It looks as if Katrine has
arrived. Shall we go out to meet her?"

Han tossed down the newspaper and looked at Harry.
"It is going to begin now, is it not?" he asked with a
rueful smile. "How long will it be until I have you to
myself again?"

"With a lifetime ahead, surely you will not begrudge
a few days?" she teased, wincing slightly at the look in
his eyes. Han had grown too attentive during their brief
engagement. Far too attentive. Harry welcomed the advent of the wedding guests, for they would keep her
busy, and away from Han. She refused to think about
what that portended for their marriage.

She heard Katrine's and Alasdair's voices in the hall
and mentally fortified herself for the meeting. She was

the daughter of a marquess. She must remember that, and act accordingly.

"Harry, there you are," Katrine exclaimed as her friend entered the hall. She quickly embraced Harry. "It is so exciting to be here. I can almost believe everything is real at last."

Harry smiled. "More than real, I am afraid. Wait until you see the last-minute decisions you will have to make."

Katrine laughed. "I do not care a whit. Oh, Harry, only five more days!"

Harry glanced toward Alasdair. He was talking with Han, an uneasy expression on his face. "Welcome to Highbury, Lord Kintail," she said.

Alasdair looked toward her, and for a moment she thought she saw pain in his face.

"Thank you, Lady Harriet," he said. "I am certain your hospitality will be warm."

To her relief, Han drew Alasdair away. Harry took Katrine's arm in her own and led her up the stairs. "We have put you in the room next to mine," she explained. "It has a lovely view of the park. I hope you like it." She knew she was babbling, but she could not stop.

"I am certain I will," Katrine assured her. "Tris is not here yet, is he?"

"No," said Harry. "He said he will not arrive until the day before the wedding. But he wishes me to assure you that he has made all the arrangements for your trip and that the house in Norfolk is ready for your arrival."

"I cannot wait to see it," said Katrine wistfully. She looked about her with interest as Harry drew her into the commodious bedchamber. "Goodness, how elegant! I feel like a princess."

"I fear you will have to look higher than Tris if you wish to have *that* rank," Harry said laughingly.

"Oh, Harry, I cannot believe the wedding is almost here."

Katrine turned to her with such a look of joy that Harry glanced away. "I can," she said matter-of-factly.

Katrine blushed. "You have done so much work . . . and not even for your own wedding. How can I ever thank you?"

"Take good care of Tris," Harry said. "That will be quite enough. Now," she continued, "shall we return downstairs for tea? I doubt Han has thought to show your brother to his room yet."

"Oh, Alasdair is not staying," Katrine said. "He is going back to London to wait for the others."

"The others?"

"Dougall and the others from Kintail," Katrine explained. "Alasdair is determined to bring a bit of Scotland to the wedding"

"How nice," said Harry, relieved that she would not have to endure his presence all week after all. The thought buoyed her so much that she was able to endure Alasdair's short visit with calm equanimity. She would be able to save her strength for the wedding.

Yet once he departed she was surprised at the disappointment she felt. Every moment in his presence had been torture. She should be relieved to have him gone. But she was not. Despite the pain it caused her, she wanted to be with him, knowing that this would be the last time.

The day of Katrine's wedding dawned with a clear sky and warm sun—a perfect spring day. Alasdair and his Highlanders had not descended on Highbury until the previous day. Their most welcome contribution to the wedding was several kegs of whiskey—no doubt Kintail's illegal product. Alasdair also brought his piper, insisting that one could not have a proper wedding without one. Harry shook her head. It looked to be a very interesting event. It brought a smile to her face. What would the English guests think of all this?

Harry barely had time to catch her breath in the flurry of final details. Someone had forgotten to polish the salt cellars. A batch of cream had curdled. The extra candles could not be found. Harry dealt with each and every crisis with calm detachment. It was the only way to keep her sanity.

In spare moments she dashed up to Katrine's room, to make certain the bride-to-be was maintaining her composure. Katrine alternated between nervous excitement and sudden moments of silence during these brief visits, but Harry felt confident she would endure. If only she could say the same of herself.

Somehow she found time to don her new gown of sea-foam Levantine silk. Critically assessing her appearance in the pier glass, Harry pinched her cheeks to bring a little color to them. She prayed everything would go smoothly—and quickly.

Harry helped Katrine with her last preparations, supervising the arrangement of her hair and the final details of her dress. When all was done, they went downstairs to meet Alasdair.

He was in full Highland regalia again, as he had been that fateful night at the ball in Edinburgh. Harry could not look at the imposing picture he made without thinking of all that she had gained—and then lost—on that fateful trip to Scotland. Her gaze drifted to his face and she saw Alasdair regarding her, a curious expression in his eyes. He turned quickly toward Katrine.

"You look lovely, *a phiuthar*," he said. "Very much like *Maman*."

Katrine smiled and gave him a hug. "Thank you," she whispered.

Lord Egerton entered the room. "Is everyone ready?" he asked impatiently. "The coaches are waiting."

Harry quickly crossed the room, eager to escape from Alasdair's presence. "Come, Katrine. I will help you with your gown."

Harry settled Katrine in the coach, carefully arranging her dress so it would not be crushed. She gave her a swift hug then exited. Ignoring Alasdair, she brushed past him and her father, standing in the yard, and climbed into her own coach. Egerton climbed in beside her and the coach lurched into motion.

At the church, Harry gave Katrine's dress a last critical examination, then made her way to the Egerton box, where she took her seat beside Han. All too quickly Katrine was coming down the aisle on Alasdair's arm. Harry focused her gaze on Katrine, willing herself to ignore the kilted man who stood so rigidly beside her.

Harry struggled to keep back tears of mingled joy and

despair. Katrine looked so lovely, Tris so handsome, and they both appeared as happy as two people could be. Yet all her pleasure for them could not push back the hollow ache in her own heart. Why could she not have found such happiness too?

The ceremony passed quickly, and before Harry knew it, Tris and Katrine were sharing a kiss in front of the altar, then dancing gaily down the aisle. As the doors of the church were thrown open, the first startling notes of the pipes were heard, playing a salute to the newly wedded couple. Harry smiled to herself. Trust Alasdair to insert his little bit of Scotland into the wedding.

There was a rush of confusion as the guests made their way back to the house for the banquet. Harry had tossed up her hands at the impossibility of maintaining any sort of protocol in the seating arrangements, and she held her breath at the sight of Alasdair's kilted Highlanders sitting amidst the English aristocracy. Particularly since they were all armed with those wicked daggers. She observed them carefully during the meal and they all behaved with proper decorum. Alasdair had probably drilled them for hours in preparation.

She pushed her barely tasted food aside when her father stood to begin the toasting. Champagne and whiskey were already flowing freely about the tables, and Harry felt a touch of nervousness about exactly what could happen. She prayed nothing would disrupt this special day for Katrine and Tris.

Egerton led the first toast, wishing his favorite nephew and his new wife a long, prosperous life together.

"Slàinte mhath!" cried Alasdair, and all the Highlanders lifted their whiskey glasses high. *"A h-uile latha sona dhuibh, gun latha idir dona dhuibh."*

Harry saw Katrine whisper something in Tris's ear and he stood. *"Mo bhrathair ùr,"* he said in salute to Alasdair, stumbling over the unfamiliar Gaelic words. He smiled at Katrine. "And to my lovely wife." He sat down amidst much applause.

Harry felt as if she were watching everything through a veil of mist. She reached for her glass, taking another sip of champagne. Surely the meal would be over soon and they could retreat to the ballroom. Time seemed to crawl with incredible slowness. Would the day never be over?

Han, sitting next to her, nudged her slightly and nodded toward Tris, who was standing again.

"Another toast," he cried, turning toward Harry. "It is an old saying that one wedding begets another." He beamed broadly at his cousin. "May your wedding day be as happy as mine, Harry."

Harry blushed. Inexorably, her gaze was drawn across the table to where Alasdair sat. He raised his glass in silent salute and she quickly averted her eyes.

In a short while her father announced the meal was finished, and the guests drifted into the ballroom. Tris led out Katrine for the first waltz.

Harry watched them with a creeping sadness. They looked so happy, their new life together just beginning, with everything before them. Why could she not stop thinking that her own marriage would mark an ending, rather than a beginning, in her own life?

Tris caught her hand and led her out for the next dance, while Alasdair swirled Katrine about the floor. Harry quickly slipped into the crowd when the dance was over. She did not want Alasdair to partner her. She found Han and stayed by his side. She felt safer there.

The dancing continued for some time, waltzes and giddy country dances that brought a flush to everyone's face. The Highlanders gathered in one corner, around the whiskey bowl. Harry saw the other guests watching them with mingled amusement and curiosity.

When the musicians took a break, Tris stepped forward. "My new brother-in-law, while graciously consenting to allow his sister to be married in England, insists that it is not a proper wedding without some Scots dancing as well. He tells me this is a dance of celebration, which is done in honor of Lady Katrine and myself." He nodded to Alasdair.

Harry watched with growing curiosity as Alasdair and Dougall stepped forward, each carrying a long, wicked-looking sword. This must be the sword dance he had spoken of to her! Both men removed their coats, the stark white of their fine lawn shirts contrasting against the brilliant plaid of their skirts.

They laid the swords in an X pattern in the middle of the floor. Removing their shoes, they stood in their stocking feet and bowed low to Katrine and Tris. The piper, who had slipped in unnoticed, began his eerie music. Alasdair and Dougall bowed to each other, then began their strange dance.

Harry watched with growing fascination as the two men cavorted over the swords with feet as nimble as any opera dancer's. Their plaid skirts swayed side to side in a rhythmic motion. But it was their feet that kept her attention, leaping nimbly over those sharp pieces of metal, first one foot, then the other. Just when she thought that one of them would falter because of such intricate steps, the pace of the music quickened and they began dancing even faster, their feet stepping from one side of the X to the other so fast that her eyes could barely follow.

She looked up and sucked in her breath at the sight of Alasdair, his arms raised high over his head and a broad smile on his face. He loved doing this, she realized. Just as he loved the land and the language of his homeland, he loved the music and the dance as well. Never before had she had a truer sense of the gulf that lay between them. However could she have thought that she could fit into his life?

Yet she could not tear her gaze away from him. As he leaped and twisted, she watched with rapt attention. There was nothing feminine in this dance. He exuded raw male power. In his actions, she saw his Scots ancestors celebrating their victories in battle, their personal triumphs, their family successes. She wanted to reach out and touch him, to absorb some of that power, to feel it in her hand. Maybe then she could understand him.

She almost cried aloud when the last notes of the pipe died and the dancers bowed again. Wild cheers swept across the room. Harry was too dazed to even speak.

Blindly she slipped through the crowd of guests, seeking only to escape the room. She fled to the privacy of the library and flung herself into one of the old winged chairs that flanked the fireplace. With a low moan, she buried her face in her hands.

Why did love have to hurt so much?

Harry did not know how long she sat there in the dark. She jumped when the door was flung open and a shaft of candlelight illuminated the floor.

"Harry?" Han inquired.

"I am here," she said wearily.

He walked into the room and sat the candles on the table. "Why did you run off? I have been looking all over for you."

"I am sorry, Han," said Harry, quickly rising. "I was tired."

"You did far too much work on the wedding," he said, chastising her. "Now you are too tired to enjoy it." He kissed her on the cheek. "It was a wonderful wedding, Harry. I only hope ours goes as well."

Until that moment, Harry had fought against the urgings of her heart, listening instead to the voice of reason. But the battle was lost. She took a deep breath. "I do not think there will be a wedding, Han."

He stiffened. "What do you mean?"

She turned away. "I never should have agreed to marry you, Han. I have been terribly unfair."

"Weddings usually make people want to get married," he said lightly.

Harry turned back to him again, knowing she could not be a coward. "Han, you are a dear friend. I am afraid I would make you miserable as your wife."

"Is that not for me to decide?" he asked.

"No," she said, and took his hand. "I think I was caught up with Tris and Katrine's happiness, and thought I would find my own in the same way. But I realized today that I was fooling myself. I am only sorry that I have to hurt you in the process."

"If you wish to postpone things . . ."

"It is not a postponement I need, but an end to our betrothal." Tears sprang to her eyes at the stricken look on his face. "Oh, Han, I am so sorry. I never meant to hurt you. I have behaved abominably."

"You are tired," he said. "We can talk in the morning."

"No," she said. "Things will look the same in the morning." She shook her head wearily. "I only hope that someday you can forgive me."

"Harry, I—"

Tris barreled into the library. "There you are! Come on, coz, we are leaving!" He grabbed Harry by the hand and dragged her out into the hall.

After Tris and Katrine departed, Harry wished she could wave a magic wand and make all the guests disappear. It was far too difficult to paste a smile upon her face and act as if nothing was wrong. Thank goodness Han was staying away.

Over the next few hours, the guests gradually slipped away. Only a handful of close friends and relatives remained, and Harry felt comfortable in making her excuses to them.

Instead of going upstairs, however, she went back to the library. To her surprise, her father was there, savoring a late-night glass of port.

"Hello, Papa." Harry dropped a kiss atop his head and took the seat opposite him.

"Do you have time to sit like this?" he teased her. "Are there not more wedding details that demand your attention?"

"None at all," Harry said emphatically. She accepted the glass of wine her father poured her.

"You worked too hard," he said. "You need to rest."

"There will be time enough for that now that Tris is safely wed," she said. "I do not have a care in the world."

"Ah, but then you will have to begin working on your own."

Harry sat silently. She did not wish to spoil the joy of Tris's wedding with her own news.

His eyes twinkled. "What did you finally decide to give your cousin for a gift?"

"A pianoforte," Harry said. "Perhaps Tris will develop some appreciation for music if it is Katrine playing."

"A good choice." Egerton nodded his approval. "I had

thought of such a thing myself, but I decided to give Tris some more land. There is a good farm property in Norfolk."

"Tris is on his way to being a gentleman of wealth," she said. "Land in Norfolk, land in Dorset, land in Scotland."

"I did not give Tris the Scottish land," Egerton said with an enigmatic expression.

"Why not?" she asked, puzzled. "Now that he has wed Katrine, it would be most suitable. I certainly do not want it."

He glanced at her thoughtfully. "Is there a curse on the land?" he asked. "I have been getting all manner of requests to give away that land. It seems that nobody desires to own it."

Harry looked at him in confusion. "What do you mean?"

"Last month I received a letter from Kintail. He seemed rather familiar with the terms of your dowry— and suggested there was another piece of land in Scotland that might suit you better. Did you not find it to your liking?"

Harry stared in disbelief at her father. Why would Alasdair ask such a thing of him? Then realization struck. He feared that once she married Han, the land would be lost to him forever. "And did you comply with his request?" she asked coldly.

"Not yet. I thought to discuss it with you first." He leaned forward. "Lord Kintail suggested that such a trade would be acceptable to you."

"He only fears that he shall never get it back," she said with a trace of bitterness. "News of my engagement must have driven him to write."

"He did not renew his request to purchase the land," Egerton said. "From the tone of his letter, I rather think he has abandoned that effort."

Harry refused to believe that. Whyever would Alasdair give up his claim to the land? It made no sense. That horrid piece of land meant everything to him. He had driven her away with it. Why would he now give it up?

She sat up in a sudden shock, the thought that just

occurred to her jolting her to the core. Because it *had* come between them. Now he was offering to give it up forever. Did he want to prove that he regretted their last argument, that it was not the land he wanted, but her?

A cold chill surged through her. Oh, dear God, what had she done? She gripped the arm of her chair until she thought the marks of her fingers would show in the wood. She might have made the very worst mistake of her entire life, and what hope did she now have of unraveling it at this late date? She had broken with Han, but that did not mean she could run to Alasdair. She had little hope he would welcome her with open arms.

Yet why had he said nothing to her about his disavowal of the land? She would not have gone to Han if she had known. Bitterly, she acknowledged the reason. His damnable pride. Alasdair always allowed it to get in the way of everything between them, and now he was doing it again. Except now the price was far higher.

The bleak despair she felt must have shown on her face, for her father reached out and covered her hand with his. "Can I do anything to help?" he asked.

Harry glanced fondly at his kind expression, but shook her head. "There is nothing you can do, Papa," she said. Unsteadily she rose to her feet and walked to the door.

Once outside the library, she leaned weakly against the wall. What on earth was she going to do?

She had to talk with him, of course, but she cringed at the very thought. What if her theory was wrong? What if he did despise her? She would throw herself at his feet and look like the veriest fool. Winterbourne pride forbade that course. But had she not berated him for the same fault? Could she be the one to take the first step?

If only she could engage him in conversation, she might get an inkling about his feelings. She had spent so much time and effort avoiding him these last two days that it seemed ironic that she now wanted to speak with him. But she had to know.

She summoned a footman, and sent him off with a message to have Alasdair meet her in the drawing room. But the man returned with the intelligence that Lord Kintail was not in his room.

Panic swept over her. Had he left for Scotland already? Learning that his bags were still here, she breathed a sigh of relief. She would awaken with the dawn tomorrow and lay in wait for him. She had to try to talk with him one more time. To discover whether all was lost forever, or if there was some hope left in the world. The tiniest spark of hope blazed within her.

21

Will ye gang to the Hielands, Leezie Lindsay?
Will ye gang to the Hielands wi' me?
Will ye gang to the Hielands, Leezie Lindsay,
My pride and my darling to be?

Robert Burns,
Leezie Lindsay

Alasdair awoke early, bleary-eyed, with his head pounding. It seemed as if only moments before he had stumbled to his bed. Too much *uisge-beatha*. But that had been the only way he could endure being so close to Harry.

He sat up, quickly closing his eyes against the dizziness. It would not be a wonderful day to travel, he thought ruefully. But travel he must, to get away from Harry.

A quick ride would clear his head, he decided, and make the thought of travel more palatable. Hastily he drew on his clothes. The rest of the house was surely asleep after yesterday's festivities; he need not make himself presentable.

In scant minutes he was galloping over the Kentish Downs, the wind streaming through his hair and the fresh air clearing his head. Soon he could leave for home. It would be a great relief to leave England behind—for good, he hoped.

Katrine's wedding had gone smoothly. Too smoothly. Some minor disaster would have distracted everyone and thrown the beautifully orchestrated reception into chaos. Instead, it had proceeded like clockwork. Which meant that he was always far too aware of Harry's presence—across from him at the table, chatting gaily with her guests, or dancing with Lord Hanover. The last had been the worst.

He had nothing against Lord Hanover. He seemed a nice enough fellow. But Alasdair could not like him, simply because he had Harry. And worse, he had virtually driven her into that man's arms with his stupid anger. There was nothing worse than having yourself to blame for folly.

By the time he returned to the stables, his head felt better. He glanced at the windows of the house, seeing no signs of life in any. He did not want to go back inside just yet, where he would be forced to enter into polite conversation with everyone he met. He started toward the back of the house, where he knew the gardens were. Not until he was halfway there did he remember how Harry had described the gardens as her mother's favorite place.

How long would it take to forget her? It had been months already, and he was no closer to forgetting every word she had ever uttered to him than he had been when she left Scotland. Would another year be enough? Five? Or would he carry this weight within him for a lifetime? Just how much would he have to pay for the folly of turning away the woman he loved?

Harry, who received the intelligence that Lord Kintail had gone riding early in the morning, stationed herself in the hall, where she could be certain to intercept him on his return. She was surprised, but relieved, when a footman told her Alasdair was walking in the gardens. She thought it odd, but did not cavil. It was better that this interview took place in private, for she had no idea what the outcome would be.

Harry drew on her cloak and slipped out the side door. Would he think her too bold, deliberately seeking him out like this? She was woefully uncertain of what she would say to him. She knew she could not bring herself to ask what was foremost in her mind—why he had requested that her father dispose of the Keppoch land. And worse, she could not ask what she hoped—was it a sign that he did love her?

Alasdair was a goodly way down the garden path, and Harry nearly had to run to catch up with him. When she stopped a few feet behind him, she was breathing hard, but not only from the exertion.

"Lord Kintail," she called.

Alasdair stopped at the sound of that agonizingly familiar voice. What did she want now? To torture him further? Reluctantly he turned to face her.

"Lady Harriet." He nodded solemnly.

"Walk with me a pace," she requested.

Alasdair fell in beside her, but did not take her arm.

"Were you pleased with the wedding?" she asked.

"It went well," he replied laconically.

"Katrine and Tris seemed particularly happy," she said, her eyes riveted to the path below her feet. "I have not asked you why you finally relented."

"Katrine wished it so," he said.

A rather simplistic answer for such a dramatic turnabout, but Harry dared not probe further. Confronting him now, all her courage faded.

"Do you not fear to find it lonely at Kintail now that she is gone?" she asked.

Alasdair shrugged. *It is not my sister's face that haunts my days. You are the one I cannot live without—and cannot have.* As if to drive the knife in further, he asked the question. "When is your own marriage to be?"

Harry blanched. "There will be no marriage," she said quietly. "Han and I have broken our betrothal."

He said nothing, merely continued walking at her side.

Harry stopped, and turned to face him. She reached out and touched his sleeve, daring to look into his eyes. "Alasdair, do you still hate me?"

The expression in his eyes softened. "No, Harry. I do not hate you. I never hated you."

"And did you ever love me?" she whispered so softly he could hardly hear.

His face contorted in anger. "Jilted by one suitor and on the lookout for another already?" he demanded harshly. "Of course, the great Lady Harriet still requires a full court of admirers."

Harry bit her lower lip to keep it from trembling.

After he saw the torment in her eyes, his anger quickly faded. "Are you in love with him?" he asked.

"It was I who broke the betrothal," she said.

"Why?"

She looked at him for a long moment, hardly daring to breathe. "I did not love him," she said at last.

Alasdair stared at her, dumbfounded. "It was not in love you were? Then why, for God's sake, did you plan to wed?"

She shrugged. "Not many marriages in our class are based on love. It often works out better that way."

He stepped in front of her and put his hands on her shoulders, shaking her roughly. "You are a fool, Harriet Winterbourne," he said icily.

Her blue eyes flashed with anger. "I am quite aware that you do not think highly of me, *Lord* Kintail. You need not spell out all my faults in detail."

"Anyone who agrees to marry without feeling some form of affection for her spouse is a foolish creature."

"But at least I would have been spared the pain of not having my love returned," she cried.

His face softened. "You are a stubborn and infuriating woman, Harriet Winterbourne, but I am going to tell you what I came to England to say." He grabbed her arm and spun her around. "I made a terrible mistake when I allowed you to leave Kintail. But I am not going to let my mistake ruin your life."

"Do you think it will?" she asked.

"Damn it, Harry, listen to me. I love you. I was stupid to drive you away, but I could not help it. I was frightened by what you were doing to me. You scared me."

"I scared you?"

"I needed you too much," he explained. "And I have never needed anyone before. It was frightening to know that I could no longer be content by myself."

"You have a deucedly odd way of showing it," she said.

"I know. That is what I wanted to do when I came south with Katrine—to try and explain things to you, to tell you how I felt and how wrong I had been. But by the time I arrived . . ."

"That is why you wrote to my father about the land."

"He told you?"

She nodded. "Last night. Why did you not tell me yourself?"

"I planned to when I brought Katrine to London," he said. "But you were betrothed by then."

He caught her hand in his. "Harry, I do not want to cause you grief. I wrote that letter to prove to you that the land did not matter to me—you did. I cannot change what I am—a Scotsman. Yet we can overcome our differences, I know. I cannot allow you to walk out of my life again."

"And how can you stop me?" she challenged him.

He grinned. "I shall toss you across the back of my saddle and carry you over the border," he said. "A time-honored Scottish custom."

Harry burst into tears.

"Do not cry, *mo ghraidh*," he said, gathering her into his arms.

"I cannot help it."

"We do not have to elope," he said.

Harry laughed through her tears. "But only think how it will scandalize English society."

He kissed her softly. "We will marry in any way you wish, *mo ghraidh*."

She looked at him archly. "You are so certain that I will marry you, Lord Kintail?"

He nodded. "Let me remind you that it is the ancient Scottish practice to kidnap an unwilling bride," he said. "One way or another, *mo leannan,* you will find yourself my countess."

She looked at him, her eyes troubled. "But can you truly bring yourself to wed an English bride?" she asked.

"You could be the granddaughter of Butcher Cumberland and I would wed you," he said. "I cannot be happy without you, Harry."

"I love you," she said, a radiant smile on her face.

"And I you," he replied, tightening his arms about her and lowering his lips to hers again.